BEING ADALIZA
A Maison du Lemorque Novel

Primrose Hugh

Copyright © 2024 Primrose Hugh

All rights reserved.

ISBN: 9798338473238

For Emily

1

As soon as the cloaked figures enter the shop I know that they don't usually frequent the Ruelle de Gargouille. It is a dismal October afternoon, and a whistling wind whips the door back on its hinges with a bang when the first figure unlatches it. The sound catches all three of them by surprise and they stop, flinch, visibly have to gather their nerve as they cross the threshold and enter the Maison du Lemorque.

I regard them silently from behind the counter as they file in out of the rain. They wear dark cloaks with voluminous hoods that shadow their faces, and none of them move to pull them down. I can't see their eyes but I can feel them appraising me warily. Like many of our human clients they are shifty, suspicious of their surroundings and unwilling to reveal their identity. I don't blame them for that. The Lemorques have long made a business out of stolen identities, after all.

"We ... We're here for ... We need a decoy," one of the

cloaked figures says, taking a jerky step towards me at the counter. Her voice is female.

"Then you've come to the right place," I say.

I am wearing the form I often take when I'm front of house: a skinny, sullen girl with lank black hair and a disinterested tone. I have found that it's the best way to avoid unwanted attention from the less scrupulous punters who prowl the Ruelle de Gargouille. Throsne may be a beautiful city, but every city has an underbelly – a place where the peacemakers fear to tread, where laws are bent to breaking point and shadows hide secrets that the good folk pretend to ignore. Until, that is, they venture into the shadows of the Ruelle de Gargouille for our help.

I reach out and tug sharply on a bell pull, making one of the cloaked figures – the shortest one nearest the door – jump and let out a soft squeak of surprise. The floorboards above our heads groan as someone crosses the room on the level above us and makes a slow, noisy descent down the creaking staircase. When she emerges onto the shop floor, my grandmother wears the shape of a humpbacked crone. She is wizened and tottering, every bit the fairytale villain selling sorcery that these fine folk were expecting. Her eyes, like mine, are entirely black – pupils, irises and whites all. She turns her unsettling gaze on the cloaked customers.

"Yes?" she asks in a feeble, croaking tone. I roll my eyes at her theatrics.

"Are you Madame Lemorque?" their leader asks warily.

"For my sins," Grandmére replies, giving them a devilish grin that lacks a number of teeth.

"We are in need of your services." I hear the woman inhale under her hood, as if steeling herself. "We require a decoy right away."

"For whom?" Grandmére asks.

Being Adaliza

"For me," the leader says, her voice growing bolder. She reaches up and pulls the wide hood off her head, revealing the pretty face of a young woman, expression set with determination. "Princess Adaliza of Belforet."

I stare at her in shock. The princess is a long, long way from the palace. What on earth could have prompted her to evade her guards and wander the Ruelle de Gargouille? The second cloaked figure sighs and pulls down her hood, revealing an older woman with an expression of exasperation on her face as she cuts a narrow-eyed look at the princess. The third figure quickly follows suit. She is young and round faced, and she looks half terrified. My grandmother shoots a sideways glance at me, and I know what she's thinking. It's not everyday that a princess walks into the shop in need of a decoy. This assignment will be mine.

Grandmére steps one foot forward and lifts her arms, shifting her form mid-curtsey into a tall, elegant lady with sleek silver hair. She still takes the form of an older woman but she wears the years much more easily; her back is straight, her air is regal, her voice is rich and alluring when she purrs, "What a pleasure, your Highness. Manon Lemorque, at your service."

All three of the women stare in amazement at her transformation. Perhaps they didn't truly believe that the Lemorques are changelings with the power to shift their shape at will. There are precious few of the faefolk left in Belforet. It has been 100 years since the gateway to Faerie was barred, separating the realms for good. My ancestors had the misfortune of being stuck on the wrong side of the gate when it happened, marooned in a human land that saw them as untrustworthy fairy tricksters. We, at least, had the capacity to blend in. Many other faefolk were hunted to extinction or pushed to the margins of the kingdom, to hide in murky lakes or misty bowers. The Lemorques quickly learnt that the best way to survive among humans was to be useful.

"Shall we go somewhere a little more private?" Grandmére asks, pointing towards the door at the back of the shop with one elegant hand.

Like me she wears a billowing black houppelande, a long, full gown with flared sleeves and a hemline that rustles the floor. Its loose and flowing fit allows us to change our form without worrying about the restriction of the garments we're wearing. It also swishes and eddies dramatically as one moves, allowing Grandmére to indulge her love for theatricality around humans who expect the sinister and strange from us.

She leads the three women into the parlour behind the shop room, where they take a seat on the large settle against the wall. I follow silently behind, unnoticed. It is warmer here, away from the draughty windows and the cold that seeps through the cracks around the shop door. A low fire crackles in the grate, casting a soft glow over their faces. Both the princess and the older woman sit straight backed with their hands clasped neatly in their laps. I realise that it's not just their posture that they have in common; they share the same face shape, the same lustre to their brown hair. It is the older woman who talks first.

"What we tell you next is to be treated with the utmost discretion," she says stiffly, reluctantly. Her voice is crisp and cultured.

"Of course," Grandmére assures smoothly. "We respect and maintain the privacy of all of our patrons. Our business depends on it."

"We wouldn't be here if we had any other option. But time is running out, and he won't be dissuaded."

She pauses, and Grandmére waits for her to explain

Being Adaliza

herself. The woman sighs and glances at the princess to her right.

"As you may have heard, there is a plague ravaging the continent. It is incurable and unstoppable. Many of our neighbouring kingdoms have had their populations devastated by the disease. So far we have managed to keep it from penetrating the borders of Belforet – and we may still succeed. But my husband, the king, grows more paranoid every day. Princess Adaliza is his sole heir. He is terrified that any day now the plague could spread to Throsne and wipe out his family, his line.

"He has convinced himself that the only way to keep Adaliza safe is to send her away. There is a tower hidden deep in the heart of the Old Woods of Belforet. He wants Adda to stay there in isolation, out of the path of any plague, until it is safe to return to the capital."

I read the defiance in her daughter's expression, the rebellion in her stiff posture. I know that my grandmother sees it too.

"And why is it that you need our services?" Grandmére asks mildly.

"Because I'm not going." Adaliza's statement is absolute. "I won't sit idly in a tower, regardless of whether a plague comes to Belforet. I don't need to be kept safe or hidden away from the world."

"So you need a changeling to take your place in the tower? Where will you be?" asks Grandmére.

"Far away," the princess vows. "I have never seen the world outside our castles in Belforet. If I were a boy my life wouldn't have been nearly so sheltered, and yet I'm still expected to rule one day. How can I speak for a kingdom that I barely know? How can I protect its borders when I'm barred from knowing what's beyond them?"

"Your father loves you," her mother says, and I get the impression that this isn't the first time they've had the conversation. "He's doing what he thinks is best for you."

"And we both agreed that he's wrong in this," the princess replies firmly.

She has already won the argument – they are here, after all. The queen and princess of Belforet are seeking a changeling decoy in defiance of their king. My grandmother's smile is wide and her black eyes gleam, as if the situation is delectable.

"How long will you need our services?" she asks.

"For as long as necessary," Adaliza replies.

"And when will the assignment start?"

"Tomorrow."

Tomorrow? It's too soon. Being a decoy is more than just imitating another person's face. It means learning their mannerisms, predicting their reactions and understanding their back story to make the deception believable. I can't become Princess Adaliza in less than a day. Anyone who knows her will see through it in a heartbeat.

"As you wish."

Grandmére's calm reply surprises me and I raise my eyebrows at her in silent protest. She's not thinking about the difficulties of the job – she's picturing the gold that will make its way from the royal coffers to the Maison du Lemorque.

"Aster, come here, child," she says in my direction, even though I'm eighteen years old and far from an innocent child.

The three women turn to look at me, surprised to find I have been in the room the whole time. None of them meet my midnight black gaze.

"This is my granddaughter, Aster," Grandmére tells them. "She will be a fine match for the princess."

The queen and the princess stare at me with obvious

skepticism. I don't take it personally. It suits me to be underestimated, overlooked. I've been doing this job since I was slipped into another baby's cradle when I was just a month old. I've been a duchess, a prostitute, a long lost daughter. I've been both bait and bodyguard. The princess is just another face for my collection.

I bob a courtesy in their direction.

"Your Highness, would you mind standing?" I ask Adaliza.

The princess purses her lips but rises to her feet. I stand opposite her, my head slightly cocked as I observe her keenly. Princess Adaliza's hair is long and mink brown, with enough of a natural, restrained wave to ripple over her shoulders and tousle in soft curls at the ends. She has a heart-shaped face with broad cheekbones and a pointed chin. I have noticed that her lips are quick to pout or quirk at the corners, and generally express her feelings with arresting panache. Her stormy blue eyes are wide set and long-lashed, and are currently narrowed with intelligence – almost challenge – as they watch me. All in all there is an alluringly feline way about her. I know she is a little younger than me but she has an air of confidence, as if she is comfortable in her body. It's rare in one her age.

I let the magic flow through me in a warm glow that spreads from my face to my feet. My body feels soft and pliant as I massage it into shape from the inside like a baker kneading dough. Shifting requires intention. My spine lengthens, my breasts swell, my flesh becomes fuller yet firmer. My lank hair thickens, lightens, curls. Adaliza's eyes flare wide and her mouth drops open as I shift into her mirror image.

"It's a little disconcerting the first time," I say in a perfect imitation of her voice.

She blinks once, twice, then shuts her mouth with a clack. "What about the eyes?"

While a changeling can alter almost anything about their appearance, there are limitations to our powers. We can't alter our age or gender, and we can't shift our distinctive all-black eyes. This is a well-known fact about changelings and brings a degree of comfort to the human populace, who are assured that they would recognise a shapeshifter if they ever tried to take the place of a loved one. But we are Lemorques, and we haven't survived this long in the human world without a few tricks up the sleeves of our houppelandes.

"The eyes require an extra degree of trust," Grandmére says.

She presses on the wooden panelling of the opposite wall and a compartment springs open at her touch. Inside is what looks like an array of jewellery: bracelets, necklaces, earrings, all set with gemstones in shades of blue, green, brown and grey. Grandmére takes an oval of clear, colourless glass from a drawer and brings it over to me, dropping it in my palm.

"Princess Adaliza of Belforet, do you give permission for me, Aster Lemorque, to bear your true likeness?" I ask.

The princess looks confused as I offer her the small piece of glass, but she takes it and nods solemnly.

"Yes, I give my permission," she says.

The moment the words come out of her mouth, the glass oval in her palm changes colour. It turns the deep, stormy blue of lapis lazuli – the exact shade of the princess's irises. I reach out my hand to take it back, and when Adaliza tips it into my palm and looks up at me she gasps in surprise. As long as the stone is in contact with my skin, I can mimic her eyes to perfection. No one would suspect I was a changeling decoy, not even her own father.

"At the end of the job you will get the gemstone back – as

a sign of good faith," Grandmére reassures the queen, whose expression walks the edge between fascination and outrage.

It's an important stipulation that we offer our patrons. Once they take away the gemstone they are reassured that we can't fully imitate them without their knowledge in the future.

"This could actually work," Adaliza says under her breath as she looks at me with something like ... excitement.

She isn't disconcerted by my appearance anymore.

"If you want Aster to start tomorrow, she will need some way of getting into the palace to take your place," Grandmére says.

"We have already thought of that," Adaliza reassures her.

She glances to the third member of their party, who has stayed completely silent throughout the exchange.

"Delphine is my most trusted handmaiden and the only servant I am permitted to take with me to the tower. It is not unusual for her to leave the palace on an errand for me. No one will question you if you enter wearing her form."

I study Delphine, who is practically quaking in fear. She rises to her feet, attempting to swallow down her nerves under my scrutiny. She is shorter than her mistress, buxom and rounded, with blonde hair the colour of butter pulled back under a cap. She looks as harmless as a dormouse. Her face is expressive and honest, and her wide brown eyes give away her unease in my presence.

I shift my form, my eyeline sinking a few inches until it's level with hers. I still have the lapis lazuli stone in my hand, and I know it's utterly disconcerting for her to see herself with her mistress's blue eyes.

"I need to hear your voice, Delphine," I tell her, using Adaliza's confident tone as well.

When I'm not impersonating someone specifically, I often

end up as a patchwork of composite parts. I can only take the form of a real person who I have met in the flesh, but once they're in my mental library I can pick and choose which bits of them I wear. I might want the height and strength of the young midwife but the forgettable face of the beggar girl in the gutter, the strident voice of the duchess and the blue-green eyes of the baker's daughter who died before she could ask for the bracelet back that keeps her turquoise stone pressed against the skin of my wrist. The jewellery in Grandmére's cabinet comes from those people who never came back to claim their gemstones. It's not uncommon – we deal in a dangerous game of deception, after all.

"W-what d-do you want me to say?" she asks in panic.

I try to give her a reassuring smile from her own lips.

"That's enough," I say, matching her pitch and inflection.

We repeat the trust vow process, resulting in a tiger's eye pendant the same colour as Delphine's golden brown irises that will allow me to wholly take her form. I remain as Delphine as we put together a plan for sneaking into the palace tomorrow. By the time our three patrons leave the Maison du Lemorque, Adaliza is triumphant and excited, the queen is clearly suspicious and Delphine is downright terrified by the part she has to play.

I turn to my grandmother once the door latch falls, shifting from Delphine's form back to the sulky shop girl.

"One day, Grandmére?" I ask accusingly. "How am I supposed to prepare in one day?"

She waves a hand at me dismissively. "Don't be so dramatic, Aster. All you're required to do is sit in a tower on your own all day until the plague passes. It's not like you'll be impersonating the princess at court. It will be the easiest job you've ever taken.

"Besides," she smiles wickedly, "I wasn't going to let this

one pass us by. A royal patron – and a royal scandal! The information we are party to is just as valuable as the gold they are giving us."

Her eyes, black and glistening as pitch, are bright with avarice. I am under no illusion; I know that I am a precious commodity to my grandmother, the only female changeling in the family under the age of thirty. I am expected to serve the Maison du Lemorque unquestioningly. And I do – because what else is there for me?

"Yes, Grandmére," I say, and I can blame my sullen tone on the girl whose stolen form I wear.

2

A day later I sit straight backed with my hands clasped in my lap as I stare out of the coach window. The narrow streets and morning jostle of Throsne is long behind us; we are rumbling through the rolling pasture land of southern Belforet. The fields look rather soggy and forlorn in the grey of the October day. Sheep stare at us as we pass noisily, the only movement in the landscape the rhythmical circling of their jaws as they masticate. It isn't much of a view, but I know that Delphine feels more comfortable when I'm looking elsewhere.

She sits on the bench opposite me, the only other occupant of the coach. There are two armed horsemen riding alongside us for protection, but nowhere near the pomp, pageantry and security that would normally accompany a royal party. There are no royal crests emblazoned on the sides of the coach and no uniformed guards to give away the identity of who travels inside. The king would not gamble with his daughter's life by broadcasting her movements across the kingdom. Very few of the royal court know that Adaliza has been sent away. Only three people – the princess, the queen and the handmaiden – are privy to the true extent of the deception.

Getting into the palace and being smuggled out again as Adaliza was surprisingly straightforward. The princess had already said her goodbyes to her parents – and made her displeasure about the arrangement known – so I didn't speak to anyone when we switched places just as she was due to enter the coach. Once I was on board and waving from the window, no one suspected that the cloaked figure who slipped unobtrusively from a side door might be the princess.

I would guess that we have been travelling for around four hours now. The roads are uneven and it makes the carriage rattle and shudder; the constant bouncing up and down on the seat is already making my backside ache. I have studied enough maps of our continent, Oramundi, to have a clear idea of where we are going. The kingdom of Belforet is mostly landlocked and roughly diamond shaped, with its capital city, Throsne, situated near the southern tip close to the border with the neighbouring kingdoms of Paillevalee and Herza. We are travelling north from Throsne to the wild heart of the kingdom, far from the borders, which is still thickly forested in ancient woodland. It will take a number of days on the road to get there. I grimace at the thought of so much time stuck in this rattling box.

The first few drops of rain spit against the coach window. I suppose it could be worse – we could be on horseback. Most animals are suspicious of changelings, and horses are no exception. I have been kicked, bucked and whinneyed at more times than I care to count by stubborn horses that refuse to let such an unnatural smelling creature ride on their back. Adaliza, however, is known to be a keen horsewoman. I'm relieved that this assignment won't require any riding – I doubt I could keep up the deception for very long.

I glance at Delphine and pretend not to notice that she has been staring at me with a wary expression. Her gaze quickly falls to her lap and her cheeks redden.

"It's starting to rain," I say conversationally.

"Yes, Your Highness," she squeaks automatically in reply.

"You can call me Aster when it's just the two of us," I offer.

I see the struggle in her face as she chances another look at me, trying to reconcile the familiar appearance of her mistress with the knowledge that I am not what I seem. Her eyes settle on the lapis lazuli stone that lies between my collarbones, held in a silver cuff necklace at my throat.

"Delphine, I'm not here to deceive you. It is my job to serve the princess, just as it is yours. I hope that we can become friends."

I give her a small smile that just seems to unnerve her further and sigh inwardly. It will be a lonely few months – years, even – if the only person I'm allowed to have contact with is terrified of me.

"Yes Your— I mean, m-mistress," she says, correcting herself but not quite managing to use my real name.

I reach into the pocket of my gown and pull out a necklace, its tiger's eye pendant hanging down between my fingers. It's the gemstone that allowed me to mimic Delphine's eye colour, the one I used to gain entry to the palace.

"This is yours," I say to Delphine and hold it out for her to take.

She blinks down at the necklace as if it's a snake that

might bite her.

"You can touch it – there's nothing magic about it now. It's just a piece of jewellery that matches remarkably well with your eyes. I won't impersonate you again without your knowledge," I reassure her.

She nods, swallows and gingerly takes the necklace from me, her fingers wrapping around the golden brown stone before she folds her hands in her lap.

The rain is getting heavier. It run in branching rivulets down the window and drums softly on the roof of the coach. I return my gaze to the blurred view of the murky landscape and we sit in silence once again.

On the third day of travel we reach the edge of the Old Woods. Centuries ago this woodland swathed all of Belforet, before the trees were chopped down to make ships and houses and their roots pulled from the soil to make way for farmland. Now the ancient forest grows in a thick band around the heart of the kingdom, making travel from north to south by land almost impossible. Traders and travellers alike make the journey by boat on the River Fluet, which flows deep and wide through the woods. I have sailed the route myself a number of times. I've never taken the old track through the forest as we do now.

I expected the woodland to loom with sinister intent, ready to swallow any foolish wayfarer into its ancient depths. It is still a wild place, untamed by humans and their straight lines, unchanged by time. When I peer out of the window as we approach I am taken aback by how utterly beautiful it is. The foliage of the trees is a riot of autumnal colours above us, russet and crimson and gold, and a carpet of leaves turn the ground beneath the coach's wheels into a sweep of fiery orange. The trees tower upwards around us, their trunks so thick it would take three people holding hands with their arms outstretched to circle them. It doesn't feel gloomy under their canopy; it feels warm and safe, like they're offering their protection. Or maybe that's the fairy in me feeling a connection to the natural world.

A number of times the coach is forced to halt while the horsemen clear the path of debris or hack away at overgrown branches to allow us to pass. It is a gruelling final leg taken at a much slower pace than the rest of our journey, but I hardly notice as I stare out of the window, enchanted. It must be well past midday by the time we turn off the track down a wide gully and end up in a sunlit glade.

The door is opened for me and I step down from the coach, stretching my protesting legs for the first time in hours. Ahead of us is a tall stone tower that looks as if it has happily stood in this glade for centuries. The grey stonework is all but covered in creeping ivy that has turned blood red for the season. A conical roof with a crooked chimney poking from the top crowns the tower, and just below it is a large balcony that must offer a wonderful view of the tree canopies. Narrow windows wind up the tower in regular intervals but I can't see a door. At ground level I noticed a well and a neat kitchen garden with beds laid out in orderly rows.

"Your Highness?"

I turn my gaze to the three people standing in a line just ahead of me. They immediately lower their heads and bob a courtesy or bow.

"I am Marie, Your Highness," a plump older woman says. "I am the cook. This here is Claude, the woodsman, and Annette, the housemaid."

I nod to each one as she introduces them. Claude is tall

and broad shouldered with a ruffian's nose and a bristling black beard. Annette is slender and pale, with the kind of unremarkable face that I find infinitely more useful than a striking one.

"Princess Adaliza is pleased to meet you," Delphine says in a superior tone on my behalf, and I glance at her in surprise. Gone is the nervous mouse of a girl I shared a carriage with for the past three days. So she can act, then.

"I am Delphine, the princess's handmaiden. The princess has been sent here by the king for her own safety. Only I will be permitted entry to her chambers."

Marie nods. "Aye, we were told as much. We are happy to welcome you both here."

"Thank you, Marie. Claude, Annette," I say.

The old cook looks taken aback for a moment before giving me a warm smile. Perhaps Adaliza wouldn't have talked to the servants directly, but I am not going to ignore the only other people who will live alongside me here.

"If you will follow me," Marie says.

She leads us towards what I assumed was a shrub-covered mound but turns out to be a hidden door hatch that leads to an underground tunnel.

"This is the only way into the tower," Marie tells us as we step down through the doorway. There are a couple of lit torches burning in brackets along the tunnel to light our way. We pass what looks to be a food store before we climb a set of stone steps and emerge blinking in what I assume is the room at the base of the tower.

"This is my domain," Marie says proudly, spreading her hands to show off a large working kitchen. "If there's any food you particularly fancy, Your Highness, you just tell me. We don't have all the ingredients that the palace has access to but we make do quite nicely."

Primrose Hugh

I see a wire basket piled with plump pears, bunches of carrots and parsnips hung from the central beam like hands with swollen fingers, a tray of fat, floury rolls cooling on the side. The room smells delicious, like herbs and freshly baked bread. It makes my mouth water.

Marie points through a doorway before heading towards a stone staircase at the back of the kitchen.

"Through there are Claude's quarters," she says. "The next level houses the female servants, there's no need to stop there. Go on up, Your Highness."

She stands by to let me pass her and I continue up the staircase. It opens out into a double height space that makes me blink in surprise. It's ... a library. Floor to ceiling bookcases line the curved walls, and a ladder leads to a small mezzanine level where a large armchair is positioned under a round stained glass window. Every shelf is densely packed with books, from hulking tomes to slim pocket books that make my fingers itch to explore the collection. I adore reading. The room also has a large stone fireplace and a writing desk, an easel and paints, a beautiful harp with a cushioned stool and a music stand. There is a dressmaker's dummy and an embroidery hoop.

I go back to the main stairwell and climb again, finding myself in another double height room made even taller by the conical roof criss-crossed with wooden beams. The walls are wrapped in richly embroidered tapestries and a large four-poster bed with sumptuous hangings hulks against the wall with a settle at its foot. A round table with two chairs has been set up by the fireplace, as if two friends have just got up from a game of cards. I notice a dressing table with a mirror and a set of silver combs and brushes, a large armoire and a painted dressing screen. There is a small door to the left and inside I glimpse a washroom with a copper tub.

Being Adaliza

My eyes sweep the bedchamber but my attention is quickly caught by the large doors that lead out onto the balcony. I throw them wide and revel in a view that's even more impressive than I imagined from the ground. The gentle afternoon light sets the forest aflame all around me in reds and yellows. I breathe in deeply and smell earth and air, clean and cleansing. I've never felt further from the Ruelle de Gargouille, or been happier for it.

I don't know why I'm surprised by the luxuriousness of the tower – it's not as if the King and Queen of Belforet would send their daughter off to live in rustic squalor. Of course it has all the trappings one would expect of a royal residence. For the first time I feel a bubble of excitement in my chest at the thought of this assignment.

In truth, I'm already tired of decoy work. It's not just the danger, although there has been a fair amount of that on my last two jobs. The work is often grubby and morally questionable, and it's exhausting to always have to think before you act or speak, to always play a part. Eighteen years old and I'm already sick of it – not that I would ever admit any of that to my mother or grandmother.

I have to admit that Grandmére was right. This will be my easiest assignment. All I have to do is stay in the tower and allow myself to be waited on hand and foot. There will be no armed assassins, no carefully planned heists or double-crossing allies or greedy masters. I look at the large bed with its layers of blankets and sit down on the sinking mattress. No more sleeping with one eye open, fearful of a treacherous knife in the ribs or the wandering hands of a drunk husband. I let myself fall back against the blankets with my arms spread wide and my eyes closed, a small smile playing on Adaliza's lips.

3

The First Autumn/Winter

It surprises me how quickly I fall into the gentle routines of the tower. Delphine wakes me every day, throwing open the shutters to let in the morning light that wanes a little each day as the year draws closer to the winter solstice. One night a fierce storm blows many of the leaves from the trees, turning their branches from red and gold to bare and spindly. I still find the vista beautiful, and even more so when the first snow falls and dusts the glade white overnight.

I eat my breakfast tray in bed while Delphine prepares my outfit for the day. The huge armoire is full of linen chemises and fitted kirtles, silk surcoats and fur-lined cloaks. When Delphine isn't around I sometimes stroke my hand along the garments in fascination, watching the light play off the sheen of green silk, pink brocade, blue wool embroidered with vines and flowers. It's a jewel box of colour. I let

Being Adaliza

Delphine dress me in whatever she deems most appropriate, and often find myself tightly laced into beautiful gowns that I would prefer to see from a distance than wear myself.

I study Adaliza's body for clues about the princess I barely got to meet before I took her form. I have never understood why humans are so shy about their own nakedness – I have no qualms about standing in front of the looking glass and examining every inch of myself. When I took Adaliza's form I didn't just replicate her face by looking at it. Our magic works much more subtly than that. Every part of me mirrors every part of her on the day that I met her. Her body is strong and straight, her upper arms and thighs toned by many hours of horse riding. Her skin is pale as milk all over, as if it has been carefully kept out of the sun. The most notable blemish is a ragged scar that bisects the flesh of her left forearm, and I wonder how she got it.

For a while I'm fascinated by Adaliza's fingers. I expected her hands to be soft as silk, but when I skim over my fingertips with the pad of my thumb I can feel calluses on both hands. It can't be from weapons training – there's no way a princess would be allowed to handle a knife or a bow and arrow for long enough to develop calluses. I ponder the mystery until I come across the cause in the library on the lower floor of my chambers. Adaliza is a harp player. When I skim my hand past the strings my fingers reach to pluck as if they know what to do, but I have no idea how to play the harp. Muscle memory is a funny thing.

Once I am up and about I spend most of my days in the library. I have conducted a full inventory of the shelves, and although there are a number of prayer books and law texts that I have no interest in, there are plenty of histories, romances, epic poems and foreign language almanacs that capture my attention. I have a particular love of languages; I know the Common Tongue of Oramundi, of course, plus all the dialects of Belforetian and Herzan, two variants of Orphish and the three ancient languages that the Common Tongue was based on. All of the Lemorques are educated well beyond normal expectations, especially for women. It angers me that most human females aren't even taught to read and write. For once I'm glad that I don't have to feign ignorance on a job – Adaliza is at liberty to read whatever she wants. I make a cosy nest for myself in the armchair on the mezzanine and spend hours with my head buried in a book.

True to their word, Marie, Annette and Claude never set foot in my chambers but I feel their presence everywhere. Annette sees to the cleaning and washing, somehow keeping the rooms spotless without ever crossing paths with me. Sometimes when I peer out of a window I see Claude heading out into the woods with his axe, and I know that his firewood keeps the hearths burning and the tower snug as winter encroaches on the woodland glade. Marie is endlessly inventive with the ingredients at her disposal and serves up some of the most delicious meals I have ever had the privilege to taste. Changelings have notoriously large appetites, and I don't know if Marie is suspicious or approves of the fact that the princess voraciously consumes everything she sends upstairs in the dumbwaiter. After a few weeks of eating alone at every meal time I persuade Delphine to join me, and the hearty food tastes even better when the experience is shared.

Delphine is my ongoing project. We have settled into such a mundane routine that she no longer outwardly fears me or flinches when I move too quickly for her liking. She's trying to keep a formal-feeling distance between us while I simultaneously work to erode it. A few times I've coaxed a genuine smile out of her and felt jubilant at my progress.

Being Adaliza

It's the first week of December when a lone rider appears in the frosty glade. Delphine and I watch with interest from a window as Claude approaches him warily. The two men speak for a time, then the rider reaches into his panniers and passes Claude a number of parcels.

"Go and find out what they are," I tell Delphine, nudging her in the ribs, wishing I could descend the tower steps and find out for myself.

When she comes back her cheeks are flushed from the cold and she is carrying a small box in her hands.

"It was a rider from the palace," she explains. "He brought provisions that the queen thought would be useful – salt, soap, a box of the princess's favourite marzipans. And a letter."

I draw back the lid of the wooden box and see the neatly packed items inside. An emotion twinges in my chest, one I can't precisely identify. The box is ... thoughtful. A care package from a mother to her daughter, to remind her that, although she is far away, she is still loved. The queen knows that I am not her daughter. Maybe she only did it to keep up appearances, but ... she knew that *my* hands would open the box, and she sent it anyway. Someone is thinking of me. I've never had that kind of reassurance from my own family while working a job.

The letter that sits on top of the items is neatly folded and sealed with purple wax. 'The princess in the tower' is written on its front in a bold, feminine hand. I break the seal and unfold the letter, curious about its contents.

Dear Aster,

May I call you Aster? I hope it's not too impertinent, but I didn't get the impression that you care overly much about social convention. I'm sure you got the impression that I certainly don't.

Primrose Hugh

I realised I didn't get the chance to thank you properly when we last met. I promised my mother that I would write to keep her updated about my movements while I'm away, so I thought I would write to you too. Maybe we can get to know one another a little better.

When I left the palace I boarded a boat on the River Pompone and sailed straight out of Throsne. When I was a girl my mother told me that the river flowed through the capital cities of four different kingdoms in Oramundi, and ever since I have dreamed of seeing them all by boat. I'm currently in Stuol, the most prosperous city in Herza. Its buildings are taller and its streets are wider than Throsne, with hawkers on every street corner selling pelts, pies, charms, nosegays. I find that I can't resist their calls and often end up buying trinkets that I give to the beggars and street urchins who have no money to buy such things themselves. One thing I have bought for myself is a pair of new fur-lined boots ahead of the winter snows. When I've seen all that Stuol has to offer I will take to the river again, to the next grand city that sprawls along its banks.

So, I wanted to say thank you, Aster. Thank you for giving me my freedom and allowing me to see things, do things, that I never thought would be possible for me.

How is life in the tower? I'm sorry you have to endure that prison on my behalf. Give Delphine my very best regards – if she has mustered the courage to talk to you yet.

Yours in friendship,
Adda

I find myself smiling as I finish the letter. I hear Princess Adaliza's voice so clearly in my head as I read her words. No, not Princess Adaliza – she signed off as Adda. I like the nickname. Adaliza sounds like a pretty jewel in a cushioned velvet box, but Adda has bite.

I look up to see Delphine watching me quizzically, clearly

curious about who has written to me.

"It's from Adda," I explain. "She says to give you her best regards."

Delphine's brown eyes widen. "She is safe? She is well?"

"Oh yes – and enjoying herself, by the sounds of it," I reassure her.

Delphine nods. "The rider said he can take a letter back with him if you wish. I thought he meant a letter to the queen, but perhaps she has a way of contacting the princess?"

"Yes, I think she does. When does he leave?"

"Marie is plying him with rabbit cassoulet, he won't leave until his belly is full. You have time to write a response."

I sit at the teak writing desk, which is stocked with creamy parchment, bottles of ink and a handful of goose feather quills. At first I wonder what to say in the letter, but after a few lines the thoughts and questions are flowing out of me. I tell Adda that being in the tower is no hardship and describe all the lovely things at my disposal. I confess my love of books and how content I am to simply while away the day in the well-stocked library. I ask her how she got the scar on her arm, and whether she misses playing the harp. I have her face and her voice – maybe I'm greedy but I want to know her history too, and her plans for the future.

Delphine takes the folded and sealed letter downstairs when I'm finished, and it's not long before I see the horseman reluctantly leave the warmth of the tower and mount his steed in the frozen glade.

Christmas passes in the tower with very little fanfare – at least for me, alone in the upper apartment. I don't mind. My family and I don't observe the human religious holidays. We keep the old fairy custom of celebrating the Turns of the Year at spring equinox, summer solstice, autumn equinox and winter solstice. My celebration of the longest night is a quiet and solitary one. I wrap in my warmest clothes and stand on the balcony, my face tilted to the winter night sky. I feel peaceful as I stare out at the cloudy sky, pregnant with snow.

I tell Delphine to make sure that she, Marie, Annette and Claude celebrate Christmas together downstairs. I don't usually hear any sounds from below through the thick stone walls of the tower, but as I read in the library I can hear their merriment from the kitchen. Chatter made a little louder by wine, chuckles, teasing, singing along to the tune of a fiddle. I reach for a marzipan from the box next to me, a sweet but sad weight in my chest as I pop the treat in my mouth.

I feel ... lonely. Not because I want to go downstairs and join in with the Christmas celebrations. Even if I did, I would still feel alone, apart, other. I am not human, no matter what I pretend. I can't eat and laugh and sing along with them, not without feeling the artifice of it. I am far, far away from the Maison du Lemorque and, for the first time since I arrived at the tower, that distance weighs on me.

Then I shake myself. I don't have the right to feel maudlin, not while I'm dressed in a princess' finery and eating sugary delicacies in front of the fire. I think of the Ruelle de Gargouille, how the winter winds roar down the street like vengeful spirits, strong enough to strip the skin from your bones. How the snow falls white and soft but ends up grey and churned with grime underfoot. That feeling of always being watched by hungry, malevolent eyes. No, I don't miss it.

Delphine is flushed and giddy when she comes to help me undress. Her tongue is looser than I've ever known it in my presence as she tells me of Claude's skill on the fiddle. I smile and make encouraging noises to keep her talking, warmed by her happiness. I'm not the only one who left

Being Adaliza

Throsne for the isolation of this tower. I sleep soundly as snow falls in the night, blanketing the glade in sparkling white stillness.

4

The First Spring/Summer

Winter feels like a hibernation and I take comfort in the warmth and safety of the tower, content with books and stews and quiet card games with Delphine in front of the fire. When the snow starts to melt, however, I feel a part of myself thawing too. A part I had buried and ignored when I found myself in such luxurious isolation.

As much as I craved a rest from the trials of decoying when I arrived, I feel restlessness start to skitter down my bones. I was not made, not trained, to live a life of leisure. While my mind may have been stretched and expanded while I read voraciously over the winter, my body – Adaliza's body – has grown soft and lethargic. I no longer feel the strength in her horsewoman's arms; her toned legs have lost their muscle definition. It would only take a whisper of magic to stroke down my limbs and firm them up again, to revert to the exact state her body was in when I first beheld her, but I don't want to shapeshift. I want to stretch and jump and use this body, to deserve the vitality I had initially felt in it. As the spring sunshine strengthens, as daffodils and crocuses sprout in colourful clumps under the trees, as Marie's vegetable garden grows green and leafy again, I watch from my balcony and I want to *move*.

I know that Adda would approve. I received her reply to my letter in late January. She spent Christmas in Kral, the next capital city eastward along the River Pompone, and described ice skating in the central square, drinking mulled wine long into the night, accidentally starting a brawl in a tavern and fleeing the scene before she could get caught. She told me that she got the scar on her arm when she tried to ride her father's prize stallion at the age of eleven and was immediately bucked from its back. The real Princess Adaliza was not sedentary – she would understand my need to appease this itch in my bones, would have appeased her own months earlier.

One morning I ask Delphine to dress me in my least restrictive gown and braid my hair back off my face. I fetch the dressmaker's dummy from the floor below and place it in the centre of my bedchamber. I circle the target, imagining a hostile sneer on the blank-faced mannequin head, and let my training take over. I snap out a series of blows – to the nose, the wind pipe, the solar plexus – before grabbing the shoulders and wrenching the dummy down onto my upraised knee. I spring back, bouncing on the balls of my feet, ready for an imagined counter attack. I strike in swift arcs from a sideways stance, backhand, knifehand, palm heel, the mannequin wobbling on its wooden feet. I kick out defensively as I jump back and stumble slightly.

It feels awkward and I frown down at my straight skirts,

missing the flowing fit of my houppelande for the first time since I arrived at the tower. But it's more than just my clothes. Even when it was fit, Adaliza's body isn't used to fighting. Just as my hands wanted to play the harp but my head didn't know how, now my head knows how to be a formidable fighter but my body doesn't quite understand how to make it happen. It's why we usually insist on more time to prepare for a decoy assignment. We need to get to know the body before we can be expected to fight in it.

It's my own fault for not training sooner. I push down the frustration and work through the series of combat movements that my two older brothers, Errol and Inigo, drilled into me years ago. They taught me how to assess a body's strengths and weaknesses, to understand my centre of gravity and test my reach and grip. I've spent too long curled up in the armchair eating marzipans. I'm sweaty and breathless within a few minutes, my dress feeling heavy and oppressive around my limbs.

I frown at the dressmaker's dummy as I try to regain my breath. I haven't touched the sewing kit or embroidery hoop since I've been in the tower, but ... if there aren't any suitable fighting clothes in the packed armoire, I suppose I will have to make some myself.

For the next few days I cut and pin and sew with a focus that disturbs Delphine as she sits quietly with her needlepoint beside me. I'm no master tailor but I manage to fashion myself a pair of lightweight trousers out of the skirt of one of my underdresses, and I trim down the top to make a long-sleeved blouse to go with it. Delphine is horrified when I try it on and turn this way and that in front of the looking glass, enjoying the freedom of movement it gives me.

"You can't wear that!" she gasps, her brown eyes round and her cheeks colouring. "It's ... indecent!"

I shrug at her. "It's not like anyone is going to see me, and I need something to train in."

"Train for what?" she asks.

"For any eventuality," I say grimly as I crack my knuckles, teasing her.

She isn't scared of me anymore, hasn't been for a while, but she looks at me warily again as if remembering who I really am and why I'm here.

"But ... but we're safe here?" she says uncertainly. "The only thing we need to fight is the plague, and your kicks and punches won't be any use against that."

"When an invading army marches into the glade and tries to scale the tower, you'll be glad that I got some practice in while we were here," I tell her.

Delphine makes herself scarce whenever I don the makeshift outfit and train with the dressmaker's dummy, and I'm glad of it. Her little winces and crows of surprise as she watches me are very distracting and I can do without it. After one dinner I slip the serrated steak knife from my empty plate and hide it in the folds of my skirt, knowing that Delphine will make a fuss at the thought of me training with a blade. I add knife manoeuvres to my combat routine.

I settle into the feel of Adaliza's body at my command, until I don't have to think about the length of my reach or the accuracy of my blows. One morning, after gazing up at the ceiling thoughtfully, I climb onto the canopy of the four-poster bed and reach up to grab the closest beam, heaving myself up onto it. Thick wooden trusses spread out from the centre of the conical roof like a wheel far above the floor of my bedchamber. The rafters make excellent balance beams. I practise running and jumping from one beam to another, catching myself and swinging in the open space above the room, strengthening my arms and my core.

But no amount of physical exertion can distract me for long. I stare out at the glade from my balcony and yearn to explore the woodland around me. The trees glow a luminous green in the spring sunshine, branches spread majestically as they bask after the cold winter. Sometimes the breeze carries the scent of grass and freshly turned loam up to the balcony, and I breathe the smell of the forest floor deep into my lungs. I watch enviously as Claude enters the wood with his snares and comes back with rabbits and pigeons slung over his back, as Marie potters in her vegetable patch, her hands muddy and her complexion growing ruddy after hours outdoors.

I can't leave the tower. It's the one and only stipulation of this assignment. Princess Adaliza is to be sequestered in the tower for as long as it takes for the threat of plague to pass. It doesn't matter that I think the restriction is unnecessary, here in the heart of the Old Woods so far from the possibility of human contact. When the weather is warm, Delphine sits with me on the balcony and tries to coax me out of my sullen mood.

"Could you turn into a bird and fly around for a bit?" she suggests. "Technically it wouldn't be the princess leaving the tower."

I shake my head. "I can't turn into a bird. I'm a changeling, we're not true shapeshifters."

"What do you mean?" Delphine asks.

It's a mark of our strengthening friendship that she dares to ask anything about my fairy heritage.

"True shapeshifting is the ability to change every part of yourself. We can alter our skin, hair and bones until we mimic another person, but we can't fundamentally change ourselves into something other. I will always have my brain, my bottomless stomach ..."

"Your heart?" Delphine asks softly.

Being Adaliza

"Yes, for whatever that's worth," I say dismissively.

There is a pause as Delphine thinks about this.

"So when you became me ... you didn't, I mean, you couldn't ..." She stumbles over her words, her cheeks reddening.

Somehow I understand what she is trying to ask. "I took your appearance, not your thoughts or feelings. Those are yours and yours alone."

She nods, staring out at the rustling canopy of the tree line.

"What do you look like?" she asks.

The question catches me unaware and I don't answer straight away.

"I mean ... what does Aster Lemorque look like when she isn't impersonating anyone?"

She glances over to me as I try to string together a reply.

"I ... I don't know."

Her brow creases. "You mean, you've forgotten?"

I have worn so many faces, used so many arms and legs, borrowed from countless bodies in my mental library. I was shifting before I could walk. I'm a Lemorque – we're praised and encouraged for our ability to mimic, not reminded of whatever we had been before.

"Maybe. Maybe I never had my own form."

My reply is softer, sadder, than I intended it to be. I feel exposed. Delphine frowns at my response.

"Of course you did. If you have your own brain and stomach and heart ... at some point you had your own body too."

I stay silent, willing her to drop the subject, knowing how close she is to rooting out my biggest insecurity: that Aster Lemorque doesn't exist. That I'm nothing more than a patchwork girl of stolen body parts.

Spring warms into summer and my restlessness only grows. I've read all of the books in the library, even the deathly boring ones. My daily exercises and combat training can only distract me for a few hours before the sunshine beckons from the balcony, the pull of the woods.

My frustration at my captivity is not wholly on my own behalf. How could Adda's father possibly think that this is the best way to protect his daughter? He must not know her at all. The Adda I know from her letters is fearless and headstrong, clever and impulsive. Prone to getting herself into risky situations but somehow always managing to come out of them laughing. I understand why she couldn't stand the thought of being cooped up in this tower for months on end. Although I've received regular care packages from the queen at the palace, she has sent no word about the plague. Is it wending a path of destruction through Belforet? It's hard to even imagine that deadly threat here in the woods, where all is serene. Serene and green and interminably the same.

The summer solstice is ushered in with a balmy, lazy heat and searingly blue sky. I wear only a linen chemise as I sit on my balcony, having grumbled at Delphine that it's far too hot to lace a stifling kirtle over the top. She no longer baulks at my unusual fashion choices, knowing that it's a battle she won't win. I am touched when she lets herself through the balcony doors behind me and passes me a flower crown. The circlet winds together white roses and daisies with fragrant stalks of lavender and myrtle sprigs.

"You made this?" I ask her softly, turning the beautiful wreath in my fingers.

"Midsummer night is important for the faefolk, isn't it?" she says in reply.

I nod.

"Thank you," I breathe, placing the flower crown on my head and smiling at her.

My chest feels tight and my eyes smart. I'm so grateful to Delphine for the small kindness. She shrugs bashfully.

"I wish you could see the woods. Not far from here there's a wildflower meadow. I think it's the most beautiful place I've ever seen. Claude showed me ..."

Delphine doesn't finish the sentence as her cheeks flush red and she avoids my curious gaze.

"You went into the woods with Claude, did you?" I ask innocently.

He is the person I see most from my balcony, striding out across the glade on his way to chop wood or hunt game. He is a reserved man with an unsmiling, brutish countenance, more at home in the wilderness than in human company. I thought him rather coarse when I first arrived at the tower, but Delphine has let slip a few details that make me re-evaluate him. He plays the fiddle beautifully. He takes her to pick flowers in hidden meadows.

"It's not like ... I don't think ..." Delphine stutters, her face still bright red.

I don't want to tease her, not about this. "Tell me about the woods," I say instead.

When our dinner is sent up in the dumbwaiter, Delphine brings it onto the balcony and we continue to talk, our plates balanced on our knees. We talk until the longest day wanes and the insects buzz dreamily below us in the long grass. Delphine goes downstairs to bed but I stay outside in the dark embrace of midsummer night, my flower crown still atop my head. The night sky feels so much bigger here than it does in Throsne, and I want to be closer to it.

I glance behind me at the tiled roof that peeks over the

door back into my chamber, rising to a point at its centre. I am limber as I scale the door frame and easily pull myself up onto the roof. The tiles are still warm from the sun as I lie back on the slope, my head near the point, and chart the constellations in the sky above.

5

The Third Summer

Adda's letters sit in a dog-eared pile on the writing desk in the library. There are dozens of them, and I've read them so many times that the parchment is worn and pliant, the ink faded. The letters chart her adventures all across the continent. Every time I read her words I hear them in her bright, confident tone, the princess I know so well and yet only really met for a few hours three and a half years ago.

    It's been three and a half years. I've never spent so long on one job, never spent so long in one *body*. I can't remember the last time I was tempted to lengthen Adda's arms to increase my reach while swinging from the beams in my bedroom, or swap her hair for a shorter, thinner style that was less stifling in the summer heat. I have forgotten my changeling tendencies in my seclusion, settling into a human life tethered to one form. When I regard my reflection in the looking glass I only ever see Adda's stormy blue eyes staring back at me, and the silver collar necklace that keeps the lapis lazuli stone pressed to my throat. I never take it off. I think my changeling eyes, those unearthly, empty pools of black, would unnerve me if I saw them again.

I fiddle absentmindedly with the curled corner of Adda's most recent letter to me. She sent it four months ago, and my reply went back to her immediately. Usually I would have received her response by now, along with one of the queen's care packages, but there has been no word from the palace in months. Delphine told me that Marie has lamented the lack of salt and wheat flour that she usually receives as part of the regular deliveries. Perhaps, after all this time, we really have been forgotten. Without the palace's horseman there is no way to get word to Throsne, to check whether anything is amiss. And even if I could, who would I appeal to? There is no point trying to contact my grandmother at the Maison du Lemorque – they are paid so handsomely by the royal family that I have no doubt she would leave me here for fifty years if required.

Adda's last missive was sent from Brillermare in the far north of Belforet, the upper point of the diamond-shaped kingdom. The few miles of coastline are home to Belforet's only sea port. Adda had gleefully recounted a flirtation with a handsome sea captain who had no idea who she was.

He says he loves me, Aster. I don't love him but I like him well enough. He says the way I laugh at the wind makes him want to kiss me – so I kiss him back, just to know what it feels like. I'm not naïve enough to think that it would ever be more than just a tryst ... but perhaps the trysting would be worth it. I know this freedom won't last forever. If I'm going to be with a man for the first time, I want it to be on my terms. Have you ever trysted with anyone? Tell me truly, did you enjoy it?

I had been contemplative as I composed my response.

I can't say I've ever really trysted with a man. I've been swived and bedded while decoying as someone else. There wasn't any choice in the matter, at least not for me, and it hardly made me eager to repeat the process. It was just part of the job. But as Aster Lemorque? No – most of the men who know what I really am are afraid of me, and those who aren't ... well, they're not the trysting type.

I want to know what happened next. Did the princess of Belforet give up her maidenhead to a sea captain in a Brillermare tavern? I hope Adda is looking after herself. I have no idea what system she and her mother have in place for exchanging letters, but I assume it relies on Adda being in a certain place at a certain time. Perhaps she has taken to the seas? I try not to dwell on the dangers she may be facing as I smooth the letter against the desktop and sigh, rising to my feet.

It's early in the day but already the heavy heat of August is building. I feel it as I take the stone steps up from the library to my bedchamber, pressing down on me like a storm cloud. Delphine is studying the open armoire critically as I enter, choosing my outfit for the day.

"Just the training clothes for now," I tell her, as if this isn't our daily routine.

"What have you been doing all this time? You're going to be boiling," she observes. "Surely it's too hot for training?"

I should have started my exercises sooner while the top room of the tower was still cool, but there's nothing I can do about it now. I shrug at Delphine.

"I'll have a bath ready for when you're done," she says.

"Thank you," I tell her with a smile.

Primrose Hugh

It's a pain to fill the copper tub in my washroom, requiring buckets of heated water sent up in multiple trips in the dumbwaiter. Most of the time I make do with a wash cloth in the basin so that Delphine and Annette aren't put out, but I love a long soak in the bath to ease my sore muscles after training.

Delphine bustles about while I don my training outfit and pull my hair back off my face, securing it with a ribbon. I stretch, lunge and bounce on my feet before I face the mannequin, my long-suffering opponent. The combat routines – jab-jab-cross, duck-jab-right hook, duck-jab-shuffle back – are second nature to me. My breath settles into a steady rhythm, my movements are fluid and lethal. I introduce strikes and kicks, dancing around the dummy, then draw my knife to stab and slice. Delphine pointedly ignores me as I shimmy up the bed post and swing out onto the beams to test my strength and balance. She doesn't think it's safe or princess-like. I do a few cartwheels just to rile her, my feet precise and sure.

My face is bright red and slick with sweat by the time I'm finished, but the exercise has left me feeling grounded and calm.

I groan with contentment as I slip into the bath, the tepid water like cool silk against my sweaty limbs. Delphine has scented the water with lavender and rose petals and the gentle perfume caresses my nose before I close my eyes and sink under into blissful, cool quiet.

By the time I've finished soaking, my bedchamber is awash with streaming summer sunlight, hot as a baker's oven. I can't bear the thought of being laced into a dress, so I pull on my lightest chemise and pad barefoot to the balcony, throwing open the doors. It lets in the gentlest suggestion of a breeze. When I lie down on the bed covers, limbs akimbo, it dances over the sheer fabric of my chemise and whispers against my face, cooling my still wet hair. I'm warm and tired and relaxed and comfortable, and within minutes I'm asleep.

Some time later my eyelids flutter open and ... there is a man. A man is in my bed chamber. A man is standing over me, his face hovering barely half a foot away from mine, and I *shriek* with surprise.

He cries out in return, a strangled sound that ends in an unmanly squeak, and immediately backs away, green eyes wide and hands out in front of him in a placating gesture. My heart is hammering like a horse's hooves in full gallop, I blink and blink and try to make sense of what is happening. There is a man in my tower. How is there a man in my tower?

"Please!" he says, his hands still spread in front of his chest as if in surrender, "I didn't mean to startle you! I'm not going to hurt you."

"What were you doing?" I ask breathlessly as I sit up with a hand on my chest, trying to will my heartbeat to calm.

He blinks and looks abashed as he says, "I ... I saw you there and I thought you might be ... I didn't know you were sleeping ..."

I frown in confusion. "You thought I might be ... dead?"

He shakes his head quickly, his cheeks flushing. "No, I didn't know if you were ... you know. Enchanted."

"Enchanted? Why would I be—" I trail off as I realise: a princess trapped in a tower, lying prone on a bed in the middle of the day ... He thought I was in some kind of enchanted sleep. Which means ...

"Were you going to *kiss* me?" I demand, outraged.

He has the good grace to turn even pinker and can't meet my eye as he says, "No! No, of course not! I mean ... well I wasn't sure – that is, I was only ..."

I cut off his blustering as I ask the question that should have been my first. "What are you doing here?"

He meets my gaze then, his expression as bewildered as mine must be. "I'm a knight. I'm rescuing you."

I notice that he is indeed wearing armour – and that he must be sweltering in this heat. Metal plates encase his arms and legs, accentuating the breadth of his shoulders. A sword is sheathed at his waist. He may even be wearing a chainmail shirt under his surcoat.

"But ... I don't need rescuing," I tell him sharply.

I must be dreaming. There is no way that this is real. Not a single person other than Delphine has stood this close to me in three and a half years. This thought spurs my next question.

"How did you get in here?"

"I shimmied up a rope and climbed in through the balcony," he explains.

I frown as I trace the route with my eyes. The balcony doors are still flung wide, and I see a rope tied to the balustrade. "Why on earth did you do that?"

He blinks a few times in confusion. "Well ... there wasn't a door, so ..."

"Of course there's a door," I say archly. "Who would build a tower without an entrance?"

I can't stop myself from being peevish. He may have all the noble intentions in the world, but that doesn't change the fact that neither I nor the real Adaliza need saving. I simply can't fall into my carefully rehearsed courtly manners in such a situation, and I'm certain that Adda would react similarly. Well, that's not entirely true – she would have punched him in the nose the minute she opened her eyes and saw his face hovering above hers.

Being Adaliza

The thought of Adda centres me somewhat. I lean across the bed and tug on the tasselled bell pull to summon Delphine before addressing him.

"Look, Sir ... What's your name?"

"Sir Finton Prest," he says quickly.

"Sir Finton – clearly you're operating under false instructions. And as much as I'd love to sit here debating the matter, I really ought to get dressed first."

I raise my eyebrows at him and he seems to realise suddenly that all I'm wearing is a scandalously sheer chemise. His cheeks immediately flood red again and he looks anywhere but at me.

"Of course, Your Highness," he stammers, and I have to admit that I delight a little in his discomfort.

Delphine then appears at the doorway and lets out a terrified scream that makes Sir Finton flinch and raise his hands in supplication again.

"Delphine, please can you show our unexpected guest to the library and then come back to help me dress?" I say calmly as my handmaiden stares in disbelief and opens and closes her mouth like a fish.

She obeys dumbly, leading the disconcerted knight down the stairs. I let out a long breath when I'm alone, smoothing back my loose hair. My pulse is still racing. No one is supposed to know where Adda is sequestered. How did Sir Finton find me? And why is he under the impression that I – that Adaliza – need rescuing? Surely the queen wouldn't let this happen. She knows that the real Adaliza isn't here.

What am I to do? How should I act? Grateful? Imperious? Outraged? I'm not prepared for this. If I pretend to be the real Adda I would turn him out on his ear – but should Princess Adaliza, heir to the throne of Belforet, act differently?

"What is going on?" Delphine squeaks as she hurries back

into the room and shuts the door with a slam.

"I don't know!" I confess. "He said he came to rescue me ... rescue Adaliza, I mean. We haven't heard from the queen in months. Something must have changed."

Delphine ushers me behind the dressing screen and throws a pretty silk gown over my head. It's lilac with wildflowers embroidered up the waist and lining the train that trails softly on the floor.

"What are we going to do?" Delphine frets. "What if he finds out ..."

"He's not going to find out," I reassure her. "This is my job – I play other people. We need to gather as much information as possible before we decide what to do next."

She nods, smoothing my skirts with shaking hands. "Ok. Ok, we can do this."

We. It's rare, to have an accomplice when a plan goes awry. I am more grateful than ever for Delphine's friendship.

I take her hand and squeeze it. "Yes, we can."

She pulls a face as her eyes trace the tangle of my hair, slept on while still wet.

"But first we need to sort out this bird's nest."

6

When Delphine and I descend the stone stairs and emerge into the library, I am the picture of regal grace. Delphine has braided my hair into an elegant coronet, finished with a silver diadem. Just as he is wearing his armour in preparation for battle, I am wearing mine. I am a vision in lilac and silver, pretty and feminine and composed. Sir Finton is standing with his hands behind his back facing the fireplace, and when he turns his eyes flare at the sight of me. "Your Highness," he says, dropping to one knee and bowing his head respectfully. "May I apologise once again for my intrusion."

"Rise, Sir Finton," I say coolly, and he straightens as I step closer to him.

I appraise him carefully. He stands a head taller than Adaliza and carries all that gleaming armour lightly, as if it is a part of him. He is young to be a knight – only a few years older than me and Adda, I suspect. His features are strong and his expression is open, unused to courtly scheming or subterfuge. Green eyes, full lips, freckled skin. A head of thick chestnut hair cut short at the back and sides and long in the front, bouncing up into a quiff over his forehead. Young and gallant and idealistic, I surmise. Easy to manipulate.

I lower myself into a chair and sit straight backed, gesturing towards the opposite chair with a wave of my hand, but Sir Finton doesn't take it. He continues to stand before me, and I can't decide whether he looks more like a man on trial or a naughty boy prepared for a scalding.

"I believe we are working at cross purposes," I tell him. "I haven't heard from the palace in months, since my mother's last package. How did you know to find me here? And why do you think I need rescuing?"

Sir Finton's eyebrows pull together and his lips press into a line before he speaks. An expression of ... pity. My stomach sinks in preparation for bad news.

"I'm sorry to be the one to tell you this, Your Highness," he says gently. "The plague reached Throsne at the turn of the year. The queen – your mother – passed away three months ago."

Delphine, who has come to stand by the side of my chair, lets out a shocked intake of breath and presses her hand over her mouth. I blink rapidly as I try to process the news.

"What?" I breathe.

The queen had been kind to me. And now she is gone – taken by the invisible threat that has haunted Belforet for years. It was the king's worst fear, now realised. The reason he sent Adaliza away. But ... for me, for Adda, the death of the queen has more pressing ramifications. No one else knows that I'm a decoy. No one knows that the real Adaliza is off adventuring in goodness knows where, unaware of the tragedy unfolding in Throsne.

"Your father, the king, has also been gravely ill," Sir Finton continues. "He escaped death but his lungs are thought to be permanently damaged by the plague. He sent out an announcement proclaiming that whichever nobleman could find and rescue Princess Adaliza from her tower could have her hand in marriage."

I stare at Sir Finton in shock for a few long moments.

"Marriage?" I ask faintly.

The knight looks abashed – it's an expression I'm already used to seeing on his face. He's here ... to *marry* me. To marry Adaliza, that is. He expects ... how can I go through with this? How long will I have to be Adaliza before the real Adda comes home to Throsne? There's no way that she will accept this turn of events.

"And if ... if I don't wish to marry?" I ask him stiffly, my gaze cold and piercing.

Sir Finton blanches under the weight of it, and I'm glad. What did he expect? To have swept Adaliza into his arms and rode off into the sunset with her, no questions asked?

"Your Highness ... in order to ascend the throne, you must marry," Sir Finton reminds me carefully.

I know the laws of Belforet. A royal female can inherit the throne, but only if she's married. If the king is ill and demanding this stupid rescue contest now, he must be fearful that Adaliza needs to secure her accession before he dies and rival claimants attempt to usurp her.

"And you're first, so you've *won* me? I don't get any say in the decision?" I fume.

"It would be my pleasure – my privilege – to have your hand in marriage," he says, but his pretty words illicit nothing but a scowl from me. "I am a Knight of the Order of the Ivory Maiden, dedicated to the protection of women. When I heard of the contest I immediately took up arms to find you. There are many others searching for you, some with ... unscrupulous intentions. I sought to protect you from that, from them."

He's a romantic – I want to roll my eyes at him. But he makes a valid point. Adaliza's husband would be made king consort when she took the throne, an extremely powerful position that most would see as a way to wrest rule from a feeble woman. If the king launched an open contest for her hand in marriage, there must be scores of noblemen willing to try their luck at finding her. Refusing Sir Finton will not make this problem go away. How long will it be before other knights discover the tower? It's no longer a refuge – it's a homing beacon. And I'm the prize for finding it.

I have to play along. I have to go back to Throsne with my knight in shining armour, to play the rescued maiden, and somehow track down Adda before the wedding can go ahead. It is up to her to decide how to proceed – it's not my right to make those decisions on her behalf.

I try to settle my roiling emotions, my whirling thoughts, as I take a steadying breath and address Sir Finton again.

"So ... what now?"

He is looking at me warily, as if afraid I'll snap at him again. Good. Adaliza is not a spineless pushover, and neither am I. We will not go easily. The young knight clears his throat.

"Now we return to Throsne, to your father."

I have no allies in the palace, no one who knows my true identity other than my family at the Maison du Lemorque. Perhaps I can contact them on the journey back and beseech them for an extraction plan? Or I could bolt from Sir Finton when we're on the road and try to find Adda myself? Both are better options than barricading myself in the tower and sitting tight while vultures in shining armour gather around me.

"Very well," I say coldly, making my displeasure at the situation known.

With that I get to my feet, stride to the stairs without a backwards glance and leave him in the library.

We leave the tower in the early afternoon. Delphine and I share a final lunch together in my bedchamber, both of us quiet with apprehension. I assume that Marie, who can't help but feed anyone who comes within shouting distance of her kitchen, is seeing to Sir Finton, but I don't bother to check. He can starve for all I care.

Delphine helps me to change out of the lilac silk dress, swapping it for a more durable travelling outfit in cobalt blue that brings out the colour in Adaliza's eyes. I spin and kick in the gown and find that my limbs are relatively unhampered by the loose skirts – good. I refuse the embroidered slippers that Delphine sets out for me, choosing a sturdy pair of boots instead. I need to be ready to run or fight. There are deep pockets in my skirts and I assemble the things I want to keep close: the steak knife, Adda's letters, a spare hair ribbon. The other items I will need for travelling are packed into a bag by Delphine.

My heart pounds as I descend the stone stairs of the tower for the last time. I continue down past the library, down past the servants' quarters, down past the kitchen I haven't set eyes on for years. Delphine leads me along the dark tunnel and up out into the open air of the glade. I shut my eyes for a moment and breathe deeply, rooting my feet in the grass, feeling the warm breeze on my face. I'm free. How many times have I imagined emerging from that trap door? I'm leaving. It's what I wanted. It's not what I want at all.

Marie, Annette and Claude are standing in a line just as they did when I arrived at the tower. They bow and curtsy smartly when I turn to them, but I ignore the rules of conduct as I embrace Marie, whose eyes are glassy as she hugs me back.

"Oh, Your Highness, I'll miss you," she says, and my chest aches a little at her genuine tone.

"You're the best cook in Belforet, Marie," I tell her. "This isn't the last you'll see of me, not if I can help it."

She gives me a watery smile as we pull away from each other. I smile warmly at Annette, who is still shy with me, and look to Claude. His attention is entirely fixated on Delphine at my side. The intensity on both of their faces, as if they're having some kind of silent conversation, makes me look away. After years of infatuation, I know that Delphine finally discovered that Claude returned her feelings a few months ago. She has been floating on air ever since. And although she knew that one day she would return to her old life in Throsne, I don't think she was prepared for it to happen so suddenly. I wish I could give them a private moment to say goodbye.

My gaze lifts to the two horses tethered in the shade of an oak tree on the edge of the clearing, and my expression immediately turns cold. Sir Finton is watching me, one hand resting on the neck of his huge chestnut destrier. A boy of maybe fourteen stands with a second smaller horse, a dappled grey. I try not to grimace as I approach. Urgh, horses. There will be no carriage ride back to Throsne, it seems.

"Sir Finton," I say coolly as I near.

"Your Highness," he says with a respectful bow of his head. "May I introduce you to my squire, Rollo de Sommette."

Being Adaliza

The boy bows deeply and I get a view of his mop of dark hair. "It's an honour, Your Highness."

I nod in response. He is gangly, as if he has recently had a growth spurt and isn't quite used to the length of his limbs yet. It's a feeling I can sympathise with.

"May I assist you?" Sir Finton asks politely, gesturing towards the massive horse at his side.

Two horses for the four of us – me, Sir Finton, Delphine and Rollo. I suppose he expects me to share the saddle with him, to cling to his back as he rides. I will do no such thing.

I try to hide my swallow as I size up the destrier. Convincingly riding any horse would be a challenge for me, but a huge war horse? It towers over me, all gleaming chestnut over thick muscle. I take a step closer and its nostrils flare. The horse startles backwards a pace, throwing its head and giving a warning snort in my direction.

"Alezan!" Sir Finton chides, reaching for the horse's bridle and looking to me apologetically. "I'm sorry, he's usually solid as a rock."

The horse's loam brown eyes are fixed on me. *What are you, untrustworthy one?*, it seems to say. *Wrong. You smell wrong. You are wrong.* I glare straight back at it. There's no way I'm risking my neck on that beast's back.

"I will walk," I tell Sir Finton.

His brow creases. "All the way to Throsne? Your Highness, I must insist ..."

"I have spent nearly four years sitting around in that tower, wishing I could walk through these woods," I interrupt him. "I don't intend to sit again for some time. I will walk."

Sir Finton exchanges a look with his young squire, but shrugs. "As you wish. I will walk alongside you."

"There's really no need, take your mount," I say

dismissively.

Delphine has approached us and is also staring warily up at the destrier. Her gaze flicks to her slippered feet, as if weighing whether she too can insist on walking, but we both know she won't last more than an hour in the forest without proper boots.

"My Lady," Sir Finton says gallantly, cupping his hands and bending down to allow her to step into them.

With little effort he boosts Delphine onto the huge beast's back, where she straightens her skirts and looks down at me nervously. Rollo untethers both horses and mounts his own steed. Sir Finton, standing with Alezan's reins in one hand, looks back at me with a crooked smile.

"Into the woods, then," he says, and I follow reluctantly as he leads us out of the glade and into the shade of the ancient trees.

7

It's blessedly cool in the shade of the forest, sheltered from the heat of the late summer sun. I drink in the sheer size of the trunks all around me, the rustle and snap of the forest floor underfoot, the smell of moss and soil. I let it fill my lungs, basking in the freedom of walking in the woods as I have dreamt of doing for so long. My legs are moving, my lungs are working, my eyes can't stop roving around and upwards as I take it all in. For a while I am so delighted by my surroundings that I can almost forget about who walks by my side and all that he represents.

Sir Finton tries to strike up conversation with me a few times but he gives up after receiving dismissive one-word answers. We walk the overgrown track through the woods mostly in silence for hours, stopping only once to rest and water the horses by a small stream.

I sit on a mossy log, bending and straightening my feet under my long skirts to stretch out my legs. I'm aching, but I won't let him know that. Sir Finton passes me a waterskin and I thank him without making eye contact, swallowing down mouthfuls of the spring water greedily.

"We're still a few hours out from the edge of the forest," Sir Finton says. "Are you sure you don't want to ride, Your Highness? I would rather we're not caught in the woods at night. This is a wild place. There is no telling what beasts might roam these parts."

Delphine looks at me in alarm from where she sits by the stream bank, a plea clear in her wide brown eyes. I twist my lips as I consider. My legs are sore and my feet are heavy already, and as much as I love the woods I really don't relish the idea of making camp in here at night. I have heard the howl of wolves drift to my balcony on a night-time breeze. But ... the thought of having to mount that giant, unpredictable destrier – not to mention being pressed up against Sir Finton for hours – makes me even more uncomfortable. There is so little choice left to me in this situation that I need the sense of control that this decision gives me.

"Then let's walk faster," I say.

I rise to my aching feet, meeting Sir Finton's eye for the first time since we left the tower, raising my chin in a dare to object. His green eyes narrow slightly and he gives me a small smile as if he knows how much my body is already hurting.

"As you wish, Your Highness," he says politely.

Rollo appears from behind his horse, eating an apple. "All ready, Fin," he tells Sir Finton.

"It's *My Lord* to you," the knight corrects quietly, as if I can't hear every word, but Rollo just gives him a casual shrug and a grin.

"Old habits die hard," the squire says, throwing Sir Finton

an apple with his free hand. "Would you like one, Your Highness?"

I try to hide my smile. "Yes, please."

Rollo produces a third apple from his saddlebag and throws it to me. I snatch it out of the air with one hand.

"Rollo!" Sir Finton hisses before turning to me with an apologetic look on his face. "I'm sorry about my squire. He's ... new to the post. And yet to learn his manners."

"But she caught it!" Rollo says in defence.

Sir Finton shakes his head in disbelief and turns back to me. "Our family estates are side by side. We grew up together," he explains.

I much prefer Rollo's easy-going attitude to Sir Finton's unwavering politeness, which is getting on my nerves. But I just take a large bite out of my apple in response and stride back out onto the track.

Hours later, the light in the forest under the tree canopies turns from luminous green to twilight blue. I've set a punishing pace since our rest stop but we're still not out of the woods. I listen keenly to the sounds of the forest around us, unnerved by the scuffling, chittering and snapping that had seemed a harmless accompaniment to our journey during the daytime. The fading light throws shadows that could hide any number of dangers. A crow's caw sounds close by and I startle, stepping closer to Sir Finton's side on reflex, before shaking myself mentally and deliberately stepping away again, chin high.

"We're close to the edge now, we'll be out before nightfall," Sir Finton reassures me, his tone kind with understanding. I don't look at him. "There's an inn on the Forest Road where we can stay for the night."

Indeed, by the time we break through the final line of trees, the wide sky opens up around us and we can watch the last watery purples and blues of the sunset fade into darkness. I sag a little with relief, feeling every tight muscle in my legs and each blister on my feet.

The inn, which has a swinging sign above the door emblazoned with 'The Wayfarer's Rest', is the single beacon of brightness and noise along the road. Light streams from each of the windows, along with the sounds of loud male chatter, clinking tankards and bawdy tavern music. Rollo leads the two horses to the stables and Delphine and I trail Sir Finton through the front door into the hubbub of the taproom.

Other than a few serving wenches carrying platters and avoiding the wandering hands of their patrons, everyone in the taproom is male. There are weary travellers in tattered tunics, local workmen with craggy, sun-darkened faces, a few smartly dressed merchants eating magnanimously at the wooden tables, ignoring the rowdy company around them. And ... there are knights. A number of them, most without their armour but still wearing their surcoats and weapons strapped to their sword belts. One tall and gallant, one portly and ruddy with drink, one old and serious-faced, one pock-marked and leering. Sir Finton freezes in front of me and Delphine when he sees them, squaring his shoulders to block us from view. He quickly herds us back out of the door.

"Those knights," I ask him, "are they questing to find me?"

Sir Finton's expression is grave. "Yes, I suspect so. And if they see another knight travelling with young women ... They might guess who you are and try to take you for their own."

My eyes widen at that, both in alarm at the casual brutality of the notion and in indignance that I might be taken by anybody against my will. Those men ... they feel they are entitled to me, entitled to Adaliza. I think of their searching eyes, their cheeks flushed with ale. It makes me want to shudder.

"When Rollo is back from the stables, I'll go in and get us some rooms for the night," Sir Finton reassures us.

I nod, glancing at his surcoat. It's pale green, emblazoned at the chest with a female figure in cream. He is a member of the Order of the Ivory Maiden, sworn to protect women. I had scoffed at that, back in the tower. Now I realise how lucky I may be to have been found by him first, rather than any of *them*.

Sir Finton goes back into the taproom when Rollo appears, although I'm pretty certain that I could take on and beat more fighters than the skinny youth could. No one exits or enters the inn before Sir Finton emerges again with an iron key grasped in his fist.

"There's only one room left, if the two of you don't mind sharing?" he asks me and Delphine.

"That will be fine," I confirm. "Where will you sleep?"

Sir Finton throws a look towards his squire. "Sorry, Rollo, you're in the stables tonight."

Rollo makes a show of objecting but good humour flashes in his dark eyes.

"And I'll keep watch outside your door," Sir Finton continues, turning back to me and Delphine.

"Is that really necessary?" I ask.

I'm not the only one who has spent hours walking through the forest – and in full armour, too. He must be as tired as I am. It makes me uncomfortable to think of him standing in a draughty corridor all night while I sleep soundly in a comfortable bed.

His expression is honest and wary. "It's my responsibility

to keep you safe. I don't trust the drunkards in this tavern."

There's no room for discussion in his tone. And besides, there's only one room left – where else would he sleep? Certainly not *inside* the room with me and Delphine.

I nod to him, unsmiling. "Very well."

I'm a little nervous when we enter the taproom for a second time, walking straight to the large staircase at the back that leads to the rooms above. I keep my head down, not looking towards the men leaning against the bar, sitting at the tables, standing in groups with their hands wrapped around their tankards. It makes me wish it was winter so that we could hide our faces with hooded cloaks – at this time of year, it would be more suspicious to wear the extra layers.

If anyone notices us, they don't vocalise it. I breathe a little easier when we're clear of the taproom.

Our room is tiny but relatively clean, with a large wooden bed and a round table with two rickety chairs taking up the majority of the floor space. Sir Finton apologises for the rustic room but it's far from the least glamorous inn I've ever stayed in. He disappears to bring some supper up to us from the kitchen and I collapse on the bed, abandoning all decorum.

"My feet!" I groan.

Delphine smiles as she perches next to me. "It serves you right for being so stubborn. You should have got on the horse."

I kick off my boots and sit up to pull off my stockings and inspect my sore feet. There are angry blisters on the back of both heels and at the side of my big toes.

"Horses hate me. I'd be in more danger of injury if I got on that huge beast of a destrier."

I stroke my magic down my feet and feel it lick against the skin in a soothing wave. Within moments the blisters are gone. I toughen up the skin around my heels a little with half a thought in the hope of preventing the torture tomorrow.

"Oh stop, he's a pleasant enough horse," Delphine says.

She smiles at me a little wickedly. "And from his back I get an excellent view of you staunchly ignoring poor Sir Finton as you stomp through the forest."

"Poor Sir Finton?" I scoff. "Whose side are you on?"

"Yours, of course. But he can't tear his eyes away from you. It's rather sweet, actually."

I ignore her observation. He can't tear his eyes away from *Adaliza*. It has nothing to do with me.

A large bowl and ewer sit on a creaking sideboard against the opposite wall. We take turns washing our faces and hands, and I feel less travel weary by the time I hear Sir Finton's tread on the stairs. He enters with a tray of food and the savour wafting off it makes my mouth water. There's a huge meat pie, a tureen of greens, a small cob loaf and a bottle of wine with two glasses. Sir Finton sets it on the table and says he's going to find Rollo. The minute he's gone I set upon the pie with single-minded ferocity.

Delphine serves herself a more modest plate of food and eats in small, elegant bites. I am too hungry for that charade, shovelling in as much as I can before Sir Finton comes back and I have to pretend to be ladylike.

"Do you ever get full?" Delphine asks me as I dunk a hunk of dense bread into the pie juices.

"Rarely," I shrug.

It's my magic. It burns through energy at a rate faster than a normal human diet can sustain, even when I'm not shifting all the time.

There is nothing more than a pie crust left in the large dish by the time Sir Finton returns. He blinks at it in surprise.

"Oh, I didn't expect you to ..."

He cuts himself off before he can insult either one of us. If he thought he would be sharing the pie with us, he can think again.

"The princess has a legendary appetite," Delphine says sweetly, and I elbow her surreptitiously in the ribs.

He smiles. "I'm glad to hear it. Well, I'll get something for myself in the taproom. Are you well settled in here for the night?"

"We are," I say, and, "Thank you," as a begrudging afterthought.

"Very well. One of us will be outside your door all night. Just call out if you need anything."

I nod.

He fixes me with those well-meaning green eyes. "Good night, Your Highness."

He bows his head and leaves the room. I don't need him – need anyone – to stand guard over me. I am quite capable of looking after myself and Delphine if trouble stirs under this roof. But ... as I lie in the bed and hear the slight creak of floorboards outside the door, I can't help feeling ... reassured. It isn't long before I fall into a deep, exhausted sleep.

8

The next morning, after breakfast and dressing, we descend the staircase into a considerably subdued taproom compared with last night. It is still busy – most of the round tables are occupied by groups of travellers eating their breakfast before they continue down the Forest Road, or to the nearby town of Sudferry which offers the last chance for passage up the River Fluet before the road disappears into the Old Woods. Judging by the heads hanging heavy in the room, I guess that there are more than a few who are feeling the after-effects of all the ale they drank last night.

A number of gazes swivel to us as we take the final few steps down the staircase. I try not to stiffen under their attention. Without the distraction of lairy drinking partners and loud music, they are much more likely to notice two young women and the protective knight trying to shuffle them out the door. I look away, relaxing Adaliza's regal posture, making my body language convey that I'm harmless, inconsequential, not worth noticing. I don't have to shift my form to change my entire bearing. I hope it's enough.

The stables are bustling. Rollo leads our two horses towards us, their coats shining in the morning sunlight. Sir Finton runs his hand along the neck of the destrier, murmuring to the horse affectionately. His chestnut hair is a remarkably close match to the colour of the horse's coat. I wonder whether he chose his mount for that reason.

Sir Finton turns to me. "My Lady – may I help you into the saddle?"

I narrow my eyes at him and then the destrier, who is staring back at me with distrust. "No, thank you. I will walk."

"But we are out of the woods now, and the road ahead is dusty. Surely you would prefer to ride?"

"If *you* would prefer to ride, Sir Finton, please don't let me stop you."

I don't mean it as a challenge, but he pauses and the muscle in his jaw flickers as he clenches his teeth, and I can see that the knight takes it as one. "I will walk by your side."

I shrug, and Delphine gives me a look that says *"stop being obstructive for the sake of it"* before she is assisted onto the back of the destrier.

When we leave the inn, the road is busier than I've ever seen it as travellers set off on their various journeys. It soon quietens down. Our small party is overtaken by riders on horseback, walking, trotting or cantering depending on their urgency, stringing out along the road. Sir Finton was right; it is unpleasantly dusty at ground level. I can't help but cough when other horses pass us, their hooves kicking up clouds of dust from the road, which is parched in the heat of summer. Before long I'm hot and filthy and in a simmering bad mood. Rollo whistles a good-natured tune from the back of his dappled grey, and I resist the urge to snap at him to be quiet.

Being Adaliza

We're alone on the road when it all happens so quickly. I hear the sound of rapid hoof beats behind us but I keep my gaze on the road beyond my boots, assuming we'll soon be overtaken by another cantering rider. A familiar sound makes my head snap up in alarm: the whistle of an arrow sailing over our heads and a *thunk* as it embeds into the trunk of a roadside tree. Sir Finton immediately pulls his horse to a stop with the reins in his left hand, while his right hand goes to the hilt of the broadsword sheathed at his waist.

"Behind the horses!" he shouts to me as Rollo guides his own mount to corral me in. I see a group of armed men galloping towards us down the road. My heart is hammering, my breath is jagged as I see how quickly they are advancing. They will be upon us in moments.

Delphine, sitting high above me on the destrier's back, is staring at the attackers in shock, her eyes wide and face wan. Sir Finton reaches a hand up to her.

"Get down, My Lady," he orders, and she looks to him in terrified incomprehension for a second before she leans forward on the horse's neck to manoeuvre her leg over the saddle. Her limbs don't seem to cooperate and she wriggles on her stomach, taking too long – because before she can slide off the horse's back, one of the attackers rides level with the destrier and an arm catches her around the waist. Delphine screams as the man drags her from the saddle and holds her dangling in midair from the side of his horse as he rides past us down the road.

"No!" I howl, reaching my arms out towards Delphine as if I could pluck her back. Her keening wails slice through me as surely a blade.

"After her, Rollo!" Sir Finton commands, and his squire takes off in pursuit.

Sir Finton and I face the oncoming riders. There are three

of them, all with their weapons drawn. Sir Finton steps in front of me defensively and withdraws his broadsword with a *shing*, but I back up a few paces and sink into my own fighting stance. Shock and anger makes my hands shake as I lift them into a guard, but I ball my fists and grit my teeth. I will not let this happen. These men will not succeed today.

The first rider swings his sword at Sir Finton as he passes, which the knight blocks with a mighty clang of metal on metal, quickly swivelling to unbalance the rider and use the momentum to force him off his horse. The attacker keeps his seat, but I don't see what happens next because the second rider is heading for me at speed, one arm reaching towards me as if he intends to sweep me off my feet and take me with him. I have barely a moment to rue the fact I'm not carrying a proper blade before he is upon me, and I let his arm slam into me and hook under my armpit. I am dragged behind his horse for a pace or two before I kindle my magic, sending it to my bones, my muscles, making them as dense and heavy as possible – like steel, like stone. The man grunts at the unexpected weight, so heavy that it yanks him down and backwards. He drops the reins and his horse startles and rears, sending him out of the saddle and on top of me in a heap in the road, dust swirling around us.

I manage to shove the startled man off me and scramble back a step, leaving him in a heap. He is wearing a full chainmail tunic with a hood and leather gauntlets at his wrists, leaving no part of his body exposed other than his face. My hand-to-hand combat skills will be of no use here – I'm more likely to hurt myself on all that metal than land a debilitating blow. I pull the steak knife from the pocket of my gown as the man rolls onto all fours and glowers up at me, panting.

He opens his mouth to say something to me – something

unseemly, judging by the hateful look on his puce face – but I don't let him speak. I know that as soon as he heaves himself to his feet, I'll be at a disadvantage. So I strike, quick as an asp, and he gives a shrieking, gurgling cry of pain as I sink my small knife into his right eye socket. I leave him writhing on the floor and spin, panting, to assess the others.

One of the assailants is on his knees on the ground, close to unconsciousness, and Sir Finton is trading sword blows with the other. He moves beautifully, graceful despite the weight of his plate armour, and I can see that the attacker is outclassed. I turn to look back up the road, but I can't see the galloping figures of either Delphine and her captor or Rollo in pursuit. A movement in the corner of my eye makes me turn back to the men locked in deadly swordplay. The second man, the one I thought was barely conscious, has staggered to his feet and unsheathed a knife from his weapons belt. He is striding unsteadily towards Sir Finton's back, and I'm moving in an instant. I leap on the man from behind, tearing his attention from Sir Finton, and kick viciously at any part of him that comes into contact with my boots.

"You bitch!" the man grunts.

He spins, trying to dislodge me, but I cling on with all my might, pulling my forearm into his windpipe and managing to kick his fist – he drops the blade with a clatter. He roars, and with a ferocious shake my hold around his neck loosens and I fly backwards. I only manage to stumble back a step before he is on me, with wrath flaming in his eyes. He throws a gauntleted fist into my jaw, snapping my head back – and everything turns black.

My eyelids are heavy as I force them open, blinking at the grit in my eyes and the brightness of the sun. I'm flat on my back, facing the bright summer sky. My head bangs like a drum and I let out a groan of pain. Suddenly there are two faces looking down at me, dirty and fraught with worry.

"Your Highness!"

Sir Finton lays a hand on the side of my face, stilling my movements.

"You're ok – gently now. No need to move."

His tone is soothing, as if he's speaking to a nervous horse. My eyes trace his face as I fight the disorientation that makes me feel slow and dizzy. Blood wells in his hairline from a small cut. His face is streaked with dust, making his eyes look very green in contrast. People think that eyes can express all sorts of feelings, but they're wrong. It is the way that the skin around the eyes tightens and creases, the shape and tension of the brows, the many complex muscles of the face that convey emotion, not the eyeballs themselves. I read the relief that I'm awake in the wideness of his eyes, the tense worry in the set of his mouth, the thrum of battle still evident in his stiff posture.

And then I remember.

"Delphine?" I gasp.

He shakes his head, his brow creased, and I look to Rollo, who is kneeling next to Sir Finton. The boy's skin is pallid, his lips bloodless, and then I notice the arrow shaft stuck in his shoulder.

"I chased them, but there were others up ahead – one found his mark. I'm sorry, Your Highness ..." Rollo's voice is tight with pain.

I grimace and pull myself up onto my elbows.

"Slowly," Sir Finton warns, his hand supporting the back of my neck.

I look around us, blinking against the brightness again.

There are two bodies slumped in the dust – Sir Finton's opponent and the man who punched me. A pool of blood is all that remains of my would-be abductor, the one I stabbed in the eye. Sir Finton follows my gaze.

"That one fled. You've been unconscious for less than five minutes."

My face feels stiff and swollen. I try to move my jaw from side to side; a jolt of pain lashes down my face, making me squeeze my eyes shut and grimace. I summon my magic and let it bloom under my skin, decompressing the nerves in my head and draining the excess fluid from my jaw, fixing the tissue and soothing the bone. I make sure not to touch the capillaries in my skin that were ruptured on impact with my attacker's fist. I can't come out of this completely unscathed – I keep the bruise. The banging drum in my head is muted, but the headache doesn't go away completely. I'm tired and thirsty.

"We need to go after Delphine," I rasp, trying to push myself up, but Sir Finton catches my arms gently.

"Not yet," he says.

"What do you mean, not yet?" I snap. "We can't leave her with those men!"

The longer we wait, the further they will flee. Delphine must be so scared. I can't stand the thought of abandoning her.

Sir Finton's response is calm but firm. "You're in no state to gallop off after them, and neither is Rollo. Acting on impulse when we're not fit to fight will only get us killed."

"Then you go," I insist.

He shakes his head. "I'm not leaving you."

"But ... but ..."

My voice chokes, there's an unbearable weight in my chest.

"It's my fault," I say, barely more than a croak.

Sir Finton's hands are still on my arms. Although they are strapped into fearsome metal gauntlets, he holds me lightly in place and his thumbs skim over the fabric of my sleeves in whisper-soft reassurance.

"None of this is your fault," he says softly, but he doesn't understand.

There's only one reason why they would have snatched Delphine and not come back for me. They think that *she's* the princess. Of course they do – would the princess really be walking in the dusty road, or fight back like a hellcat when attacked? I remember all those watchful eyes at the inn. If I had played my part properly, she would never have been taken in my place. *I'm* the decoy, not her. She's not equipped for this. I think of how she always cringed away from my combat manoeuvres, how she can barely say boo to a goose.

I bite my lip to stop it trembling and try to swallow down my emotions. My eyes settle on Rollo, who still has an arrow sticking out of him. I'm being selfish. We need to see to his injury and make a plan. Sir Finton is right.

"Ok," I say unevenly, then repeat it again to be sure of myself. "Ok. What next?"

9

We agree that it's best to leave the road. Whoever took Delphine was working in a group and we don't know if they have more accomplices who might come back to finish us off. We consider going back to the inn to clean ourselves up, but decide against it. Rollo can't trot or canter in his condition and it will be at least an hour's walk back the way we came – plus, we want to avoid any potential entanglements with the knights we encountered there. Sir Finton says that he remembers a village nearby. We will surely be able to find clean water there at the very least, and maybe even a healer for Rollo.

Sir Finton carefully helps his squire onto the dappled grey before turning to me.

"Can you ride with him? He might hurt himself further if he has to take the reins, or even fall out of the saddle if he faints."

I look at Rollo's pale, pain-pinched face and the shaft still sticking out of his shoulder. He must be in agony. Sir Finton didn't want to attempt to wrench out the arrow on the dusty road.

I nod. "Of course."

I step into Sir Finton's laced hands and mount the grey horse in front of Rollo, snatching up the reins. The beast beneath me takes a few nervous steps, flicking its ears and blowing out a huff of displeasure. The jolt of movement makes Rollo groan in pain behind me. Sir Finton takes its bridle and settles it with a few murmured words before turning to his own horse. He steps up into the stirrup and mounts the destrier in one easy movement.

"All ready?" he calls to us, and I nod back at him.

He leads the way over the verge and through a gap in the hedge into a barley field. I nudge the horse with my heels and try to keep my balance as it lurches into movement, following the destrier. My back is stiff, my knuckles are white as they hold the bunched reins in a death grip. As we turn to round the hedge, I wobble dangerously. My stomach plummets and I'm convinced I'll tumble out of the saddle, but arms reach out on either side of me to steady me.

"It's ok, Your Highness," Rollo says quietly, too quietly for Sir Finton to hear. "I won't let you fall."

He shouldn't have to do anything, he's the one with an arrow sticking out of him. I'm pathetic, to be so disconcerted by a horse.

"Sorry," I mutter back. "Horses don't like me, and I don't like them."

"Colombe is a good horse. She'll—" he hisses in pain as we walk over an uneven patch and it jostles him in the saddle, "She'll follow Fin without any trouble."

Thankfully it's hardly any time at all before we reach a fast-flowing stream. We dismount, both Sir Finton and me helping Rollo down onto the ground and settling him on a felled tree trunk.

"What can I do to help?" I ask the knight as he rifles through the panniers on his horse.

"Are you squeamish?" he asks.

"No," I reply truthfully. I've dressed wounds and reset bones, even if my own ailments can mostly be fixed by magic.

He nods approvingly and we both walk back to Rollo. Sir Finton examines his shoulder. His squire is not wearing the plate armour that could stop an arrow from entering the body – only a tunic in the same pale green as his own. There is only a little blood, which is why Sir Finton didn't remove the arrow immediately – it's keeping the wound closed. Luckily the arrow has gone straight through the shoulder; I can see the barbed arrow head protruding out the back. The nasty head is designed to cause as much damage as possible if it is pulled out of a wound. Luckily we can break off the fletching at the front and pull out the shaft from the back.

I glance down at the items that Sir Finton has assembled. A knife, a saucepan, a bone needle and a length of what must be catgut, a bundled up old undershirt with yellowed cuffs and stains flecking the sleeves.

"Wait," I say and rise to my feet.

Both men look up in surprise and watch as I dig through my own pack tied to the destrier. I return with a linen chemise. It's much newer and cleaner than the shirt, and it offers more fabric.

"There's no need ..." Sir Finton starts when he understands my intention, but he stops as I use the knife to tear down the seam of the chemise in one long motion, and then rip the fabric into strips.

"Ok, continue," I say when I have a pile of bandages ready.

Rollo swallows thickly in apprehension.

"Can you hold him while I break the shaft?" Sir Finton asks me.

I nod and kneel behind Rollo, holding him under the armpits to try to keep him still. Sir Finton doesn't give any warning before he snaps the arrow shaft. Rollo cries out in pain and flinches, but I hold him still.

"Well done, Rollo – we're halfway there," Sir Finton reassures him.

He moves to Rollo's back and I take up position in front, my gaze fixed on Rollo's ashen, sweaty face. His eyes are roving everywhere, he's breathing heavily.

"Look at me, focus on me," I tell him.

His dark eyes, pupils dilated, settle on my stormy blue ones and I hold him there. He looks so young – a boy, not a man. Again, Sir Finton doesn't give any warning, no opportunity for him to tense, before he yanks out the arrow from behind in one clean movement. Rollo gives out another gargled, pain-addled cry and tears track down his dust-caked cheeks.

We have to move quickly now that the arrow is free and the wound is open. Sir Finton uses the knife to cut away Rollo's tunic, exposing a skinny, pale torso and a cascade of blood that flows from the front and back of his shoulder. I hold a wad of fabric to the entry wound while Sir Finton sews the exit wound together, then swaps positions with me to sew up the front.

I grab the saucepan and go to the edge of the stream. The water is clear enough that I can see every rock on the stream bed and the tiny fish that dart just under the surface. I fill the pan and return to Rollo's side. Sir Finton nods at me as I soak one of the squares of linen, wring it out and then gently sluice the blood from Rollo's back and chest. The water in the pan is pink by the time I'm finished. Together, Sir Finton and I dress the wounds and use the long strips of fabric I tore off the chemise to wrap Rollo's shoulder.

"How does that feel?" Sir Finton asks.

Rollo's eyes are closed and his face is still grey, but his voice is steady when he replies, "Better. Thank you, Fin. And thank you, Your Highness."

Sir Finton's green eyes lift to mine, as if remembering that I am a princess and not a healer's assistant. We have hardly spoken since we dismounted, but we've been working harmoniously side by side, anticipating each other's movements. He had dropped his gallant, overly polite ways and ... I hadn't actively disliked him for it. I know better than to hope he will drop them forever.

"We should clean up too," I say pointing at the stream, rising to my feet and walking over before he can answer.

I scoop up handfuls of stream water and dash them over my face, my breath hitching at the shock of cold. I run my hands over my skin, scrubbing off the grime of dust, and round the back of my neck. My hair is a mess. The braided updo that Delphine secured against my head this morning is sagging and tousled. My heart lurches at the thought of her – she's gone. She's been stolen away and I'm here thinking about the state of my hair. I pull at the pins angrily, letting the locks fall around me in a snarl. I don't have the patience to sit and comb it all through. Instead I extract the length of ribbon from my pocket and gather my hair back off my face, securing it with a bow the way I do when I'm exercising.

A splash to my right makes me glance up and I see Sir Finton washing himself in the stream a little further down the bank. His surcoat, armour and chainmail sit in a pile by his side. I haven't seen him without the many layers of metal and fabric covering his body before. He has the sleeves of his undertunic pulled back to expose his forearms. They are muscled and dappled with freckles, I notice. Like his face. I look away.

My blue travelling gown isn't ripped after the fight but it is filthy. I beat at the skirts with my hands but it doesn't make a huge difference. It needs to be washed, but there is no time for that.

"We need to change our clothes," I say to Sir Finton.

"What?" He looks over at me, water dripping off his face.

"You are clearly a knight with a squire, and I am clearly a noblewoman. If we want to avoid suspicion on the road, we need to make sure we don't stand out so much."

He frowns slightly at the heap of armour he has stripped off. "I can't forgo all of my armour."

"No," I concede, "but you don't have to ride around in all of it, surely?"

"It came in very useful not so long ago, if you remember," he says archly, before catching himself and adding, rather apologetically, "Your Highness."

"Enough of that, too. Nothing more formal than My Lady," I order. "That applies to you too, Rollo. If anyone hears the two of you calling me 'Your Highness' all the time, we won't stay incognito for very long."

"Understood, My Lady," Rollo calls over wearily.

"Then you must call me Fin," Sir Finton says, and his cheeks immediately redden.

I nod, ignoring his blush. "Very well ... Fin."

There is an awkward pause.

"So it's agreed – we find the nearest village and try to acquire some less attention-grabbing clothes," I say. "Then Rollo can get some rest while we go after Delphine."

Sir Finton – Fin – shakes his head. "*I'll* go after Delphine. It's too dangerous for you to be there."

Being Adaliza

I raise my eyebrows at him. "In case you didn't notice, I know how to fight."

"Where did you learn to fight?" Rollo asks, peering at me from his seat on the felled log.

I shrug, not letting the question rattle me. "When a woman lives alone, she must learn to defend herself."

"Is that what you were doing in that tower for four years?" he asks, his tone somewhere between disbelieving and impressed.

"There wasn't much else to do. But ... we're getting distracted."

I turn back to Fin, who has crossed his arms across his chest obstinately.

"Let's just find a village first?" I ask in a compromising tone, even though I don't intend to compromise one bit.

He nods once, relaxing his arms a little. "There is a settlement around here – it might be a large village or a small town. We skirted it a few days ago before we entered the forest."

Good – it sounds like the kind of place we might be able to find a room to rent for Rollo to recuperate, and maybe a market to purchase some new clothing.

"Let's go, then," I say, ready to leave here. Ready to move, ready to get my friend back.

Again Sir Finton helps both me and Rollo onto the same horse. Again it snorts and tosses its head in disapproval when it catches my scent, but I take the reins in my hands with determination. I have accepted the fact that I'm not going to get back to Throsne on foot. These horses have to put up with me, whether they like it or not.

We follow Fin on the destrier as they splash through the stream and lead the way down a grass path between rustling rows of golden barley, almost ready for reaping.

10

It is quiet as we approach the village green, the clip-clopping of our horses' hooves echoing off the nearby buildings. Most are thatched and timber framed, but there are a few larger houses and public buildings made from honey-coloured stone surrounding the green, which is actually more of a baked yellow in the heat of summer. It has a pond, and we tether the horses to a willow tree at its edge to allow them to drink.

The sun is at its zenith in the sky – it's midday. It's only been a few hours since we were attacked, but it feels like days. I'm ravenously hungry, from both the adrenaline and using my magic to heal my head injury. There appears to be a tavern across the green, which seems like the best place to head for first.

As we walk past a squat building, undoubtedly the village forge, our small party is forced to stop. A man is thrown into our path, falling to the floor and cringing upwards with his hands in front of his face.

"Get out!" comes the angry voice of the blacksmith, who hulks in the doorway with a stony face. "Drunk or stupid, I don't care. Be gone with you!"

He turns away dismissively and disappears into the dim exterior of the forge. Collectively we turn to look at the man sprawled in front of us. He is middle aged, thin and bearded, with a travellers staff and a straw hat lying close by, knocked from him in the fall. He looks shaken and upset.

"Sir, are you well?" I ask, and he blinks up at me.

He tries to speak but only strange, moaning sounds come out of his mouth. He frowns, frustrated at my lack of comprehension and the alarmed, slightly wary look that must be on my face. Sir Finton makes a gesture with his hands, pulling the man's attention away from me, and his face lights up in excitement. The man's hands move quickly, making a complicated series of gestures, accompanied by exaggerated facial expressions: eyebrows down, pursed lips, eyebrows up, open mouth. I'm astounded when Sir Finton seems to understand them and replies in kind.

After some back and forth, Sir Finton turns to me.

"The man's name is Benoit. He is here visiting his sister, who lives in the village. He says that she will help us."

"How do you know that?" I ask.

"Benoit is deaf," he explains. "He only speaks sign language."

Sign language – that's what the hand movements are. Benoit beckons us forward, an excited smile on his face, and we follow him. I cut a sideways glance at Sir Finton. Fin. I find myself ... impressed. Both by the fact he knows how to sign – a language I've never even come across before, and I'm something of a polyglot – and at the kindness he showed the distressed man, whose delighted reaction made me suspect that he didn't often encounter it.

Benoit leads us down a lane to a thatched cottage draped in an overgrown climbing rose. There is a woman in the garden, hanging out washing on a line. A look of relief comes over her face when she sees him.

"There you are!" she says, at the same time as her hands gesture.

She is plump and friendly looking, with a crisp apron over her kirtle and a white cap on her head. Certainly not wealthy but clean and well kept.

He signs something back to her, his hands moving so rapidly I can hardly keep up, and she looks at the three of us.

"Thank you for helping him," she says, her eyes round with gratitude. "Folks around here aren't used to deaf people. They don't trust him. I told him not to go to the blacksmith's alone, but does he listen to me?"

I think of what the blacksmith said: *I don't care whether you're drunk or stupid.* Benoit was neither, he just couldn't communicate with him. It must have taken a lot of courage for Benoit to leave the safety and familiarity of his home to visit his sister.

"It's quite alright, Mistress," Sir Finton replies politely, moving his hands at the same time as he speaks. So as not to exclude Benoit from the conversation, I realise.

"Benoit says you need help?" she says, also signing at the same time.

"We were attacked on the road – my companion was shot through the shoulder with an arrow."

The woman's face creases in horror, settling on Rollo with his pale face and hunched shoulder. "Oh, you poor things! Come in, of course, come in!"

The woman, whose name is Ysabel, fusses over Rollo like

a mother hen. She sweeps him into her cottage and checks his wounds, complementing me and Fin on our handiwork before taking a small pot of something down from a shelf.

"This is a salve I make myself – it helps to stop the wound from festering," she explains.

She carefully applies the pungent paste to the front and back of Rollo's shoulder, clucking all the while. I am passed a different jar of ointment and told to put it on my jaw – it is bruised, I remember. I dutifully comply.

When Rollo is bandaged up again and Ysabel is fully satisfied, she clears the scrubbed wooden table and lays out a spread of bread, cheeses, chutneys and boiled eggs, along with a jug of fresh milk. I pile a hearty selection on my plate and have to force myself to pick at it in moderation rather than wolfing down whatever I can reach at first sight. The food is fresh and filling. By the time my hunger is sated, the last of my headache has dissipated.

Once we have eaten, Ysabel asks us to tell her our story. Fin opens his mouth but I speak first. I suspect he is not an accomplished liar.

"My husband is a merchant. We're from northern Belforet."

I glance to Fin, who tries to hide his surprise as a red flush creeps into his cheeks. I don't know why he's alarmed by the notion of being married to me – he's the one who set out to win Adaliza's hand. He catches my eye briefly and then signs what I said for Benoit's benefit. I continue, flattening my accent just a little to sound like a well-bred northerner.

"We were travelling south to Throsne on the Forest Road when we were attacked by four men on horseback. They took a number of our possessions, including a prize horse that we were supposed to be selling to a local lord."

Ysabel's face is pinched with sympathy. "Oh, how terrible. I told you these roads aren't safe, Benoit," she says to her brother, signing as she speaks.

"We can't continue to Throsne without that horse," I say, letting desperation lace my tone. "My husband wants to chase it down, but we can't force Rollo on such a dangerous journey, not in his state."

Rollo, we had already established while Ysabel was tending to his wounds, is supposed to be Fin's younger cousin.

"Rollo can stay here with us, of course!" Ysabel offers immediately – which is exactly what I had hoped she would say.

A wide, grateful smile blooms on my face. "Oh Ysabel, that would be wonderful – you're so kind."

"And you, Mistress?" Ysabel asks. "You're not planning to go after the thieves too, surely?"

I hesitate. I want to – I desperately want to get Delphine back – but I weigh the reality of the situation. Fin will be quicker without me, as I would either have to share the saddle with him or awkwardly ride Rollo's horse alongside him. This isn't about what I want, it's about getting Delphine back as quickly and safely as possible.

"No," I confirm. "I was hoping that I could replenish our supplies. Is there a market nearby that sells clothing? All of ours were taken by the thieves."

Ysabel nods. "Not here, but Charcuire, the next town over, has a market today. It is three miles – you could walk it."

I nod. At least I will have something to occupy my time while Fin is off saving Delphine. The last thing I want to do is sit around and fret while I'm unable to help. I have done enough sitting around for a lifetime.

Being Adaliza

Rollo is sent off to rest by Ysabel, and I walk Fin back to the horses on the village green.

"You ... you were brilliant back there," he says, pointing back in the direction of Ysabel's cottage. "I almost believed you myself. How did you know I'm from northern Belforet?"

I shrug. "There's a hint of it in your accent. And you speak Sea Belforetian to your horse."

There are three local dialects of our language. Sea Belforetian is spoken in the north; I've always thought it sounds weathered, as if the consonants have been smoothed by an ever-present sea breeze. Wood Belforetian is spoken in the centre of the country, including where we are now. It sounds rounder and thornier, like roots and vines and briars. Throsne Belforetian is the prevalent dialect in the city, fast and chattering, with an ever-evolving set of slang words. High Belforetian is spoken all over and preferred by the upper classes. I speak all four dialects without any trouble.

Fin's eyebrows raise at me. "And you speak it?"

I switch to Sea Belforetian when I answer. "Yes. If we're northern, it gives us an opportunity to talk privately in Sea Belforetian if we need to. They don't speak it here."

"Clever," he admits with a grin. I smile back.

We have reached the horses. Fin strokes his destrier's nose affectionately, not noticing how it surveys me warily with its ears pricked. That's an improvement on snorting and stamping in my presence, at least. Fin checks the horse's tack and the saddlebags that now contain his armour. When he is satisfied he turns to me.

"Get her back, Fin," I say quietly, seriously.

I'm trusting him. I've known the knight for all of two days, and yet I trust him to do this. He is sworn to rescue damsels in distress, after all.

He is equally serious in his reply. "I will. Stay safe, My

Lady. I'll return soon."

As I watch him leave the village, sitting straight and bold on the back of the chestnut warhorse, I realise that ... I'm alone. For the first time in years I'm entirely at liberty to go where I please. It's exactly the opportunity I had hoped for when I agreed to go with Sir Finton – a chance to slip away unnoticed, to venture north to track down Adda or flee south to the Maison du Lemorque. I could leave this unforeseen entanglement behind.

But ... I can't bring myself to leave now, not while Delphine is paying the price for my mistakes. Maybe I can trust Fin to rescue her and look out for her even if he returns to find me gone, but could I live with myself knowing that I abandoned my friend at the first opportunity? Delphine knows me – the real me, Aster Lemorque – and sees more than just the changeling trickster. I think she's the only human who ever has.

So I borrow one of Ysabel's sunhats – "You must protect that lovely face! The sun is so fierce at this time of year ..." – and follow her directions to the market of Charcuire.

11

When night falls, Fin isn't back. I try to stay awake as I sit propped on pillows in the large bed that Ysabel insisted I take. She and her husband Jean gave up their own bedchamber for me and Fin to share and wouldn't hear of it when I tried to refuse. I couldn't tell her that there was no way I would be sharing a bed with my so-called husband tonight, so it really would be a waste with so many people under one roof. Rollo is sharing a room with Benoit up in the eaves. Ysabel and Jean are sleeping on cots downstairs by the fireplace. I try to ignore the wriggle of guilt at the thought.

 I'm tired to my very bones after the drama of the morning and the six-mile round trip I walked this afternoon. I found everything I needed in Charcuire. I selected light linen tunics for Fin and Rollo, to replace their easily identifiable surcoats emblazoned with the ivory maiden. Fin's is forest green and Rollo's is tan.

It's rare that I ever buy any clothing for myself – I usually wear either my black houppelande at the Maison du Lemorque or the borrowed clothes of whoever I'm imitating. I chose a butter-yellow linen kirtle, simpler than anything I had access to in Adaliza's armoire. The colour makes me smile. No need for sinister black, not here. It's sleeveless, revealing the neckline and billowing sleeves of my chemise underneath, and I bought a leather belt to secure at my waist. I also purchased a fine linen veil to cover my hair – I won't pass as a respectable married woman without one.

Now I sit with my back against the headboard, just a thin summer blanket pulled over my chemise, and wait for Fin to return. How far could the abductors have ridden before Fin caught up with them? Maybe he galloped for hours – or maybe they disappeared and he didn't find them. Maybe he has been caught, maybe he has been killed ... I try to calm my restless thoughts. This endless fretting isn't going to get him to return any quicker, I scold myself.

Despite my best efforts to keep vigil all night, I must have nodded off because I jolt awake as the latch lifts on the door to the bedchamber. When I see Fin's face peer around the door, illuminated from below by a candle, my stomach swoops in relief.

"I'm sorry, I didn't mean to wake you," he whispers as he edges around the door.

"Where is Delphine?" I ask, alert at once.

Fin sets the candle down on the dresser and scrubs his face in exhaustion. I wonder how late it is – night fell hours ago.

"I tracked them down. They must have slowed to a trot when they realised we weren't chasing them, because I caught them up by the time dusk fell. They stopped to make camp – I saw Delphine."

He reads the question in my face and answers before I can interrupt.

"She looked well – terrified but not hurt. Given food and treated with courtesy. But ... there was no way to get her out. There were six men in the group, two of which kept watch over the camp. I couldn't see any way to make a rescue attempt on my own."

My stomach writhes. Poor Delphine – she must be so scared.

"So ... we go together?" I ask.

He looks at me for a long moment, as if he's going to refuse to allow me to help him.

"Fin, I can fight," I reassure him. "Or create a distraction, or run, or do any of the things you might require of me. Please, let me help."

He still looks dubious. His gaze settles on the bruise on my jaw. "Your head ..."

"Is fine!" I interrupt. "I feel fine, honestly."

I'm going to heal that bruise as quickly as I can without it looking suspicious. Every time he looks at my face he is reminded of that fight. I shouldn't have allowed myself to get knocked unconscious. It was sloppy.

Fin sits down on the edge of the bed with a sigh. I feel his weight make the mattress sink and I pull my knees up to my chest, making myself take up less space on instinct.

"Please, Fin?" I ask again, my voice quiet in the hush of night.

He glances over to me and I know by his expression that he will concede. "Alright. Let's discuss it in the morning."

I can't help but smile. I have to count my victories, however small.

"There's more," Fin says. "I think I know who took her – and it's not a rival knight seeking her hand in marriage."

I frown in apprehension. "Who, then?"

"The Duc d'Eschecs," he says.

The duke is the king's younger brother – Adaliza's uncle. I am only surprised for a moment. The king instigated the rescue contest as a way of ensuring Adaliza's legitimacy as heir to the throne. When she marries there will be no grounds for a lawful challenge to her ascension. It follows that the duke, who is next in line to the throne of Belforet – as Adda has no siblings and no children of her own – would stand to gain a great deal if she never marries.

The duke intended to kidnap Adda to prevent her from marrying and inherit the throne himself. What he plans to do with his niece, I have no idea. Imprison her? Kill her? Marry her himself? It's a disgusting thought and I am pretty sure that the church would frown upon it, but the man is a widower and history tells us that a little issue like incest can be smoothed over when faced with the task of securing royal bloodlines.

The thought makes me seethe. Delphine is still at the hands of these people. But ... that doesn't make sense.

"But ..." I say to Fin, my mind working furiously, "the duke knows what I look like. All of my father's courtiers do. I haven't changed *that* much in four years. Why would they mistake Delphine for me?"

Fin seems to have thought about this already, because his response is quick.

"None of the men bore his coat of arms. I suspect that the duke is trying to work covertly. They are sellswords, not his usual lackeys. They identified a suspicious-looking party and took the woman they thought was most likely to be the princess."

I nod grimly. "Which means they will have to get confirmation that the woman they are holding is the princess of Belforet before they do anything with her. So they are heading towards …"

"Escrimir," Fin finishes for me.

The Duc d'Eschecs' estate in southeastern Belforet. At least we now know where they are taking Delphine.

"We need to rescue her on the road before she is taken to Escrimir," I tell Fin, a note of urgency in my voice.

The estate is widely considered one of the most heavily fortified in the kingdom. Once she is taken inside those gates, the likelihood of being able to get her out again is massively reduced.

"We're agreed on that," Fin says.

He cracks a huge yawn, putting his hand over his mouth to stifle it. He's exhausted, and I'm not surprised. He can't have slept well last night in the corridor of the inn while he guarded our door. It's at this point that Fin, exhausted as he is, looks around the room for the first time and seems to realise that there's one bed and I'm already in it. Before he can blush and stammer, I grab a pillow and the corner of a blanket.

"I can sleep on the floor," I offer.

I know it's not princess-like but I'm getting tired of people constantly offering me the best bed. I've had months of excellent sleep in the tower – I can survive one night on the floorboards. And he just looks so utterly exhausted as he runs his hands through his chestnut hair that I will him to accept the offer, even though I know he won't. He's too damn gallant.

"Absolutely not," he says straightaway, affronted at even the thought.

He holds out his arms for the pillow and blanket and I reluctantly pass them to him. He hugs the pillow to his chest and looks at me intently as if he is going to say something,

Primrose Hugh

but he doesn't say a word. The pause starts to feel charged, awkward.

"Where did you learn sign language?" I ask quickly.

I've been wondering about it all afternoon and it's the first thing that comes out when I grope around for something else to talk about.

"My younger sister is deaf. Her name is Elinor. My whole family can sign – most of Rollo's too. She and Rollo are around the same age."

He smiles slightly to himself at the thought of her. He loves his sister, I realise.

"Will you teach me?" I ask before I can think better of it.

"What?"

"Will you teach me sign language?" I repeat. Then I add in explanation: "I love languages – I collect them, I suppose."

When I glance up, Fin's smile has grown.

"Of course," he says, and drops the pillow to make a hand gesture at the same time.

I presume that that is the sign for 'of course', then, and smile back.

Fin cocks his head slightly as he considers me. "So you like fighting, eating and languages, and you dislike horses? I must admit, it's not entirely what I expected."

I shrug and look away, feeling stung – because he's describing *me*, not Adaliza. I need to be more careful. I have inhabited Adda's skin for too long. It no longer feels like a costume, a disguise – it feels like it's mine. And that's a dangerous thing when I'm supposed to be someone else.

I search for any way to steer the conversation away from me. "So you have a sister. Any other siblings?" I ask.

If he notices the blatant misdirection he doesn't mention it.

"Yes, an older brother. Quentin. He will inherit my

father's title and estate."

Those are the rules of primogeniture – the firstborn son inherits everything, while any additional sons inherit nothing. It is a brutal practice but one that has kept Belforet's noble estates intact for centuries.

I make a guess based on the way Fin talks about it. "You love your home?"

"Very much." His eyes brighten as he pictures it. "Brisebassier is just a few miles from the coast. The sky is so large there."

I'm not familiar with Brisebassier, but I know that the last place Adda sent a letter from was Brillermare, Belforet's only seaport. I wonder if it is close by.

"Do you know Brillermare?" I ask.

"Yes, of course. Our estate borders the town. Have you been there?" he asks in surprise.

"No. I have a friend who travelled through there recently," I say absentmindedly.

I'm not sure how I can use this revelation. Perhaps I can interrogate Fin for any information about Brillermare that might help me to eventually track down Adda?

"You meet all kinds in Brillermare. Less these last few years, of course, owing to the plague. But trade routes are mostly back up and running now."

He speaks fondly of the place. I study Fin's face carefully.

"So you're a second son from a northern noble family who became a knight," I say contemplatively. "Why?"

He raises an eyebrow. "Why become a knight? Well, I need to make something of myself. And I'm good at fighting. Preferably on the behalf of people who can't defend themselves."

From anyone else that would sound like a platitude, but I think he is sincere. Naive, perhaps. But sincere.

"And now you want to marry me," I state, needling for a reaction.

We haven't talked about marriage since that conversation in the library. This is the first proper conversation we've really had, I realise.

"Yes, well ... of course I – it's, it's ..." he babbles.

Predictably there is a flush creeping up his neck and into his cheeks. I take pity on him and ask a question that he can actually answer.

"Why did you join the rescue contest?"

His hands are twisting the corner of the pillow in his lap. He takes a moment to get the words out.

"When I heard the announcement ... I was only concerned for the protection of a young woman being chased like a fox by a pack of dogs. I was intent on the rescue – on piecing together the clues and outsmarting all the other men who thought they could find you first."

I hear him swallow. His green eyes dart up to my face, just once, before returning to his lap.

"In truth, I didn't think about what would happen after. About ... you."

I say it before I can stop myself. "Most people don't."

It's not the response he was expecting. "Don't what?"

I think of the king, locking Adda in a tower for four years for "her own safety", then making her a prize ripe for the taking. I think of my grandmother, sending me out on mission after mission, the greed for gold sparkling in her black eyes.

"Don't think about the woman underneath the crown," I say.

I hear the edge of bitterness in my own tone. For me. For Adaliza. For the living, breathing, loving, hurting women shuffled about like pieces on a chessboard by the their fathers and husbands and grandmothers.

"I'd like to know her," Fin says softly. "The woman underneath the crown."

I don't look at him. I know what I want to say. *Oh Fin, if you only knew.* But I won't. Because in this room, in every room, I need to be Princess Adaliza of Belforet.

"It's late," I say. "We should sleep."

He nods and slides off the end of the bed. I feel the mattress adjust when his weight lifts. I pull the blanket up to my neck and lie down on my side, facing the open window. I close my eyes and ignore the sound of the knight adjusting himself for an uncomfortable sleep on the floor.

12

We intend to leave Ysabel's cottage first thing the next morning, but it turns out that there is still a lot to argue about. Fin and I pour over the map of Belforet he keeps in his saddlebag, quibbling over the best route to intercept Delphine's abductors before they reach Escrimir. Rollo is outraged that we plan to leave him at the cottage to recover and insists that he comes with us, despite his injuries. I make to mount Rollo's horse, Colombe, but Fin objects.

"We'll be travelling at speed," he says. "You're much more likely to jostle Rollo in the saddle and hurt him further."

I cross my arms and glare at my nemesis, the chestnut destrier. I *do not* want to entrust my life to the monstrous horse – nor do I relish the thought of sharing a saddle with Sir Finton. We may have come to an understanding yesterday, but just because I shared a room with him doesn't mean I want him in my personal space in the cold light of day. I sigh. I don't really have a choice.

"Horse," Sir Finton says.

I frown and turn to look at him. "What?"

"Horse," he repeats, balling his fists and moving them up and down as if miming a gallop with reins in his hands.

He said he would teach me sign language, I realise. I give him a small smile.

"Horse," I say and repeat the gesture.

Fin grins.

"Now horse get on," he says slowly, signing each word as he says it.

So sentence structure works differently in sign language – interesting. I opened my mouth to ask him to explain, but he points at the low wall that surrounds Ysabel's garden.

"Mount first. Then you can ask questions," Fin says and I obey reluctantly, taking his proffered hand to steady me as I climb onto the wall.

The destrier is so much bigger than Rollo's dappled grey. He's a mountain of gleaming chestnut muscle – hostile gleaming chestnut muscle, I remember as he stamps and snorts his objection at my proximity – that I'm supposed to climb.

"I've got the reins," Fin reassures me when he notices my hesitation. "Alezan isn't going anywhere."

I steel myself and step into the stirrup, throwing my other leg over the horse's back and settling uneasily into the large saddle. I shuffle back and put my arms behind me to grip the cantle where the back of the seat swoops upward, trying to leave Sir Finton as much space as possible in front of me. He swings easily into the saddle and I edge further away from him, conscious of the inside of my thighs brushing the outside of his. If he notices how I squirm uncomfortably to keep some distance between us, he doesn't show it as he waves goodbye to Ysabel and Benoit.

I try to swallow my squeak of alarm when Fin heels the horse into action and it lurches beneath us. I hold the cantle behind me in a death grip, arms straight, as we walk through the village with Rollo following behind.

"Ready, Rollo?" Fin calls to him.

I don't have enough trust in my balance to swivel in my seat and look at him, but I hear his cheerful reply.

"Ready, Fin!"

"Ok then, my lad," Fin mutters to his horse in Sea Belforetian, and with another kick of his heels the beast surges into a canter.

Immediately I slide forward in the saddle, losing the precious inches I had kept between me and Fin, and on instinct I throw my arms around his waist, clutching the only solid thing that might stop me from toppling off the horse's back. I feel a laugh rumble through Fin's chest – he's laughing at me! I grit my teeth, alarm still coursing through my body as some deep instinct screams at me to *get off the horse*, and I force myself to loosen my grip around his waist. But no – a veer to the side by Alezan and I'm hanging onto him just as desperately as before, my front pressed tightly against the length of his back.

I hate this – not just the gut-churning ride, but the fact it makes me feel so helpless, so much like the damsel in distress. I don't want to cling to a man's back with my face buried in his shirt in fear. Especially not Sir Finton's. Not when he *laughed* at me. I distract myself by thinking up idiomatic insults for him in every language I know.

You craven lover of cockroaches.
You empty-headed son of an oxen.
You stain on the linen of your family crest.

The destrier's gait becomes a little smoother when we

reach the Drover's Road. It runs eastward across Belforet and is less busy than the Forest Road, which is the main thoroughfare to and from Throsne in the south. Our plan is to head east and then cut southwards towards Escrimir over the wild heathland that characterises the area, with an aim to intercept Delphine's captors before they reach it via the easier but longer route. It will mean some hard riding and rough sleeping over the next few days, but I will not flinch from it. Delphine's absence is a constant ache of guilt and worry inside me.

With the going easier on the flat road, I loosen my death grip on Fin and sit straighter in the saddle. My legs and backside already hurt from trying to keep my seat. I am stiff and sore when we break for lunch by the side of the road. Fin leaps easily from Alezan's back and reaches up a hand to help me down, but I ignore it and slip clumsily from the saddle without looking at him. My legs feel wobbly – I welcome the sensation, relieved to have my boots back on the ground.

Rollo's face is pale and drawn as he dismounts one-handed. I watch him, concern pinching my eyebrows together, and when he sees me looking he throws me a carefree grin as if to put my mind at ease.

"It's hurting you, isn't it?" I ask him, pointing to his injured shoulder.

"No more than can be expected. I'm fine, My Lady," he says, but my concern is not allayed.

The constant jostling on horseback must leave him in constant pain, even if he is holding the reins in his good hand and has the other strapped across his chest to keep his shoulder immobile. Not for the first time, I wish I could channel my healing magic outside my own body to help him.

Fin is rooting through the saddlebags to find the supplies that Ysabel gave us before we left. She vehemently refused to accept any payment in return for her kindness, but I saw Fin leave a pouch of coins under the pillow for her to find later. Now he sets out bread, cheese and a handful of juicy plums from her cottage garden on a cloth and drops down beside the picnic.

While on horseback I had committed myself to ignoring Fin whenever possible from that point onward, but he makes it a difficult promise to keep. When he can't draw me in conversation about the food or the landscape, he takes to signing his thoughts and questions, narrating each gesture as he goes. I can't help but watch, and my curiosity about the language's grammar and sentence structure gets the better of me. By the time all the food has been eaten, I have learned the signs for bread, cheese, eat, road, grass, tree, ride, journey, yesterday, today and tomorrow. I amend my earlier vow; it's acceptable to talk to Fin if it's about sign language. Or about our mission. But there will be no idle small talk, no opportunity for flattery or getting to know each other better. He's a means to an end.

The afternoon's ride is hot and exhausting, moving at a canter and a trot intermittently to preserve the strength of the horses. The bright, sun-seared August sky shows no sign of a break in the unrelenting heat, no clouds to offer the brief respite of shade or a rain shower. I'm glad of the veil I wear over my hair, which keeps the sun off my head. Adaliza's skin isn't used to spending so long exposed to the sunshine and I feel the prickling heat of sunburn on my nose and across my cheekbones by mid afternoon. I soothe the red skin with my magic and pull the veil further up and over my face to shade it from the worst of the glare.

We have covered a good amount of ground by the time the sun starts to set. The Drover's Road cuts through a remote landscape with few signs of civilisation. There are no inns or even farmhouses close by that might offer us a bed for the night. Instead we set up a camp just off the roadside in a sheltered copse of silver birches. Although I don't voice my concern out loud, I'm nervous about sleeping out in the open. It's not wild animals or brigands that worries me. Even with the disguise of the new clothes I bought us in Charcuire, I can't help constantly checking behind us for knights on the trail of Princess Adaliza.

Fin and Rollo seem quite at home in the wilderness. Rollo takes me foraging for mushrooms and blackberries, and by the time we return to our camp, Fin is sat plucking two woodpigeons in front of a small fire. My eyebrows rise – I can't help but be a little impressed.

"How did you catch them?" I ask.

He doesn't carry a bow and arrows, and there hasn't been enough time to snare two birds.

Fin nods his head towards what looks like a length of rope and a scrap of leather at his side. "I used a sling."

"I'm surprised you managed two hits," Rollo mutters before turning to me. "I'm the true master when it comes to slinging stones, My Lady. We used to spend hours scaring off crows from the crop fields after sowing."

Fin makes a 'pffft' sound of dismissal. "Such impertinence! I taught you everything you know."

"Yes, and it didn't take long for the student to best the master," Rollo insists.

I smile at their good-natured teasing. If Fin ever thought that Rollo would make a discreet, respectful squire, he was only fooling himself. He cares for the lad – that much is obvious. They act like brothers.

We dine on a surprisingly hearty meal of roast woodpigeon and mushrooms, along with a crust of bread and plenty of blackberries to finish. Despite the storm of worries inside my head, I find myself smiling in their easy company as we watch the campfire's flames leap and flicker. I don't know if it's our nondescript clothes, our remote location or the growing familiarity that only comes with time, but the formal lines between princess, knight and squire are less distinct tonight. I'm glad of it.

When we finally settle down by the fire to sleep I find myself directly across from Fin, who is already lying down with a blanket wrapped around him. He nobly offered me his bedroll earlier, which I accepted reluctantly. Now I see the gleam of his eyes in the firelight, watching me.

He gives a thumbs up, then lifts both hands, flat with the palms facing him, and brings them down and together like a drawbridge being lowered. He taught me that one earlier.

Goodnight, I sign back, the only sound the soft crackle of the fire and the low call of a bird in a nearby tree.

13

By mid morning the next day we turn off the Drover's Road and onto the heath. I gasp as the landscape reveals itself, wide, eerie and beautiful. I've never seen anything like it. Gentle hills roll away before us, thickly swathed in pink-purple heather and yellow gorse. There is nothing else: no trees, no roads, no buildings. Just that dense, brightly coloured carpet of gorse and heather as far as the eye can see.

The horses have to slow as we pick our way through the thick, low-growing vegetation, using winding passages made by the feet of wild animals. We try to steer clear of the clumps of gorse with their sharp, needle-like foliage that might hurt the horses' legs or hooves, but the scent of the yellow gorse flowers wafts over to us on a warm breeze. It's heavenly, like a floral perfume of sunshine and cream. I inhale deep lungfuls of it, committing the smell to memory for the next time I'm stuck in the filthy back streets of Throsne.

When we crest one of the hills, Fin points across the wild

purple landscape ahead of us to a collection of squat buildings.

"That's where we're heading," he tells me. "Barbacane. It marks the start of the Duc d'Eschecs' lands. Anyone entering from the west has to stop at the Barbacane tollgate before travelling on to Escrimir."

"What if the men who took Delphine have already passed through?" I ask, squinting at the small settlement in the distance.

"They won't have," Fin assures me. "Cutting across the heath from the north has saved us two days of riding. The duke's men had a wagon with them, they can only have taken the Forest Road. We'll be there by the time they arrive."

Although we can see Barbacane in the distance from our vantage point, it takes all day to traverse the dense heather on horseback. While I marvel at the desolate heathland as we ride through it, I find that I'm glad when Alezan's hooves finally clop on the hard-baked mud of a cart track that leads into the village as the sunlight starts to fade.

The small settlement has grown up around the tollgate that flanks the road. All travellers are made to pause at the small hexagonal building and wait for the tollkeeper to inspect their party and extract payment for using the road. There is no escaping the toll; the ground drops steeply away on either side of the village, where it gives over to flat pink heather. Anyone trying to avoid making payment would be seen for miles. When we approach from the Escrimir side of the tollgate there is a queue of two wagons and a riding party waiting to be permitted on the other side. Enterprising locals have clearly made the most of this enforced break, as nearby I can see a well, a bakery, a woodcarver's shop, a stables and an inn called The Nightjar. Women carrying large trays at their hips wander along the line of travellers selling flowers, handkerchiefs, jewellery and pastries.

I understand now why Fin chose this place to intercept Delphine's captors. It's a busy spot and they will be brought to a halt at the tollgate before they can progress through to Escrimir. In the bustle of horses, travellers and peddlers it will be easier to snatch Delphine and make away with her than it would be on the open road.

It's been another long day of riding and the cheerful light and noise of the roadside inn beckons to me. Rollo takes the horses to the stables while Fin goes to arrange our lodgings for the night. I keep to the shadows outside and peer through a window to assess the inn. It seems smaller and friendlier than the one we stayed at on the Forest Road. I see a few women sitting at the tables inside, laughing as they eat their evening meals – that's a good sign. I won't stand out as much, especially in my plain kirtle. Most of the patrons wear the simple clothes of countrymen or the practical travelling wear of merchants. I can't see any armour or surcoats, the tell-tale garb of knights.

Fin exits the inn and finds me in the lengthening shadows.

"I've got us two rooms next to each other at the inn for tonight. You can have one, Rollo and I will share the other. Are you ready for dinner?"

I manage to hold back my groan at the thought of a hot meal and a comfortable seat that isn't on the back of a horse.

"Yes," I say with feeling.

We wait for Rollo to finish settling the horses before we enter the warm, close atmosphere of the taproom. We have to sidestep patrons and duck under low-hanging beams to find a free table, which could seat six but only has three stools positioned around it. The other three must have been requisitioned by the large group of merry travellers that crowd around the next table over. They are talking and laughing loudly – so loudly that it would be impossible for us to hold a conversation without shouting in each other's ears – but I find that I don't mind. The jovial atmosphere of warmth and noise wraps around me like a cloak, making me feel safe in my anonymity. A serving wench brings over a tray of drinks and I keep my hands folded around my tankard, content to watch the people around me.

We have had our fill of a hearty stew served in round bread trenchers when all of a sudden there is a surge of excitement among the patrons. A loud rumbling assaults our ears as tables and benches are pushed against the walls, their legs scraping against the flagstone floor. Fin, Rollo and I glance around ourselves, unsure why the furniture is being moved and wondering if we have to relocate. The reason becomes clear when someone starts to beat out a rapid rhythm on a drum and a pipe trills a jolly melody in accompaniment. The patrons around us, rosy-faced and smiling, clap their hands or grab the sleeve of a companion and lead them to the newly cleared space in front of the musicians to dance. It brings a smile to my face. A skin-covered cylinder and a length of hollow tree branch with holes in it is all that's needed to bring people together like this, in laughter and song.

The serving wenches fan out from the bar to pull male partners onto the dance floor, and most comply with a grin. I imagine it's a ploy of the landlord – dancing will make his patrons thirsty and more likely to spend their coin this evening. One of the barmaids, with red-gold curls and a round, freckled face, grabs Fin's hand and tries to tug him to his feet with a winsome smile. He pulls out of her grip and raises his hands in protest.

"I can't," he insists, pointing to me, "my wife!" – as if my presence is excuse enough to get him out of dancing.

"Be a good husband and take your pretty wife to the floor, then," the barmaid shouts over the music.

Fin gives me a considering look from across the table, one corner of his mouth hitching in a smile that looks suspiciously like a dare. Does he really want to dance with me? It doesn't feel right to join in with the gaiety, not with Delphine still held captive and the importance of our mission tomorrow.

"Go on," Rollo urges, nudging me with his good elbow.

Wondering if it's against my better judgement I rise from my stool, which incites a cheer from the barmaid and a triumphant grin from Fin. *What am I doing?* I ask myself as Fin takes my hand and leads me through the crowd of bodies towards the space now occupied by spinning dancers. This isn't the neat, formal dancing of the royal court that imitates the bobbing and posturing of birds in a mating ritual. It is fast and joyful and unstructured. Fin turns to face me when we're on the dancefloor, lifting the hand he has clasped in mine to shoulder height and settling his other hand on my waist. I only have a moment to blink in surprise at how intimate his touch feels before he launches us into the dance and I'm carried away, laughing.

I've grown used to being in close proximity to Sir Finton Prest; for the past two days I've been flattened against him while we rode pillion. I know his smell and the width of his shoulders. I know the deft expression of his fingers as he signs to me across a campfire. I know the soft sounds of his inhales and exhales as he sleeps. But this is something new.

We are pressed as close together as we are when we're sharing a saddle, but now we're face to face and there's no escaping the reality of his nearness. His auburn hair, shiny as Alezan's coat. His bright eyes fixed on mine, the green of his irises brought out by the green tunic I bought for him. Had I done that on purpose, chosen a colour that would complement his hair and eyes? His broad smile, the richer, grander cousin of the grin that often hovers on his lips when he looks at me. The freckles sun-scattered across his face – the ones I try hard not to notice because I don't allow myself to study his face for too long. The feel of his arm around my waist, holding me close, keeping me safe against the barging of other dancers.

And I'm confused.

Sir Finton Prest is nothing but a nuisance, a bump in the road of my mission as a decoy. I was so outraged by his presence at the tower, rankled by his presumption that he had won me and could take me where he wished like a doll with a frozen smile on her face. I have tried to hate him for it. So ... why am I feeling this way now? I don't want it, I don't trust the way my body is reacting under his touch. Maybe it's just the hot, crowded taproom, the fun of the dancing. I'm just getting carried away in the moment. Maybe it's the expression on his face as he stares, eyes only for me, as we dance and spin – as if he can't quite believe it. As if I'm a revelation.

But I'm not. I'm a liar. I'm an imposter. I shake my head slightly, as if to dispel the haze that has me basking in his attention. I forget myself. We are here in this village to save Delphine – that's what I should be focusing on. I shouldn't be dallying with a knight – a knight that is to be Adda's future husband.

I lean in to shout in Fin's ear. "I need a drink."

And then I'm pulling away out of the circle of his arm, dropping his hand and turning my back on him.

"Of course!" he says in my ear from behind, his breath stirring my hair.

Being Adaliza

I grit my teeth and he follows me from the dancefloor. He doesn't see the flat expression on my face, the one honed into careful indifference by determination and practice. I have allowed Sir Finton to get too close. I need to take a step away, to give me room to breathe and think clearly.

I take a tankard of weak ale from a tray on the bar and drink deeply. When I've drained it I turn to Fin.

"I'm tired. I want to go to bed," I say tersely, not looking him in the eye.

I don't see his face fall but I hear the slight disappointment in his tone as he says, "Oh – of course. I'll escort you upstairs."

He reaches backwards for my hand as he leads the way through the crowd to the staircase, but I pull it out of his grip. He glances back at me but doesn't say anything. By the time we reach the narrow, creaking corridor of the second floor and the two doors next to each other that lead to our rented rooms for the night, I have gathered all my scattered thoughts and reeled in my floundering feelings.

Fin leans against the wall opposite the door, his expression searching as he looks at me. I look away, keeping my focus on the key in his hand.

"Good night, Sir Finton," I say coolly, holding out my palm flat to take the key.

I glance up when he doesn't immediately hand it over. A small crease has formed between his brows. He opens his mouth to say something – I mentally prepare to rebuff whatever it is – but then he closes his mouth. I see his Adam's apple bob in the column of his throat. He drops the key into my palm.

"Good night, My Lady," he says, his voice low and quiet.

I ignore the squirm of guilt in my stomach, turn around and let myself through the door, shutting it between me and

Primrose Hugh

the knight on the other side.

14

The next day my nerves are a niggle that keep me focused as the morning warms into another baking hot day. I wrap my hand around the knife in the pocket of my dress, bounce on the balls of my feet, circle my head and wrists in preparation for a fight. We pretend to ready ourselves for our onward journey as we surreptitiously watch the road for approaching riders. By mid morning we still haven't seen any sign of them and the niggle of nerves turns into a gnaw in my gut. I want to leave this place. I want Delphine back. I've had enough of waiting.

By noon I can't sit around any longer. I can feel panic rising inside me with a lurch, surfacing all my misgivings.

"What if they don't come this way?" I ask Fin worriedly, biting my lip as I stare out at the long road that cuts through the dusky purple heathland ahead of Barbacane.

"They will," he says confidently.

"Or what if we've missed them and they're already nearing Escrimir?"

"Not possible – they can't have made the journey more quickly than we did."

"What if you were mistaken and it wasn't the Duc d'Eschecs behind the kidnapping? They might not be heading east at all," I say, my fears gathering momentum as I give them voice.

Fin puts his hands on my shoulders to stop me pacing and I glance up at him. His gaze is direct and steadying as he looks me straight in the eye.

"I know you're worried about Delphine, but we have a plan – we need to see it through. We'll get her back."

He's reassuring me. In the time I've known him I've been distant and inconsistent, curt and conniving ... and yet he still tries to reassure me. I nod and attempt to swallow the lump in my throat.

It is mid afternoon by the time we see the party far down the road on the approach to Barbacane. Two horses pull a covered wagon, flanked by four riders on horseback.

"That's them," Fin confirms, squinting into the distance with his hand shading his eyes against the glare of the sun. "Everyone knows the plan?"

Rollo and I nod.

"Let's get into position."

Rollo heads straight to the stables to collect the horses. I watch Fin sidle over to the tollkeeper, a short, portly man who clearly relishes the small amount of power that his job gives him. Fin points at the approaching party and they exchange a few words before he reaches for his money belt and slides out a few coins. They are gone, slipped into the tollkeeper's pocket, the moment they drop into his palm. I breathe out in relief, suddenly aware that I was holding my breath. We had hoped that the tollkeeper would accept a bribe to delay the party at the gate, but there was always a chance that the man would suddenly locate his morals and turn the money down. Not today, luckily for us.

Fin glances over to me and makes the sign for *all ok*. I nod in return and both of us find our hiding places, Fin near the tollgate and me by the water trough. It feels like it takes an age for the men and the wagon to reach the village. The riders look dusty and sunburnt; I see more than one of them glance longingly at the inn, clearly imagining the relief of a cool pint of ale to slake their thirst after a long ride. I try to peer into the wagon for a glimpse of Delphine but I can't see into it. As much as I long to see her, breaking into the wagon is not my part to play in this plan.

The man at the front of the party calls down to the tollkeeper from horseback, but the tollkeeper steps in front of the gate and shakes his head in apology. I can't hear what they're saying but the man is clearly annoyed by the forced delay and swings out of his saddle to land on the ground with a humph.

It's a hot August day. We thought it was safe to presume that the men would lead their horses to the water trough to drink while pausing at the tollgate. With a manufactured delay, we also betted on the fact that they would leave their mounts tethered to the trough and go in search of their own refreshment. I watch from behind a large bush as the horses drink greedily and their riders turn away, distracted by a buxom woman carrying a trayful of pasties and the pull of the inn across the road. Once they are all out of sight, I run to the trough in a crouch and squat behind its high stone sides.

At first the horses ignore me as I use my knife to slice through the tethers that tie them to hooks on the trough, too absorbed in their drinking. I let my shapeshifting magic kindle in my veins, feeling my features morph and warp as I picture various faces in my mental library, not letting any one of them fully form before shifting into the next. The horses sense the magic and look up at me, ears pricked and water dripping from their muzzles. I bare my teeth at them, my features still shifting, causing the animal straight in front of me to whinny and roll its eyes in alarm. Its panic is contagious. All six of the horses stamp and make disgruntled sounds as they survey me, unnerved by my presence. I jolt forward as if to attack and that's all it takes to make the horses bolt in terror, rearing and neighing, pulling free of their severed tethers and making their escape down the road, causing travellers and villagers to flee from their path.

I settle my features back into Adaliza's and quickly duck away from the trough, heading to where I know Rollo will be waiting with our mounts among the trees. He holds Alezan's reins as I step up onto a nearby boulder and climb onto the huge horse's back, my heartbeat hammering in my chest. There are disgruntled shouts as the six horses gallop through the village, lost to reason. Three of the men who rode in on the horses chase after them down the road. It's the distraction that Fin needs to slip into the wagon, free Delphine and bring her to us so that we can make a swift getaway.

The minutes feel like hours as Rollo and I wait for Fin. Alezan and Colombe sense our tension – and probably the remnants of my magic – and shift nervously beneath us as I grit my teeth and try to stay steady in the saddle. I wish I hadn't agreed to create the distraction rather than rescuing Delphine myself. I am moments away from telling Rollo we should head towards the tollgate and find out what's happening when Fin bursts through the trees at a run, pulling a shocked and terrified Delphine behind him.

My heart soars at the sight of her, even as a man rips

through the trees behind them in close pursuit. Rollo twirls his sling and hurls a rock at their pursuer with unnerving accuracy, despite the fact he is on horseback and only has one functioning arm. The rock finds its mark in the middle of his forehead and the man's head snaps back. He stops suddenly, his hands rising to his forehead in surprise.

Fin's expression blazes with concentration as he swings Delphine forward – Rollo reaches out to grab her hand and pull her up onto Colombe – and mounts Alezan with a deft step in the stirrups, swinging his leg over in front of me as I try to lean out of the way to make it easier for him.

"Go!" Fin shouts and then we're galloping.

I cling to Fin's back, putting all my concentration into keeping my seat as the warhorse thunders forward with all the heft of a swinging battering ram. I clamp down on my terror and work up the nerve to steal a glance backwards – I can see Delphine's white face behind Rollo's shoulder and the arms she has wrapped around his waist. Two men are running after us, shouting words I can't hear over the drumming of hoofbeats, but they have no way to catch us. Their horses are likely a mile away by now, still running scared.

I turn forward again. Alezan's long legs are eating up the road, taking us away from the commotion of Barbacane. The way ahead is clear and quiet.

"We did it," I say breathlessly, not quite believing our luck. "Fin – we did it!"

"Let's get a bit more distance between us and the duke's men," Fin calls back to me.

I understand his caution but I feel light as air, giddy laughter rising unbidden in me like bubbles. It went to plan – something actually went to plan! My life has been a series of missteps and improvisations since the morning I woke with

Fin's face hovering above mine in my tower bedroom. It feels so good to finally gain some control over the situation.

We have covered a decent distance before the horses start to tire. I may despise Alezan, but I can't fault the destrier's mettle. He has galloped far away from the men chasing us, even with two people on his back. His flanks are slick with sweat and froth whips back from his mouth when Fin eases him into a canter and then a trot. When we're finally at walking pace, Fin jumps down and stands at his horse's bridle, patting his neck and fussing over him as he walks by its side. I twist in my seat.

"Delphine!" I call backwards, and see the familiar face of my handmaiden peer over Rollo's shoulder.

Rollo takes Fin's cue and also dismounts to walk alongside Colombe, lightening the load for the blowing horse. Fin holds Alezan for a moment so that the horses can match pace and we can chat side by side.

"My Lady!" Delphine exclaims, her voice shaky after the drama of her rescue. She is wearing the same gown she wore when she was abducted, now dirty and wrinkled. Her blonde hair is mussed and her eyes are wide as she takes me in.

"Are you hurt?" I ask.

"No, not hurt – just ... rattled. You came for me," she says, still shocked, almost as if she doesn't believe it.

"Of course we came for you! You didn't think we would leave you with those awful men, did you?"

She blinks a number of times in rapid succession. "I ... I didn't tell them. That I wasn't you."

My heart jolts in my chest at her words. She was playing along – playing the decoy. So that they wouldn't find out that she wasn't the real Princess Adaliza and go after me instead. Her sacrifice ... it makes me want to cry.

"I'm so glad you're safe," I choke out.

Delphine also has tears in her eyes.

"I'm safe," she confirms, her voice lowering. "And I'm here. You're not alone anymore."

I glance at Fin and Rollo walking alongside the horses on the ground below us, trying to give us some privacy, and I realise that I haven't felt alone these past few days. They aren't bad men. I may have set off from the tower thinking of Fin as the enemy, but that's no longer the case. I'm not sure what happens now. I hadn't permitted myself to think further ahead than getting Delphine back. I'm no closer to locating the real Adda and switching places with her before she's forced into a marriage she didn't consent to. Should Delphine and I plot to run from Fin and Rollo and flee north to Brillermare? Or should we carry on south to Throsne and seek help from my family at the Maison du Lemorque?

I give Delphine a look that says *let's discuss this later in private* and we carry on in a companionable silence.

The sun is slipping down towards the horizon when the road crosses a humped bridge over a river. Delphine and I are helped down from the horses, who are led carefully down the bank by Fin to drink the slow moving water.

"This is as good a place as any to stop for a break. The horses need a proper rest," Fin says.

I nod in agreement. As ever, my stomach is growling. I think we're all in need of a sit down and a refuel. Rollo hands out the large pasties that we bought in Barbacane to eat on the road. The pastry parcel is plump with chopped vegetables and hunks of meat – it tastes just as good cold as it does hot.

As we sit on the riverbank and eat our pasties, Fin takes the opportunity to teach me more sign language. Delphine glances between us, clearly bemused by the odd turn of our relationship, which had been frosty at best when she last saw us. I've progressed from single words to simple sentences.

Primrose Hugh

I'm staring up at Fin from my position lower down the riverbank, concentrating on the fluid movement of his hands, when a shape appears behind him. Before I even have time to open my mouth in warning, a man stands at Fin's back, his broadsword outstretched towards Fin's neck. I freeze in wide-eyed shock. The man's face is red and blotchy, he hunches with obvious fatigue but his sword arm is steady as he glowers at us one by one. Delphine shudders and Rollo rises to his feet to stand in front of her.

The man's eyes narrow on Fin. "It seems you've got something of ours we want back," he grinds out.

15

The moment seems to stretch out in time. Shock courses through my veins with every beat of my heart. Fin's intense gaze, sharp with alarm and misgiving, is locked on mine. I wrap my hand around the knife tucked away in my pocket, weighing my options. Fin isn't wearing his armour or his sword, but it's very unlikely that he's completely unarmed – I'm willing to bet he has at least one dagger sheathed somewhere on his person. I move my hands in a sign that I try to make look like a gesture of distress as I stare back at him.

Get ready.

Fin's eyebrows raise slightly and then I move, springing up from my seated position lower on the bank and slashing out with my knife – slicing the man's calf just below the back of the knee. He gives a cry as his leg buckles; Fin takes advantage of the distraction, rolling away from the sword tip. I take a few running steps up the uneven bank until I'm upright, settling into a fighting stance.

The man's red face is scrunched in pain but he swings his sword at me with malice and I dodge out of its way. I don't dare to tear my eyes from him, but I sense Rollo and Delphine making their escape down the river behind me. Good – Fin and I can deal with this threat. Fin has risen to his feet opposite me and has a dagger raised, as I expected. The man is looking back and forth between us, trying to gauge his odds against the two of us. He seems to determine that Fin is the bigger threat and thrusts his sword in his direction.

We have to disarm him – he has much greater reach than either of us with our short blades. He is wearing gauntlets and dented plate armour on his shoulders and chest, but no chainmail. The man rushes Fin with a gurgled cry of effort, limping forward on his injured leg, and I take the opportunity to dart in with a thrust towards his side ribs. He twists away before I find my mark, swiping out to backhand me with his free arm, snarling like a cornered animal, and Fin harries him from the other side, his blade flashing in the sun. This time the man's flailing sword swipe slices into Fin's upper arm. The sudden gash of red across his sleeve sends a jolt of fear through me.

"Fin!" I cry out desperately.

"I'm ok," he reassures me, panting a little, intent on his opponent.

I grit my teeth. The next time the man lunges to keep Fin at the end of his sword, I advance and kick out at his injured calf from behind, making him scream in agony. His leg immediately crumples and his sword arm goes slack. Fin swiftly kicks the sword out of his grip and plunges his dagger into the fallen man's neck. A gasp, spurting gouts of blood – the man's dark eyes are wide as he loses his lifeblood, and I see the moment they go glassy.

Being Adaliza

Fin steps away from the dead man, who slumps forward onto the grass, and wipes his brow with his shirt sleeve. I go to him, my hands reaching either side of the wound in his arm. Fin's other arm wraps around me as I step close, as if on instinct.

"Just a flesh wound," he murmurs.

I look up from the gash, worry pinching my brows together, and find his face surprisingly close to mine. His expression makes my breath hitch. My heart is still thumping from the adrenaline of the fight, and I become conscious of it hammering in my ears.

"You saved me," Fin says, his voice quiet, intimate, and ... wonderous.

His eyes rove over my features, as if committing me to memory. I can feel the heat of his hand around my waist through the fabric of my dress.

"Of course I did," I reply, slightly choked. I feel like I can't quite catch my breath. His overwhelming nearness is depriving me of air.

And then, somehow, we are even closer together, his body lined up with mine. My hands move from bracing his arm to settle trembling on his chest. My limbs are tingling in a way that has nothing to do with my magic. I don't feel in control of my body as it presses closer to his of its own accord, my breasts against his broad chest, my chin rising as he lowers his face to mine, my eyes drifting closed.

He is so near; I feel the warmth of his skin across the scant distance between our faces. His breath stirs against my lips as he says, the word like an answer and a blessing and a prayer: "Adaliza."

And I freeze.

Because I am not Adaliza.

It's like being drenched with a bucketful of icy water. I

can't do this. I can't do it to Fin or to Adda, I have no place here in their story.

I step backwards abruptly, feeling cool air fill the growing space between us. I see Fin's eyes open, his brow crease in confusion, before I turn away. Walk away, breathing hard.

He has only ever called me 'Your Highness' or 'My Lady'. Somehow I let myself think – let myself *feel* – that this rising heat between us was for me, because of me, but he doesn't know me. I am not Adaliza. I am a changeling playing a princess playing a merchant's wife. It has all got so muddled. I may pretend to be human – may even wish to be, with every beat of my lonely heart – but peel back the layers and I'm nothing of the sort. I feel the keen sting of embarrassment. Stupid, to let my guard down.

"Adaliza?"

Fin's tone is confused, maybe a little hurt, but I don't turn around. He looks at me too closely – I won't let him see this, the turmoil I'm trying so desperately to push down. I glance down the river but I can't see Delphine or Rollo. They must be sheltering somewhere. I resolve to track them down and walk away from Fin.

"Wait ..." Fin says, but I ignore him.

My heart hurts and my cheeks burn and my eyes sting and my stomach is in knots. *Pull yourself together, Aster*, I tell myself savagely. *You're a professional.*

"Adaliza!" Fin shouts, his tone sharp with warning, and when I glance up from my feet I forget my self-pity.

I don't even have time to lift my arms into a guard before a second attacker, who must have been hiding behind a tree, grabs me from the side. Before I can blink he has wrapped his arm tight around my neck in a stranglehold, turning me to face Fin.

"Adaliza, is it?" he growls as I struggle against him, trying to simultaneously lash out with my limbs and shift my head to loosen my airways.

I gasp as I manage to turn my face into the crook of his elbow, freeing up my windpipe. His stench is so strong that it makes me heave.

"You owe me an eye, Princess," he bites out nastily.

So this is the sellsword from the Forest Road. I had plunged my knife into his eye socket and left him bleeding on the ground. Stupid – I should have finished him off then and there. The only thing worse than an enemy is an enemy with a personal vendetta against you.

"Let her go," Fin calls to the eyeless man, his voice sharp and dangerous as a blade.

"This one has led us in a merry dance," the man says, tightening his grip on me to stop me flailing.

I am just starting to panic about the fact that I am completely incapacitated by the man when I feel his head jolt forward against my hair and he lets out an "oooft!" of pain. I take advantage of the momentary slackening of his limbs to pull free, but he recovers quickly and his hands scramble for purchase against the back of my neck, yanking me backwards by the chain of my necklace. I yelp in pain as the silver cuff chokes me before the clasp breaks and it falls from my throat.

I gasp and spin towards my attacker, taking in his snarling face and the bloody rag tied around his head to cover his right eye. I don't hesitate – this time I won't leave him alive. I throw my small knife and it sails across the distance between us, end over end, before thudding into his eyeless socket. He screams in pain but I ignore his animalistic cries as I cross to him in a few steps and lean my weight into the short handle, sinking the blade deeper. His cries stop when the knife stabs into his brain through the back of the eye socket. I yank out the knife in a smooth, fierce motion, my chest heaving.

"Are you ..." Fin starts to ask, but the question trails off when I turn to face him.

For a moment, everything seems strangely calm and quiet next to the idyllic river. Fin's eyes go wide and his mouth falls open in shock as he stares at me. The look on his face is something like ... devastation. It hits me like a physical blow, and my stomach plunges as I realise why. He is unable to tear his gaze away from my eyes.

My changeling eyes. My traitorous, midnight black eyes that can't be mistaken for anything other than fairy trickery. The silver collar necklace that has lain against my throat for years is on the grass just out of the eyeless man's grasp, the lapis lazuli jewel gleaming in the sunlight.

"Fin," I choke, raising my hands in surrender, "I can explain ..."

"What have you done with her?" he asks, voice low with fury.

"What?" I ask in confusion.

"The real princess – where is she?"

He looks around, as if Adaliza is trussed up and hidden behind a bush. I shake my head.

"She's not here – she never has been."

He stares at me again, lips twisting with disgust, eyes shuttered with distrust. It feels like there's a wrenching, howling hole in my chest where my heart used to be. That look on Fin's face has carved it out, ripped it from me bloody and beating.

"Explain," he grinds out.

My limbs are shaking in the aftermath of the attack, I'm not sure I can breathe. And he keeps *looking* at me like that, like I'm everything that's despicable in this world.

Being Adaliza

"What's wrong?"

I glance back as Rollo and a pale, trembling Delphine approach from behind me. The squire has a sling wrapped around his fist – it must have been a stone hitting the back of my attacker's head that made him loosen his grip long enough for me to get away. Delphine gasps as she takes in the necklace on the ground and what it means.

My voice trembles when I speak, my gaze fixed on Fin.

"My name is Aster Lemorque. I ... I'm a changeling. I was employed by Adaliza years ago to take her place in the tower – it's always been me. Her father doesn't know. It was never supposed to happen like this."

Fin's expression doesn't change. "And where is she now?"

"I don't know. She's been travelling all over the continent. Her mother, the queen, was the only person in Throsne who knew about the deception and kept in contact with us both. With her gone ... I have no way of reaching Adda."

"So, what, you were just going to go ahead and marry me? Take her place and leave me none the wiser?"

I frown. "No! I ... I was going to find her and bring her back. You ... You were ... I never meant to ..."

But Fin is shaking his head, turning away from me. "I don't want to hear any more."

Tears are building inside me but I fight to keep them dammed. I look at Rollo, who stares at me as if he doesn't know me and quickly follows after Fin. Delphine rushes to scoop up the necklace and comes to my side.

"It's alright," she soothes, laying a hand on my arm. "It will be alright. I can fix this."

She is turning the necklace over in her fingers, examining the clasp. My vision blurs with tears as she fiddles with it, and then gasps in triumph.

"There!" she says, lifting the necklace for me to see before settling it around my neck.

She gently moves my hair and veil out of the way and fastens the clasp at the nape of my neck.

"There," she says again in a soft coo like a dove. "Nothing is broken."

And I fight – I strain with all my willpower – not to let that dam burst inside me. Because it's not the necklace that was irrevocably broken on the riverside.

16

Delphine and I sit close together facing the river, neither of us talking. I want to leave – there may be more than two men on our trail from Barbacane. The longer we stay here, the more likely it is that they will catch up with us. Plus there is the fact that there are two dead bodies slumped on the river bank; if anyone *else* encounters us, I don't relish the idea of having to explain that one.

But I also want to give Fin time to cool down. And maybe ... maybe I find myself nervous to face him again. He and Rollo may well decide to dump me and Delphine here with no horses and no supplies. Only the fact that I can still see Alezan and Colombe cropping the grass a little way away reassures me that they haven't abandoned us already. I rise to my feet and pace back and forward between Delphine and the horses to dispel my nervous energy.

I stop in my tracks when I see the knight and his squire trudging towards me, and I try to ignore the unbearable tightness in my chest as I bring my gaze to Fin's face. His expression is stony, controlled. There are no good-natured crinkles at the corners of his eyes, no quirk of a grin hitching one corner of his mouth. I notice that the wound in his upper arm has been bandaged.

"You said you planned to find the princess and bring her back," he says to me without preamble. "Where is she?"

"Her last letter came from Brillermare four months ago. There's no guarantee that she's still there. She said she was tempted to join the crew on one of the ships and sail the trade route to Iladiz, but I'm not sure if she was serious."

If Adda took that trip and didn't come back to Belforet, my chances of finding her are slim to none. She is headstrong but she isn't stupid. She had an agreement with her mother that she wouldn't leave Oramundi and stray beyond the queen's influence in case she was ever called back home.

"All I can hope is that she stayed in Brillermare when she didn't get a reply from her mother," I tell Fin.

He seems to mull this over. "I am familiar with a lot of the vessels that port in Brillermare. What is the name of the ship she considered joining?"

I cross to Alezan and dig around in my pack strapped to his saddle. I unwrap a chemise to find the hidden bundle of Adda's letters. I identify the right one and smooth the parchment flat, scanning Adda's familiar scrawl to remind myself of the ship's name.

"*Nicolete*," I read.

"Can I see?" Fin asks, holding out his hand for the letter, and I immediately snatch it to my chest.

"No!" I object.

There is no way I am letting him read the final letter I received from Adda – the one in which she ponders whether to give up her maidenhead to the dashing captain of the *Nicolete*.

Fin raises his hands in surrender.

"So you want to head north?" he asks.

I nod, holding his gaze, keeping my bearing confident. He doesn't need to know how ill-prepared we are for the journey. Fin glances to Rollo, who raises his eyebrows at him in question. There are so many unspoken words between us. Fin seems to make a decision and finally breaks the silence.

"We will accompany you to Brillermare."

"What? Why?"

That's not what I expected. Fin hates me. He distrusts me – that much is abundantly clear. I don't understand why he would volunteer to spend more time with me.

"Because your deception doesn't change the king's contest. Princess Adaliza, wherever she is, is still being hunted by dozens of noblemen seeking her hand."

I regard Fin with narrowed eyes. "And you still think that *you* deserve her."

The past week in my company has changed nothing for him. She's still a prize to be won – a prize he feels entitled to. I remember our hushed conversation in Ysabel's bedroom, when he admitted that he hadn't really thought the contest through, hadn't truly considered the thoughts and feelings of the woman at its centre. It turns out that he would do it all again – seize a woman against her will.

"Why do you always think the worst of me?" Fin asks, exasperated.

I blink. He has never spoken to me like that before.

"She won't marry you, Fin. If you think I was resistant, it was nothing compared to how the real Adaliza would treat you," I say, and my words have more bite than I mean them to.

What am I trying to achieve here? The man has just

offered to take us to Brillermare. I don't know why I'm attempting to sabotage that. What Fin does after we get there has no relevance to me. He can pursue Adda if he likes. I have full faith that she will humiliate and dismiss any man who tries to make her marry him.

The muscle in Fin's jaw flickers as he grits his teeth. Apparently he chooses to be the bigger person in our prickly exchange, because he takes a deep breath before replying.

"I know northern Belforet better than you. I can get us there in less than a week."

I purse my lips together and turn to Delphine, who is standing a step behind my left shoulder. Her expression is characteristically Delphine: doe-eyed, a little nervous. But she nods her approval of the plan.

"We can drop you back at the tower if you'd prefer," I tell her quietly. "You can stay with Claude until all of this is over."

I can't help feeling guilty as my gaze sweeps her ruined gown. She wasn't made for riding and rough sleeping.

Delphine shakes her head.

"I'm coming with you."

Her eyes are still wide but there is determination in the set of her jaw. I give her a small smile and reach behind to squeeze her hand. She smiles back at me.

"Then it's decided," I say, turning to Fin. "We proceed to Brillermare."

Fin nods once and busies himself with checking the straps on Alezan's saddle. When he's satisfied, he glances once at me standing at the horse's shoulder and laces his hands together to give me a leg up into the saddle. He turns his head and pointedly looks away from me as I mount. I feel him flinch slightly as I touch his shoulder to steady myself, and I try to ignore the cold that spreads through my belly at his reaction. I had prepared myself for Fin's rejection. I can't expect him to treat me the way he did before. Perhaps it will be better that way – his gallantry has always got on my nerves.

When Fin swings himself up into the saddle in front of me, he shuffles as far forward as he can to distance himself from me. He sits straight and stiff, with none of the languid grace he had in the seat when we rode together before. He may as well have a big warning sign on his back saying 'do not touch me, changeling'. I take a deep breath and blow it out my nostrils. It's fine. I won't hang onto him, no matter how fast Alezan rides. If my presence repulses him so much, I won't make him any more uncomfortable. I lean back, gripping the cantle, and hold on for dear life as Fin nudges the destrier into a trot and then a canter.

The next few hours pass in silence. The atmosphere is heavy – not just because of the strained relations between me and Fin. Clouds are gathering above us and the stifling heat of the summer feels like it's reaching a crescendo. After weeks of baking sunshine, it seems that a storm will finally break. It's fitting after the drama of the day, I think, as I lift my face to the sky and feel the static in the air, the building of the storm. I desperately want to feel the rain. For years I watched it fall from the safety of the tower, sheltered and dry.

When we reach a crossroads we turn northwards, and it settles some of the worry that constantly twists my stomach into knots. If any more of the duke's men are after us, they will assume that we are travelling south towards Throsne and the king and head in the opposite direction. It's one less threat we have to worry about. Still, this swathe of Belforet is likely to be crawling with princess hunters looking for Adaliza. We can't let our guard down.

We turn off the road and head for a quiet village that Fin

is familiar with. The inn is less likely to host knights than the larger establishments that line the Forest Road. I am utterly exhausted when we finally stop in front of the stables. My whole body hurts from the effort I have made to keep myself upright, in place and away from Fin as much as possible. I am grateful when the ostler offers his hand to help me down; he steadies me when I wobble on my feet. Running, fighting, riding and revealing my identity has drained me of the last vestiges of energy. I scrub at my eyes, trying to find the motivation to move, when I feel a reassuring hand at my back.

"Come on," Delphine says quietly, and guides me forward. "I'll get you some food. You head to bed."

I don't want to look up and see the reproof in Fin's expression or the wariness in Rollo's. I don't want to act the princess or the merchant's wife. I just want to close my eyes on this difficult day and wake up tomorrow to rain and a fresh start. So I keep my eyes on the floor as I let Delphine steer me towards the inn.

17

When we leave the inn the next morning, not a drop of rain has yet fallen from the sky. The storm clouds above are dark, oppressive, almost groaning with the need for release. The road below the horses' hooves is dry, cracked and dusty. We press on, trying to cover as much ground as we can before the inevitable deluge.

No one speaks. It makes me realise how comfortable we had become in each other's presence before the fight on the riverside. Fin, Rollo and I had gone hours without talking while we crossed the heath, occasionally punctuated by one of Rollo's whistled tunes, but the silence had never been awkward. Now it seems to echo between us, across the void that my deception created. I don't know how to span it. I don't even know if I should – why does it matter to me what they think?

No one else in my family would be so weak in my position. We're Lemorques: we're cutthroat and clever and crafty. We wear human skins and assume human lives until it suits us to toss that identity aside like a soiled shirt and don a new one, never looking back at what we left behind. Why should we? Humans will never trust us – my whole life I've been told that by Grandmère, my mother, my brothers, my aunts and uncles and cousins. We aren't required to fit into a world where we're not even welcome. Instead we manipulate it, profit from it, laugh at it, use it to our best advantage and damn anyone who gets in the way.

I am Aster Lemorque.

How long has it been since I told myself that? I was so wrapped up in being Adaliza, and then being Fin's pretend wife, when neither of those things really matters. It's embarrassing, how absorbed I have become in playing human. Would my brothers, Errol and Inigo, have cowered and cringed if their disguise slipped on a mission? No. They would have laughed at the confusion and started throwing knives if anyone got in the way of their escape.

I am Aster Lemorque.

I don't need to play human anymore. There's nothing left to hide. I won't let Fin make me feel guilty for what I am.

I straighten my spine as I look up at the sky and hear the first ominous rumble of thunder.

"Here we go," Rollo mutters under his breath from behind us.

It starts to spit with rain. Fat drops spatter on the dusty road; they land as dark speckles across the green linen of Fin's shoulders; one hits my cheek and trickles down like a tear. I breath in deeply. The air smells of lightning and petrichor, like storm and stone and dust. Finally.

I grin as the rain begins to beat down around us and a flash illuminates the clouds, followed a few seconds later by a rumble of thunder. Now it's a shower – like a child I stick out my tongue to catch the raindrops. I know that it won't be long before we're all soaked through, but I revel in it. I want to be swept up in the storm, to have rain on my cheeks and thunder in my ears.

Now it's a torrent. Rain plashes down in spears, water runs from our arms, the hoods of our cloaks and the horses' bodies like it does from gutter spouts. The flashes of lightning and crashes of thunder are getting closer together, like the ask and answer of a heated argument. Fin's face is scrunched up as he turns in the saddle, his hand shielding his eyes, and shouts back to Rollo.

"Let's get out of the open!"

Fin kicks Alezan with his heels and we lurch into a canter, the horse's hooves throwing up splashes as he runs through puddles on the waterlogged road. We turn off into a field and skirt along a dripping hedgerow. Eventually I see what Fin is aiming for: a squat barn lies ahead. It is an insubstantial and rickety thing, clad in long strips of timber with a shingle roof, but it will provide welcome shelter out of the rain.

Inside, the rain pounds an incessant din on the roof, almost loudly enough to drown out the rumbles of thunder. It is packed high and deep with straw, which must have only recently been brought in from the fields. There is just enough space to tether the two horses, and for the four of us to sit.

We share a simple meal of bread and cheese, and then settle down to wait out the worst of the storm. Delphine retrieves her small embroidery hoop from her pack and starts stitching, the picture of noble femininity despite the rustic environment. Fin sits with his plate armour at his feet and a rag and bottle in his hand. He decants a little oil onto the rag and starts cleaning the smooth metal with careful, practised strokes.

"I should be doing that!" Rollo protests and tries to take the rag from him, but Fin holds it out of his reach.

"You're still injured. I'm not so high and mighty that I don't remember how to take care of my armour," Fin says, and Rollo slumps back against the straw.

"Can I take a look at your shoulder?" I ask Rollo.

He still has his left arm strapped across his chest, and I suspect that the injury has gone from painful to frustrating. He carefully removes his tunic and undershirt, revealing the bandages that Ysabel put on a few days ago. I examine them with sight and smell, checking for any sign that the wound might have festered.

"I'm going to change the dressings," I say, and Rollo nods.

I go to my pack and retrieve the same ripped-up chemise we used last time to bandage the wounds. When I carefully unwind Rollo's bandages, I'm pleased with the neat, dark pink line beneath the stitches on the front of his shoulder. It's healing nicely. The exit wound at the back is less encouraging. The skin around the stitches is red and swollen, but there is no sign of yellow pus. There's not much I can do about the swelling. I don't have any of Ysabel's herbs, or anything to wash the wound with, like alcohol or vinegar. We should get some at the next inn.

"This looks sore," I murmur to Rollo.

"A bit," he admits, and Fin looks up from his cleaning.

"You must say something if it feels worse – or if you get a fever," I order.

"I know. I will," Rollo says dutifully as I set to work redressing both wounds.

"Thank you," he adds, and his eyes find mine for the first time since he discovered my true nature.

I give him a small smile, which he returns. When he is bandaged, clothed and sitting back against the straw again,

Being Adaliza

he manages to sit still for all of a minute before his foot is tapping against the stone floor.

"How do you do it?" he asks suddenly.

I blink and turn to look at him. "What?"

"How do you ... shift?"

His tone is slightly hesitant, as if he doesn't want to offend me by asking the question.

"It's a part of who I am. It's like asking you how you lift your hand to wave. You just do it, without thinking."

Rollo considers this. "And you can turn into anyone?"

"Not quite anyone. I have to have met them first. And, to be a convincing copy, they have to be female and around the same age as me."

"Will you show me?" he asks.

Delphine harrumphs at this over her needlework.

"Aster isn't a performing bear who will dance at your command," she chides, and Rollo has the grace to look cowed at his request.

I smile at Delphine's protectiveness of me, then turn to Rollo as my hair lightens to buttery blonde, my cheeks fill, my spine shrinks, my bosom pushes against the too-tight lacing of my kirtle.

"Quite right, Rollo. What a thing to ask," I say in Delphine's voice.

He stares at me open-mouthed as I grin back with an un-Delphine-like smile.

Delphine squawks at me and throws a hand over her eyes. "Oh stop it, it's horrible to see yourself!"

"I think you have a lovely body, Delphine," I say truthfully, and she gives a moan of embarrassment as a blush reddens her cheeks.

I decide to put her out of her misery and morph into the swerving wench at The Nightjar who had encouraged me and Fin to dance a few nights ago. My hair turns from blonde to red gold, springing into corkscrew curls that escape my bun and bounce around my face. Rollo watches in fascination. I notice Fin stealing glances out the corner of his eye while he pretends to ignore us, his hands still occupied with the rag and armour.

"Your eyes stay the same – they're blue," Rollo notices. "I thought changeling eyes were always black?"

I nod. "They are. That's a bit of extra magic that only my family knows how to do."

"How many of you are there?"

I transform back into Adaliza – her form feels so familiar to me, like shrugging on a favourite coat – as I reply. "Only a few families are left in Belforet. Many have died out. Only female changelings can give birth to changelings."

It's why our society has always been a matriarchy, and part of the reason why I'm so valuable to my grandmother. It's very unlikely that my two brothers and three male cousins will all find changeling girls to marry. The Lemorque line lives on in me, not them.

Rollo's eyes are still wide as he considers me. "Can you do anything else? Anything magic, I mean?"

"Not really. I can make myself particularly strong or light if I need to, which is handy in a fight. I can heal my own wounds – but not yours, I'm afraid."

"And you have a supernatural appetite," Delphine adds.

I roll my eyes. "Yes, and that. Oh, and most animals don't like the smell of me. But we're working on that, aren't we Alezan?" I call to the horse, who is munching inside his nosebag and staring mournfully out into the rain.

Rollo chuckles. I feel ... lighter, somehow. Buoyant. He isn't repulsed by me. He's ... intrigued. A few hours ago I wouldn't have believed that we'd be joking and laughing together. Well, three of us. Fin is stoic in his silence.

The rain is still drumming loudly on the barn roof. I rise to my feet and go to the doorway, staring out at the sheeting rain and waterlogged field beyond.

"It doesn't look like it's stopping," I say to no one in particular.

I hear someone rise to their feet and come to stand beside me.

"We need to decide whether to brave the rain now and make it to the next inn before nightfall, or cut our losses and stay here, where at least we know it will be warm and dry."

I don't turn to look at him, but Fin's voice raises the hairs on the back of my neck.

"The field looks waterlogged. Will the horses make it through without slipping?" I ask dubiously, assessing the sloping field and the runnels of water pooling in muddy dips.

A few hours of torrential rain is too much for the parched ground to absorb. There may well be flooding.

"I can't tell from here," Fin says, and steps out into the rain.

I hesitate for a moment before grabbing my sodden cloak and following him, my shoulders hunched against the downpour.

"Where are you going?" Rollo calls at our retreating backs from the doorway.

"To test the ground," Fin calls back.

My footsteps start to squelch as water and mud suck at my boots. I stop – I'm not going any further, not if I can help it. I choose the barn over another long, wet ride with no promise of a bed on the other side. Fin is still striding out, sinking deeper into the mud with each step.

"Let's go back," I say to him.

He ignores me and I put my hands on my hips and

narrow my eyes at him. Obstinate man.

I call his name again – just as he slips. His arms cartwheel, water spitting off his fingers like sparks from an anvil, and he wobbles theatrically before tumbling down onto his backside in the mud. And I can't help it – that light feeling inside me bubbles into laughter. He just looks so utterly bedraggled and stunned. My chuckle is low and burbles like a stream, melodiously infectious. I hear Rollo's bark of laughter from behind me where he watches from the doorway, and then Delphine's titter too.

Fin stares at me, surprised and outraged, and I clamp a hand over my mouth to try to stem the laughter, but I can't stop. Fin's mouth twitches and then he lets out a laugh too, finally acknowledging the ridiculousness of the situation. He throws back his head in the rain and howls with laughter. I clutch my stomach as tears of mirth gather in my eyes. I can't remember the last time I laughed this hard. Have I ever laughed this hard?

Fin finally gains enough control over his faculties to lever himself out of the mud. A wet brown smear runs up his cloak and breeches, and one hand is coated in mud up to the wrist. I'm still chuckling when he stumps over to me and reaches out a hand as if to paint me with mud.

"Don't you dare!" I gasp. "I happen to rather like this dress. You are taking a visit to the water trough before you come back inside."

Fin dutifully heads to the old stone water trough beside the barn, which must have been empty for weeks but now has a pool of rainwater inside it. I take off my cloak and mud-caked boots while Rollo fetches a change of clothes for Fin and takes them out to him. By the time they return, Fin's expression is carefully blank, all traces of good humour gone. He doesn't meet my eye.

Being Adaliza

For a moment, out in the mud and the rain, he had forgotten what I was. I know it's too much to hope that he might accept me as readily as Rollo has, and I don't expect anything of the sort. But maybe, when my betrayal isn't so raw, Fin and I might get along. Might work together. We both want the same thing, after all: Adaliza safe and back in Throsne where she belongs.

So he can pretend to ignore me while he nurses his pride at being duped – I don't care. I pull a blanket from the saddle bags and settle on the straw. Delphine sits behind me and pulls the pins from my wet hair, letting the tangled mass fan over my shoulders. She runs a comb through the snarls and I close my eyes, listening to the rain on the barn roof.

18

The next day is uneventful, notable only for the rain-fresh feeling in the air and the puddles in the ruts and holes of the road. We rise early and make good headway northwards up the Forest Road. Fin's route will not take us through the Old Woods; it will be much quicker and safer to catch a boat at the town of Sudferry on the River Fluet and sail through the swathe of forest. We arrive too late in the day to get passage on a boat big enough to transport the horses. Rather than risk another encounter at one of the busy inns nearby, we set up a small camp away from the bustle of other travellers.

    The ferry point is busy the next morning. As the primary method of travelling north to south in Belforet, the river is always crowded with vessels of all sizes. Small rowboats carry passengers and couriers; large, shallow bottomed longboats are laden with trade items in barrels, bolts and strongboxes; large rafts heavy with building materials are floated down the river and pulled by teams of mules that plod along the towpath.

Fin finds a longboat that allows horses on board – along with a few sheep, goats and an enormous pregnant sow – and we all tramp up the gangplank barely an hour past dawn. Our boat has a single mast with a square sail, and when the crew casts off and unfurls it we glide through the water at speed.

I am much more comfortable travelling by boat than by horse. The River Fluet is wide here, a murky grey-brown that makes it impossible to judge its depth or what might be living beneath its surface. I stand at the bow and take in the view as we sail downstream. It isn't long before I see the rustling green mantle of the Old Woods ahead on either side of the river. I understand why some would find them eerie – the trees are huge and twisting, the forest dense and impenetrable, with an air of ancient majesty that could easily be mistaken for menace. Even from the river I feel a strange sense of kinship with the woods.

Rollo is not so comfortable with the journey. He starts out sitting with Delphine near the mast, but soon runs to throw up over the side of the boat. He stays there, his gangly frame crumpled, his head lolling out over the water.

"Feedin' the fishes, are you, lad?" one of the old crewmates calls to him cheerily, a toothless smile on his face.

I go to stand by his side in sympathy and solidarity. It will be a whole day of sailing before we're through the Old Woods and we disembark in Nortferry, officially in northern Belforet. Poor Rollo – if his stomach can't stand a leisurely cruise down the river then he probably shouldn't attempt a rough sea crossing any time soon.

Hours pass. Rollo empties his stomach twice more, and can't face the simple meal we share out on deck in the middle of the day. Delphine and I play cards, falling into the rhythm that we established during many hours shut up in the tower. Fin continues to be distant with me. I tell myself I don't care, but I do. I miss his good humour and his reassurances. I miss the dozen touches we used to share each day: my fingers in his as he handed me up onto the horse, my arms around his middle when Alezan's pace increased, his hand on my waist as he helped me down from the saddle. Now he avoids making contact with me as much as possible. He doesn't look at me if he can help it.

I think of the silent void between us, the one I don't know how to bridge. I might not be able to shout across to Fin ... but maybe I could sign to him.

Can we sign? I ask him as all four of us sit together in silence, staring out at the unchanging view of ancient trees and winking river water. He looks to me automatically as I gesture.

His expression is reluctant, but I try not to let it dishearten me.

There is much more to learn, I sign. *How do I say ... river?*

I make up a likely gesture for river, snaking my hand forward and away from my body.

Or ... rain?

Again I guess, pulling both hands down and closing my fingers at the end as if demonstrating heavy rain falling. Rollo snorts a laugh, and I look to him in surprise. He has been morosely quiet for hours since his last bout of sickness.

What?

Rollo glances at Fin, who doesn't answer.

"That," Rollo mimics my made-up sign for rain, "means blind drunk."

My face falls. "Oh."

I had forgotten that Rollo also knows sign language. He and Fin's deaf sister grew up together.

Being Adaliza

I blink in Fin's direction. "See how much I still have to learn?"

Fin stays silent for long enough for me to give up hope that he will answer. I am about to turn away in defeat when he raises his hands and flaps them downwards twice.

"Rain," he says.

I copy the gesture. "Rain," I repeat, hiding my feeling of triumph.

By the time the trees on either side of the river thin out and we've passed through the ancient swathe of forest, I have elicited fifteen new words from Fin – fifteen words and not a single smile.

The next morning dawns bright over northern Belforet. The landscape here is quite different from the rolling pasture lands and flat, barren heath we have ridden through thus far on our wanderings around the country. This is a rugged land of craggy hills, lush valleys and lakes that shine like mirrors in the sunshine. The hillsides are scattered with hardy sheep and goats that watch us dispassionately as we ride past. The road wends up, down and around the hills, thickly hemmed in on both sides with trees that darken our path.

I'm glad we're making this journey in the summer. I imagine that the exposed peaks are lashed by perishing winds in the winter, and the welcome shade of the roadside trees would feel gloomy on a dark, cold day. I am content to sit behind Fin and take in the ever-changing views as we crest hills and descend into valleys. The stiffness in Fin's back has softened a little since we departed the river boat. He seems to breathe easier here. I suspect he's happy to be going homeward – although we're still two days' ride from Brillermare at the northern tip of Belforet.

When we stop for the night, having travelled miles over

the course of the day, Rollo is still looking peaky after his unpleasant boat ride up the river. I tell him to go to bed after our evening meal at the tavern, hoping that a good night's sleep will help him to feel better.

We continue on, the miles disappearing behind us under Alezan and Colombe's hooves. We encounter no threats, neither from knights taking part in the rescue contest nor from the Duc d'Eschecs men. Perhaps the long, uninterrupted rides are lulling all of us into a sense of security we didn't have before.

I am taken aback when Fin addresses me directly on one of our rest breaks. We are sitting near the edge of a small lake, framed by craggy hills on all sides.

"Those are asters," he says, pointing to a low bush of small, purple flowers growing nearby.

I blink in surprise, then lean in close to inspect the flowers. The purple petals are straight and narrow, fanning out around a large yellow eye.

"You're right," I say lightly, running my finger around one flower to make the petals bounce.

"They grow all over at this time of year. My grandmother used to take a tea brewed from asters – she said it soothed her chest."

It is the most he has said to me in days. It feels like a cautious step forward in a new direction. He isn't talking to Princess Adaliza – he's addressing Aster Lemorque. And there's no resentment or disgust in his tone.

"My grandmother grew asters in her garden – but only the poisonous variety. She didn't like animals trespassing on her apothecary beds, so she planted as many deterrents as possible." I am conscious that I'm rambling. "I suspect our grandmothers were very different."

I stop myself talking. Why did I say that? Fin doesn't

answer, and it doesn't surprise me.

"I like to think I'm not named after the poisonous flower. 'Aster' means *star* in Old Hellenik. I think that's much nicer."

I continue to stroke the petals of the flower, not chancing a look at Fin to gauge his reaction.

"How many languages do you speak?" he asks.

"Fourteen, I think – if you count all the dialect variants," I reply.

"Is that normal, for a changeling?"

I turn to look at him then with a small smile. "No. That's just me."

He doesn't smile back – his face still doesn't look right to me without a grin quirking one side of his mouth. He just considers me, like I'm a map he needs to carefully inspect before he plots a route.

"We should get moving," he says eventually, tearing his eyes from me.

I take a breath before I nod and rise to my feet. Delphine follows suit. Rollo is lying on his back in the shade of a nearby tree, a hat tipped over his eyes. He doesn't stir as we ready ourselves for departure.

"Come on, Rollo," I call to him.

Still he doesn't move. "Rollo?"

I move to his side and tap his arm as I pluck the hat from his head. Rollo's face is drawn and sweaty, he squeezes his eyelids closed and groans slightly at my touch. I lay my hand across his forehead – his skin is burning hot.

Worry floods my stomach as I call, "Fin!"

Fin hears the urgency in my tone and comes straight to my side, with Delphine half a step behind.

"Can you lift him while I take off his tunic?" I ask.

Fin wraps an arm around Rollo's back as Delphine and I awkwardly manage to pull his top over his head. Rollo flinches and cries out as the fabric snags over his shoulder. When I undo his bandages I know with grim certainty what I will find. The wound in the back of his shoulder is red and inflamed, the catgut stitches almost swallowed by the swollen skin around it. At one end of the wound is a swelling filled with yellow pus. My heart slams against my ribs as I survey the injury. It has festered.

I look up and my eyes meet Fin's. I read the same feelings in his expression: shock, horror, worry.

"What can we do?" I ask in a whisper.

The muscle in Fin's jaw flickers as he thinks. "We can try to find an apothecary or cunning man nearby, but it might take hours to locate one and bring them here. The other option is to ride onwards – we're maybe half a day from Rollo's family estate in Sommette. His family will be better placed to summon a good physician."

"Will he withstand the ride?" I ask.

Rollo is barely conscious. How will we keep him upright on horseback for half a day?

"He can ride with me – Alezan will be able to take the weight. Can you ride with Delphine on Colombe?"

While I'm not a confident rider, after nearly two weeks in the saddle I am at least able to keep my seat now. Delphine is a passable horsewoman, and will be able to keep Colombe in check.

I nod to Fin. "Yes."

After redressing Rollo and pouring some water into his mouth, we carefully haul him to his feet. He is weak and boneless as Delphine and I pass him to Fin in Alezan's saddle, and together we manage to get him into a sitting position in front of Fin. His head lolls from side to side, his face pale and drawn.

"Stay with me, Rollo," Fin murmurs to him, his

expression set in hard lines of determination.

Delphine and I mount Colombe, and we follow the chestnut destrier at a rolling canter.

19

We ride. With gritted teeth and hammering hearts, we ride. Past villages sheltering in the lee of the hills, along ridges with the land falling away dramatically on either side, over grass and rock and road, we ride. We don't stop or slow down, even as the light fades. I trust that Fin knows where he is going and can find his way in the dark.

The sky is deep blue and the leaping light of torches is bright in the gloaming when we reach a gatehouse, abutted on both sides by a stone wall. Fin pulls Alezan to a halt but doesn't dismount as he calls down to the guards. The destrier prances and snorts, restless after the long run.

"I'm Sir Finton Prest. I have Rollo here – he's gravely injured. I need to take him to his family. And someone needs to fetch a physician right away."

The guards seem taken aback by Fin's presence, but they obey his commands. Orders are shouted to saddle a horse for a messenger, and the men step aside to allow us to pass through the gatehouse. They peer at Delphine and I in confusion, clearly wondering why two plainly dressed women are riding Rollo's horse, but they don't question us as we follow Fin.

The path on the other side of the gatehouse is straight and flat, leading to a squat stone manor house that is a hulking shadow against the navy sky. Fin rides straight to the front door.

"Fetch the Vicomte and Vicomtesse," he calls to the servants who have come through the open door and are staring out at us in surprise.

Two of them dash back inside. The others gather around the horses, helping Fin to lower the half-conscious form of Rollo from the saddle and immediately taking him inside. Fin jumps down and follows. Delphine and I are helped down from Colombe and the two horses are led off by their bridles, presumably to the stables. We stand alone in front of the manor, the servants having scattered in different directions, and exchange a look.

What should we do? I want to follow Fin and stay at Rollo's side, but they've disappeared inside the vast house. Should we go in after them and open doors until we find where they've taken him? It feels rather invasive. We're not supposed to be here – stopping off at Rollo's ancestral home was not part of our plan. It's not a tavern where we can pass through unnoticed. Being here with Fin requires me to be Princess Adaliza, even if I'm currently wearing a commoner's travel-stained kirtle and feeling as dirty, smelly and weary as you would expect after so many days of hard riding. I briefly wonder if I could sneak off and sleep under the stars for a night to avoid the questions that will inevitably arise if I stay here.

"Don't do it," Delphine warns.

I turn to look at her and she has a narrowed gaze fixed on me.

"What?" I ask.

"You're thinking about running away. It's a silly idea – our packs are still tied to the horses, we don't have any provisions. And we can't leave Rollo."

"I don't want to leave Rollo! And I know, I was just ... being cowardly." I sigh.

A scramble of movement makes us both turn back to the front door. Four wide-eyed maids line up on the doorstep and stare at me in awe; a man pushes through the line, looking harassed. He is tall and rangy, well dressed, with streaks of grey shot through his dark hair and beard.

"Your Highness!" he gasps, bowing deeply, which prompts all four maids to curtsy in tandem. "I sincerely apologise for the lack of appropriate greeting. The Manoir de Sommette is at your service."

So this is the Vicomte, Rollo's father. Clearly Fin has only just remembered to tell them who I am and why he is travelling with me.

"No apology is necessary, really," I insist. "How is Rollo?"

The man's expression falls. "He is settled. The physician has been summoned. It is in the hands of God now."

My stomach roils at the thought – I don't believe in his god. But Rollo is strong. We got him here. He can pull through – he has to pull through. I won't contemplate any alternative.

"My wife, the Vicomtesse – she is with him now. Otherwise she would have come to greet you. I hope you understand," the Vicomte says.

"Of course," I reassure him. "It's exactly where I would expect her to be. Please don't put yourselves out on my account. This was an unplanned diversion on our journey.

We can find an inn nearby for the night if that would—"

"I wouldn't hear of it!" he interrupts, appalled by the suggestion. "You must be hungry and tired after your journey."

He turns to the maids. "Prepare the princess's rooms and have a bath drawn for her. Then send up a tray for both the ladies."

They quickly bob their assent and scurry away to do his bidding. Well, I may not have my anonymity but a bath will more than make up for it. It's been weeks since I had a proper soak – in fact, the last time was the morning that Fin climbed the tower and put this sorry saga in motion. How long ago that feels now.

"We are most grateful, My Lord," I say politely, projecting the princess in every line of my tired body as I follow him into the manor.

It feels strange, the next morning, to have Delphine dress me in Adaliza's clothes again. We choose a gown that is both beautiful and practical. It is a dusky pink silk, cut with curved seams to follow the lines of my body, with dagged sleeves that fall almost to my knees at the points. I wear no adornment other than a bejewelled belt. I don't want or need other layers of fabric to swathe and drape my form, as is the fashion at court. Delphine brushes my mink brown hair until it shines and leaves it loose to ripple over my shoulders.

When I check myself in the looking glass I'm pleased with the result: I look elegant but not ostentatious. It's the kind of thing a princess would wear when trying to travel incognito across the country, one who would forgo a tiara but refused to sacrifice good tailoring. I wonder if I'll have a chance to talk to Fin before we see our hosts. We need to get our story straight; we didn't intend to encounter anyone he actually knows in northern Belforet. It will be harder to lie to them – for him, anyway. I have more practice at it.

More importantly, I want to know how Rollo is faring. Worry is still roiling in my stomach at the thought of his wan face yesterday, the angry red of his festering wound. We heard the physician arrive last night but haven't received news of his condition from any of the maids who buzz around me like bees on a honeypot.

When we are ready, Delphine and I are led through the labyrinthine manor to what must be the Great Hall. There are a number of people gathered there; all of them turn towards me when I enter, straightening or standing, and bow or curtsy in unison. A number of them are children – presumably Rollo's younger brothers and sisters. I dismiss the formal greeting with a hand gesture.

"Your Highness, how did you sleep?" the Vicomte asks.

"How is Rollo?" I ask, ignoring the pleasantries.

A woman, presumably Rollo's mother by her silk gown and tear-stained expression, reaches out and clutches the Vicomte's arm as she speaks.

"He is ... still with us, Your Highness. The physician is attending him. I thank God that Fin – Sir Finton –" she corrects herself, "brought him home to us when he did."

My eyes travel to Fin, who is standing with the family. Unlike me, he doesn't look freshly bathed. His face is haggard with dark circles under his eyes. Colour rises in his cheeks when our eyes meet – interesting. That hasn't happened in a while, certainly not since he found out my true identity. I suppose I am looking more like Adaliza than I have in a long time. It would make sense if the thought of her makes his heart race. She is technically his betrothed.

I turn back to the Vicomte and Vicomtesse. "That is good to hear. He gave us quite a shock on the road."

They smile weakly at me. Rollo's father hesitates slightly

before he speaks again.

"Sir Finton tells me that you helped to extract the arrow and tend his wounds?"

I nod.

"Then we are forever in your debt, Your Highness."

They mean it. Their faces shine with gratitude and maybe a little awe. I shy away from it.

"I did what anyone would do in such a situation. Rollo has been unfailingly kind to me. I value his friendship. And I am also praying for his recovery."

I glance back to Fin. "My Lord and Lady, may I speak privately with Sir Finton?"

"Of course!" the Vicomtesse says immediately, and starts chivvying the children out of the room.

It isn't long before everyone but me, Fin and Delphine have vacated the hall. It feels very big and empty without all those bodies in it. I turn to Fin.

"You haven't slept?"

He rubs his face. "A little, but not much. I didn't want to leave Rollo's side. But ... he's still with us. Despite everything, he's holding on."

I nod. It's the best we can hope for.

"What have you told them about our journey?" I ask.

"Not much. I said that I found you and rescued you from the tower, but you want to see more of Belforet before I take you south to Throsne and our wedding is announced."

I hide my grimace. That is a stupid cover story. Why would he agree to let me jolly around the country with him while hundreds of other nobles are searching for me? But it's too late to change it now.

"And ..." Fin continues with a vaguely embarrassed twist to his mouth, "I'm afraid there's no way we can avoid visiting Brisebassier while we're here. Knowing how gossipy the servants are, my family will have found out by now that I turned up here unexpectedly. It would be too suspicious to ignore them."

It's ... inconvenient. We wanted as few people to know about our movements as possible. But ... I remember how fondly Fin talked about his home when we were at Ysabel's cottage. I don't begrudge him the opportunity to go home and see his family. And besides – if we find Adda in Brillermare, I won't even have to play the part of the princess by the time we go there. I can be a second handmaiden, free to explore the place without attracting any interest.

"Fine," I say evenly. "Why don't you go to bed while I head into Brillermare and track down Adda—"

"No," Fin cuts me off. "You're not going to Brillermare alone. I'll go with you."

I frown at him. "Fin, you're practically sleeping on your feet! You need to rest, and I don't want to delay another day."

"I'm coming," he insists, as stubborn as he always has been when we come to loggerheads – even though most of the time I've ended up getting my way.

I consider his reaction for a moment. "Are you worried that we'll sneak off without you?"

It would be an understandable worry – because it is a tempting proposition. Adda and I could take care of ourselves and Delphine without the need for a knightly escort. Without Adda in his company, Fin wouldn't have a claim to winning the king's stupid contest. But ... I'm not that ruthless. Rollo is close to death and Fin is exhausted from trying to save him. Taking advantage of him in our current situation doesn't sit well with me.

"No ..." Fin says, then sighs. "I just ... I want to meet her. Is that so hard to believe?"

He doesn't meet my eye – and I realise he's being

truthful. I remember how he was when he first met me in the tower, all chivalry and blushes. He's a romantic. And now he thinks he's got a second chance to woo Adda – the real Adda, this time. Is that what he was mulling over during those long hours we travelled north from the ferry?

I could retort that she won't want to meet *him*. I could tease him for his naivety. But I won't.

"Alright," I say eventually. "We'll go together. But ... maybe you could wash first?"

Delphine muffles a giggle behind me.

20

Delphine and I explore the gardens of the Manoir de Sommette while we wait for Fin to make himself presentable. It's greener here than it was in the south – the coast is exposed to more rain and wind, which must have kept the August drought at bay. Not that it feels like we're on the coast here. I crane my neck to look into the distance but there are no glimpses of the sea from the estate. I've never seen it before. All of my travels have been inland in Belforet or the neighbouring landlocked kingdoms of Paillevallee and Herza. I'm excited to finally see Brillermare and the ocean.

When Fin appears he leads us to the stables. We borrow the Vicomte's horses, leaving Alezan and Colombe to rest after their recent exertions.

"Do you want to ride your own horse?" Fin asks me as Delphine mounts a placid piebald mare.

I raise my chin determinedly as I survey the horse in front of me. It's a steady-looking dun with a messy forelock, blinking flies out of its eyes. I can do this. It's been days since I've felt like I was going to wobble out of the saddle. I can ride a horse on my own.

I step towards the animal. Its nostrils flare as it catches my scent and it whinnies at me, kicking its head back.

"Whoa," Fin says, placing a soothing hand on the horse's neck.

I pause at its show of objection but continue to the mounting block, lifting my pink skirts above my ankles to step up. I have one foot in the stirrup when the horse frights, pulling out of Fin's grip and jolting forward. With a cry I find myself falling gracelessly to the ground, landing with a hard bump on my backside.

"Aster!" Delphine calls worriedly.

"Are you ok?" Fin is at my side in an instant, reaching for me.

I squint up at him from the floor, my face scrunched in pain and irritation. "Oww!"

Pain radiates from my backside like a struck bell, and I wonder if I've bruised my coccyx. I send my magic there, soothing the nerve endings until the pain becomes a dull ache. I scowl in the direction of the horse.

"I never thought I'd come to appreciate your monster of a destrier," I tell him as I take his hand and rise unsteadily to my feet.

I realise that it's true – Alezan and Colombe hardly react to my unsettling changeling presence anymore. They're used to me. I hadn't expected that.

Fin grins. The sight of that familiar easy smile makes my stomach flip over. "You can ride with me."

Fin mounts and has tight control of his horse when I join him in the saddle. The beast dances a few steps and gives a wicker of disapproval, but complies.

Primrose Hugh

It takes almost an hour to ride to Brillermare at a leisurely pace. When we round a hill and finally see the port for the first time, my mouth goes slack in awe. The town is beautiful: wooden framed buildings with red tile roofs cluster around the curve of the seafront, penetrated by the odd spire of a church and a stone lighthouse. Stone jetties reach out into the water where dozens of great wooden ships sit majestically at rest, a forest of masts and rigging. But most astounding is the sea. It's so *big*. Undulating blue stretches as far as the eye can see, wavering into the sky at the horizon. It dwarfs the boats and buildings, those inconsequential scraps of human endeavour. It makes me feel so small in comparison. I just stare as we ride closer to the bustle of the town.

Once we're in the thick of the port, I'm begrudgingly glad that Fin is with us. He guides us straight to a stable where we leave the horses, and then out to the jetties to find the *Nicolete*. He knows each winding street and cobbled back alley. More than once he is greeted by a tradesperson who recognises him as the son of the local lord. He returns each greeting with an easy smile and a few kind words.

My stomach is in knots as I squint out at the ships, trying to read the names painted on their prows. *Saint Solange, Hippocampe, Sirene*. Adda could be here. My eyes rove every face in the crowd, searching for storm blue eyes and mink brown hair. Rather than walking the length of every jetty to find the ship – avoiding the swaggering sailors, goods pushed in handcarts and barrels being rolled towards the warehouses on the shore – Fin suggests we find the harbourmaster to enquire about the *Nicolete*.

The man in question recognises Fin and cheerfully answers us.

"The *Nicolete*? She left port more than three months ago. Was due back a fortnight past but hasn't shown up yet."

My stomach sinks at that. If Adda boarded the ship, she has been gone from Belforet for months. She won't have heard the news of the queen's death or the king's contest. And where is the ship now? Was it blown off course, floating and damaged in some far-flung sea? Or wrecked and sunk at the bottom of the ocean? What will I do if I can't find her? The chilling reality of that prospect dawns on me properly for the first time, setting my heart racing in panic. What will happen to Belforet if the heir to the throne is dead?

I feel a small hand close around mine.

"It's ok," Delphine whispers to me.

Her eyes are wide and understanding. She sees the rising panic in mine. I give her hand a squeeze in gratitude and nod my head.

"It's not unusual for a ship to come into port later than expected," Fin says. "The delay could be for a multitude of reasons: a late departure, or bad weather. It doesn't mean it won't turn up eventually."

"And we don't even know if she's on the *Nicolete*," Delphine reminds me. "She could have just holed up here when she didn't get a reply from her mother."

I purse my lips in thought. Adda is not the type to hole up and twiddle her thumbs while she waits for something to happen. The captain's offer of adventure in Iladiz would have tempted her, I know it. The *Nicolete* is our best lead – even if she didn't join the crew, the captain will be able to tell me about her movements when he saw her last. I make a mental note to ensure that Fin isn't present for that interrogation.

I take a deep breath to settle myself. I've got to be sensible.

"Let's check the town. If we don't find any trace of her, we'll just have to wait until the *Nicolete* comes into port."

Delphine nods her agreement with this plan. We sweep

the busy dockside, peering into doorways and checking each small gathering of women for evidence of Adda.

"How do I know what she looks like?" Fin asks quietly, a small frown creasing his brow as his gaze jumps from face to face.

I stare at him for a moment. "Are you serious? She looks like me."

He blinks. "Oh. Yes. Of course."

I shake my head at him in disbelief and turn back to study the crowds. Methodically we go down each street that fans out from the port. I'm hungry and irritable by the time we loop back to the waterfront for the fifth time, passing a rowdy tavern. I am about to grouse at Fin that we should stop this aimless wandering and find some food when a voice calls out behind me.

"Adda! You back, then?"

I turn in shock to find an older woman in an apron standing on the pavement, her hands on her ample hips. She has a pinched face but a keen sparkle in her dark eyes.

"You know Adda?" I ask breathlessly.

The woman frowns. "Who are you then?"

Her gaze sweeps me up and down, tallying all of the differences between me and the girl she knows.

"I'm her sister. I'm looking for her. Do you know where she is?"

"Didn't know she was a twin. Or a fine lady."

The woman's expression is still suspicious, but the similarities between Adda and I are undeniable. Eventually she answers my question.

"Still at sea, last I heard."

"On the *Nicolete*?" I ask, my heart beating fast.

"That's right. She lodges with me. Told me to keep her room aside until she comes back."

Being Adaliza

I stare at the woman, excitement flaring within me. "Can you take me there? To her room?"

The woman considers this for a moment before shrugging her assent. "Only you. I'm not letting any old person tramp through my lodging house."

I exchange looks with Fin and Delphine. Fin gives me a nod. "We'll wait here."

The woman – Adda's rough and ready landlady – leads me down a narrow street and through the door of a tall townhouse. The first storey juts out over the ground floor, and the second storey further still, giving it a precarious look as if it could fall flat on its face. We climb wooden stairs that creak loudly with each footfall as we ascend – there would be no sneaking out of this house unnoticed. My breathing is shallow and my pulse beats in my ears by the time we reach the top floor and the woman unlocks a door on the left of the landing.

"In here," she says.

I step into the room. The ceiling is low but it's surprisingly spacious, with a dormer window that looks out onto the port and the winking sea beyond. There is a bed with a pile of neatly folded blankets, a washstand with an empty ewer and bowl, and a writing desk. I step towards it eagerly; it's the only place in the room that has any sort of personal effects. Parchment and quills litter the desk, and a stack of papers is wedged into one of its cubby holes. My heart leaps when I see a familiar stick of purple sealing wax. Every letter I received from Adda had the same purple seal. This is her room. She was here.

My fingers tremble as I reach for the pile of papers. I recognise them as parcels of parchment – three of them, all sealed and simply addressed to 'Mother' in Adda's bold hand. I stroke the word, my excitement tempered. These must be the letters that Adda planned to give to the palace messenger – the one who never turned up. Judging by the overlarge size and the bulkiness, I suspect that there are letters addressed to 'The Princess in the Tower' within each parcel. For a moment I consider breaking the purple seals and looking inside, but I stop myself. These letters are for her mother. Adda doesn't know that she is dead. I won't go rifling through her correspondence like a spy.

Instead I find a clear scrap of parchment and grab a quill and ink pot.

Adda –

I'm here, I need to find you. If you see this, please stay where you are. I'll come back here as soon as I can.

– Aster

I set the note right in the middle of the desk and let out a shaky breath. It's the best I can do for now.

I leave the house, calling my thanks to the landlady as I go, and find Fin and Delphine out on the street. Fin nods when I have filled them in.

"I'll give one of the dock boys a few coins to watch for the *Nicolete* and find us as soon as she comes into port."

It's a good plan – although it does mean waiting around again. Waiting, waiting. Why do I always have to wait?

"What shall we do in the meantime?" I ask.

Fin rubs the back of his neck. "Well, there is something I need to do."

He sidles over to a woman selling flowers from a handcart. I watch him quizzically as he selects a perfect purple bloom from the collection.

"What is it?" I ask.

"Surprise my little sister," he says with a small smile,

Being Adaliza

handing over a coin to the flower seller.

21

Brisebassier is everything I expected. The small castle is built from grey stone with a hodge-podge of towers and turrets that give it more of an endearing air than a threatening one. It nestles in the hillside, facing out towards the rugged coastline and huge expanse of the ocean. Someone must have seen us coming as we rode up the coastal path from Brillermare, because the gates are wide open and there is a small gathering of people waiting for us on the front steps.

Fin's smile is wide and his eyes are bright as he leaps down from the saddle, remembering his courtly manners this time and helping me down after him rather than stranding me like he had at the Manoir de Sommette. He has only taken a step from the horse when a girl barrels into him, throwing her arms around his waist. He laughs and hugs her back, but she pulls away from him and gestures rapidly in sign language.

What are you doing back here?

Visiting you, of course, he replies, and hands her the purple flower he bought in Brillermare.

The delight on the girl's face brings a smile to mine. So this is Elinor. She looks young for fourteen, caught in that awkward stage between girlhood and womanhood. She has a profusion of chestnut hair the same shade as Fin's that is in no way contained by the cap perched on her head. Her features are rather plain but transformed with expression as she signs with her whole body, not just her hands. Benoit was the same, I remember.

Her eyes move from Fin to me and widen.

Is it true? she asks. *You did it? You found the princess?*

It is true, I sign back, and her mouth drops open in an o of surprise.

You can sign? Excitement is evident in her every movement.

Your brother is teaching me. I'm still a beginner, I explain, conscious of how much slower my hands move than hers.

Elinor beams at Fin. She would have said more but one of the other figures waiting on the steps calls out; Fin taps his sister on the shoulder and points to the speaker, and Elinor turns around.

"Well this is an unexpected delight," a woman says, signing as she speaks.

Before I started learning sign language I didn't realise how difficult that was to do. I definitely don't have the coordination to do both at once yet.

The woman is clearly Fin and Elinor's mother. She shares their chestnut hair and steps towards us with an elegant bearing, accentuated by the flow and ripple of her green gown.

"Mother."

Fin crosses to her and kisses her cheek. A man

approaches next and slaps Fin on the arm before pulling him into one of those stiff one-armed hugs that men share.

"Father."

Like Fin he is tall and broad shouldered, although he is carrying more weight around the stomach than his son. The laughter lines creasing his face look well worn, as if he rarely stops smiling.

As one all three of them turn to look at me, expectation and curiosity in the gazes of Fin's parents. I am hit with a twinge of nerves. This is the first time that Fin's family is meeting his future wife – I can't afford to mess this up for Adda.

"Mother, Father – this is Princess Adaliza of Belforet, and her handmaiden, Delphine. Your Highness, these are my parents, the Comte and Comtesse de Brisebassier." He gestures to the other people still standing on the steps. "My brother, Quentin, and his wife, Alys. And you've already met Elinor, my little sister."

They bow and curtsy. I nod in acknowledgement and smile warmly.

"It is a pleasure. Although our presence here was brought about by worrying circumstances, I am glad to have this opportunity to meet you all."

Fin signs along as I speak so that Elinor is included in the conversation.

"We heard about Rollo's accident. How is the dear boy?" the Comtesse asks, placing a concerned hand on her chest.

Fin's expression turns serious. "He is alive and still fighting."

She nods soberly. Then she seems to remember that we're all standing in front of the castle and gestures us forward.

"Come in, come in, we were about to sit down for dinner."

Being Adaliza

At that we are swept into the castle. I shoot a glance at Delphine, who gives me a look I can easily read as *See, they're feeding you, you can stop complaining.* I may have mentioned once or twice on the ride here that I was peckish.

We are led into a banqueting hall hung with tapestries and dominated by a large oak dining table. I am ushered into a seat at the very centre of the table, with the Comte on my left and Fin on my right. Elinor scrambles to claim the seat opposite me, giving me a puckish grin that I can't help but return.

Dozens of dishes are brought out on platters and placed in the centre of the table. There is freshly fried fish – I recognise mackerel and a large brill – that all sizzle and smell divine, along with bowls of peas, runner beans and broad beans. I help myself to stuffed chicken, resplendent with herbs and spices. A platter of eels sits further down the table, which I tactfully ignore. While I'll eat almost anything when I'm hungry, I can't stand eels.

Fluffy white bread is sliced into doorstops and handed around. I lick my lips at the sight of a plate of custard tarts and a creamy dessert drizzled in honey and sprinkled with almonds. It's been a long time since I had a dessert. While the food we've eaten at inns across Belforet has been hearty and plentiful, none of it has been this fine. It puts me in an excellent mood.

Fin and I answer questions about our travels from his family. They are polite and subtle, but I can tell they're desperate to find out more. I understand why they're excited. Their son is going to be the next king consort of Belforet – he has proven his bravery and bested every other noble in the land to win Adaliza's hand. If they wonder why Fin is somewhat reticent to share all the details, they don't show it. He's clearly uncomfortable pretending to his family, so I step in and shade his words with more colour when necessary.

We stick with Fin's silly story about me wanting to see more of the country before we go back to Throsne, and explain that we're trying to travel incognito so as not to attract unwanted attention.

"And what is it you came here to see?" the Comte asks.

"The sea," I say, thinking on my feet, but realising it's the truth. "I've never seen the sea before. I want to stand in the serf."

"You must take Her Highness to the beach, Fin," the Comtesse urges before turning to me. "There really is no place more beautiful in all of Belforet."

I nod. "I would love to see it."

Whenever there is a break in the conversation, Elinor pounces on me with excitement in her eyes. Hers are hazel, I notice, rather than pure green like Fin's. She signs quickly and enthusiastically, so much so that I have to ask her to repeat or explain several words and Fin tells her to slow down more than once. She rolls her eyes at him and replies something along with a sign I don't recognise, paddling her hands up and down. I repeat the gesture questioningly.

Fin jumps in to explain. "It means 'fin'. It's my sign name – a nickname so that you don't have to spell out a name by letter every time you use it."

What is your sign name? I ask Elinor.

She grins and draws her hand down and away from her nose as if miming an animal's snout.

"It means fox," Fin clarifies.

I like the nickname – it suits Elinor, and not just because of her fox-coloured hair. There's a sense of vulpine mischief and cunning about her.

What is yours? she asks me.

I shrug. *I don't have one.*

Being Adaliza

Elinor turns to Fin and scowls at him, as if this is a grave offence. He looks at me as he makes a gesture with one hand, opening and closing his fist once.

"Star," he says softly.

I stare back at him for a beat.

Star! Elinor repeats, then holds her hands to her heart and seems to melt in a gesture that can only mean "how romantic".

Fin's cheeks heat. I look away, feeling overwhelmed and wrongfooted and exposed. Because the nickname isn't for Adaliza – it's for me. My throat feels thick. It shouldn't mean so much to me ... but it does. Fin doesn't meet my eye for a long time afterwards, and I suspect he regrets choosing that particular sign name.

After hours of convivial talking and eating, Fin announces that we should be going.

"But you only just arrived!" his mother protests. "Won't you stay here?"

"All of our belongings are at the Manoir de Sommette. And I want to check on Rollo. We'll come back tomorrow."

He glances at me, as if to ask my permission. I nod. I thought that this visit would be painful and awkward as I acted the part of Princess Adaliza alongside a reluctant and embarrassed Fin, but I have enjoyed myself. I like this place, and I like these people. As long as Rollo's condition doesn't worsen, I'd be happy to stay at Brisebassier while we wait for the *Nicolete* to return.

When we get back to the manor, Delphine and I follow Fin to the room where Rollo is being tended. The drapes are drawn and a thick smell of herbs hangs in the air, making the sickroom dark and oppressive. There is a jar of leeches on the side table – I can see the black worms wriggling and writhing. It gives me an unpleasant feeling.

I don't agree with the humans' theory about the balance of humours within the body and the need to let blood to cure illnesses. I can sense no such balance within my own body, only the complex interdependent systems of blood circulation, nerves and organs. From what I've seen of the inside of human bodies – which is disgusting but rather inevitable in my line of work – they have the same systems. But I am no physician and there's nothing I can do to heal Rollo.

Rollo is propped up on a pile of pillows in bed. He is pale and his eyes are sunken into dark sockets, but he is conscious when we enter the room and an exhausted smile feathers his lips when he sees us.

"You're awake!" I say, going to the bedside and taking his hand in mine.

While a festering wound is life-threatening, it doesn't always lead to death. Rollo might be one of the lucky ones.

"You can't get rid of me that easily," he rasps, and I smile.

"How are you feeling?" Fin asks.

"Weak as a babe. But less feverish than before. How did we get here? I don't remember."

"We rode," Fin says simply.

I know that he won't tell Rollo how desperate that journey was, how Fin held him upright for hours as Alezan galloped towards home.

Rollo moves his attention to me. "Have you found Adda?"

I shake my head. "She's on a ship that is due into Brillermare any day now."

He nods and his expression brightens slightly. "Maybe by the time you find her, I'll be better."

I raise my eyebrows at Fin. Even if Rollo's health continues to improve, there is no way that he will be in any state to perform his squiring duties. He won't be coming south with us when we leave. Fin's expression tells me that his thoughts are similar to mine.

I squeeze Rollo's hand. "Let's not get ahead of ourselves. You need to rest."

His blinks are becoming slower, as if he's finding it hard to keep his eyes open.

"We'll leave you now," Fin says, and we back out of the room.

22

The next morning a carriage arrives at the Manoir de Sommette to pick us up and take us to Brisebassier. I am overjoyed at the sight – it's the one thing that I'm wholly willing to play the princess to procure. Taking the carriage to Throsne would be infinitely preferable to riding pillion down the whole length of the country.

Delphine and I are shown to opulent rooms in one of the round towers that looks out over the ocean.

"This feels disturbingly familiar," I murmur when the door latches shut behind us.

The round room, the four poster bed, the furnishings ... it could be another level of the tower in the Old Woods.

"I hope you don't feel the need to swing from the rafters here," Delphine says.

I look up. We're not on the top floor, so the ceiling is flat and uninteresting.

"Well, it depends how many days we'll be waiting for

Adda. I haven't trained in a long time. Do you think they have a spare sewing mannequin?"

Delphine gives me a disapproving look.

As soon as we are settled and head back down to the ground floor, I am accosted by Elinor.

Will you have tea with me this afternoon? she asks.

I smile. *Yes, I would love to.*

She beams back, her hazel eyes sparkling. She has taken a shine to me. I think it's rare for her to be able to communicate with anyone outside her family or Rollo's. I like talking to her. Just trying to keep up with her teaches me more than Fin has with his patient, methodical lessons. Luckily I'm a quick learner.

At tea, Elinor is inquisitive about my desire to learn how to sign. I tell her about our encounter with Benoit and how I asked Fin to teach me.

How does he know what words to teach you? she asks.

I shrug. *I don't know.*

She seems rather doubtful of her brother's teaching ability. *He probably missed lots of important words. Do you know this?*

She makes an unfamiliar sign.

No, I reply.

She spells out the word 'marzipan'.

Why would I need to know marzipan?

She grins impishly. *Because it's my favourite.*

I laugh, thinking of the care package that the queen sent me when I first arrived at the tower. *I like it too.*

What about this one?

Elinor points at herself, then lies both hands flat against her heart, then points at me. Even if she wasn't mouthing the words, I would know what that meant.

I love you.

If I had been Fin or Delphine I would have blushed, but Adda's cheeks don't betray me in that way.

He hasn't said that, I sign back, trying to keep my composure.

Elinor scowls. She wears all of her emotions so expressively.

My brother is a fool.

I shake my head. Fin won't say that – not to me. And it makes me realise that the next time Elinor meets Adaliza, the real Adda won't know sign language. I hadn't thought of that when I answered Elinor yesterday. I was too keen to show the girl that I cared, that I wanted to communicate with her. It was a silly mistake. I will have to teach Adda the basics and hope that she is a half-decent linguist.

I don't see Fin until we take our evening meal in the banquet hall. He has changed out of his forest green tunic into what must be his own clothes, the ones he wears at home when he isn't off questing for the Order of the Ivory Maiden. He looks relaxed and happy. I'm glad of it – glad he is able to spend time with his family, even if he isn't able to be completely truthful with them.

There is much talk, both spoken and signed, at the dining table. Fin's mother seems put out that Fin didn't immediately take me to the beach as she had suggested yesterday, and insists that he takes me tomorrow. We both agree dutifully. It's not like we have anything else to do while we're here. The last thing I want is to be stuck inside my chamber while I wait for Adda's ship to come in.

The next day I follow Fin out of the castle and along a narrow track that switch-backs down the cliff in front of Brisebassier. Having taken one look at the steep path, Delphine turned back to the castle and said she would prefer to return to her embroidery. I keep my gaze focused on my feet – each footfall is precarious on the loose stones, and one wrong step would send me skidding down the cliffside. We're halfway down by the time I look up.

I give a soft gasp of surprise and stop in my tracks. Below us is a small cove hidden from sight from the castle high above. The cliffs shelter a half moon of white sand, surrounded by a crescent of grey shale. The beach is lapped by gentle waves, palest aqua where they kiss the sand, strengthening to bright turquoise and then the deep blue-green of the ocean. I've never seen such colours.

Fin pauses on the path ahead when he realises I have stopped and looks back at me with a grin.

"I think your mother was right," I breathe. "It is the most beautiful place in Belforet."

I scramble eagerly down the remainder of the cliff path, my footfalls less careful than they should be. Soon the shale crunches beneath our feet as we stride out onto the beach. When we reach the sand, Fin hops on one foot to remove one boot at a time and unlace his hose underneath his tunic. I do the same, hitching up my skirts under one arm, wanting to feel the sand underneath my bare feet. It's soft and sinking and warmed by the sun.

As we near the water's edge – the sand turns from powdery and fine to wet and firm, and I leave perfectly formed footprints behind me as I walk – I am astounded again by the sheer size of the sea. I have seen large rivers before, but they really don't compare. And it's not just the water that feels endlessly huge – it's the sky. It reaches right from the horizon in a great dome all around me, blue and bright. Brisebassier has the biggest sky I've ever seen.

When the very last remnants of the waves flow over our bare feet, I give a little cry and jump back. Fin laughs at me.

"It's cold!" I squeak.

Fin takes a few steps closer to the water, and when the next wave comes it rushes and foams around his ankles.

"Once the shock wears off it will feel warm. Come on," he cajoles, holding out his hand towards me.

I step forward tentatively. The next wave flows over my feet and I can't help giving out a squeal at the rush of cold, automatically reaching out and catching Fin's outstretched fingers. He laughs again as he looks at me, his expression more open and happy than I've ever seen it. I can't help but smile back – really smile, the way you can with the sun on your face and the sea at your feet. The water isn't cold anymore; we're up to our ankles and the sensation is pleasantly warm.

We walk slowly along the length of the beach with sea water sloshing between every step, keeping at the same depth. One wave is particularly powerful; it crashes into us, soaking us to our knees and making us both cry out in surprise and lean into one another. I laugh, a low, infectious chuckle, and then Fin is laughing too, and I catch his eye as I turn. We're close, and his green eyes are so bright, pulling me even closer, and his smile is as wide as mine, and my heart is leaping, my body is tingling, and ...

And ...

He turns away and drops my hand completely naturally, as if that moment had never happened. As if he didn't feel a thing – no leaping or tingling. And that's when I realise.

I wanted Fin to kiss me.

Fin is walking off but I'm still standing there, heavy and disorientated, the serf rushing around me as the ocean seems to inhale and exhale. A feeling tightens around my insides, a paralysing squeeze of awful understanding.

I love him.

I tried not to, I ignored it and resisted it every step of the way. I would still deny it now if not for the feeling that hollows me out so brutally – the feeling that came with the realisation that he doesn't love me back.

Of course he doesn't. What was I expecting? He knows what I am now: a fairy in a borrowed body, a creature that hides behind other people's smiles. How could anyone love that? Stupid, I'm so stupid – how did this happen?

"Aster?"

Fin must have stopped a few paces away when he noticed I wasn't following. I'm still frozen, staring out to sea. My chest hurts, I try to even out my breaths but I can't seem to exhale fully.

"Are you alright?"

There is concern in his voice. I don't want to hear it. I don't want to be here. I want to close my eyes and be far away, somewhere I can cry and shout and stop pretending. But I can't – because I'm here. I'm Princess Adaliza.

"I'm fine."

I'm surprised by how even my voice sounds. It doesn't reflect any of the roiling tumult going on just beneath my surface. I turn back towards the beach and stride out of the serf.

Nothing has changed. It feels like my world has tilted but the day is still sunny and the sand is still soft. The sea still sighs in and out, in and out. I try to match my breath with it. Fin hasn't noticed any change in me. He ambles at my side, completely at ease, before throwing himself down on the sand. He pats the ground next to him, encouraging me to sit down.

I lower myself to the sand, briefly wishing that we had brought a blanket to sit on. Delphine will not be happy that there is sand all over my gown. I wrap my arms around my bent knees and stare out at the ocean. I was so happy a few minutes ago – I want to feel like that again. I want to scrub away all this heartsick nonsense, but it stays in my chest, heavy and constricting.

"Aster?" Fin asks softly.

He's sitting back on his elbows, his legs sprawled in front of him. When I glance in his direction – making my treacherous heart leap – he has his gaze fixed on the horizon.

"Yes?"

When he speaks his voice is hesitant, almost shy. "What is she like?"

I don't need to ask who 'she' is, who it is he's thinking about as he stares out at the sea. A pang of jealousy twists my stomach. No, not jealousy … Jealousy is the fear of losing something you have, and I can't lay any claim to Fin. It's envy, the fierce and bitter wanting of something someone else has. Parsing the feeling doesn't make it any more palatable.

Immediately guilt clamps down on it. It is not the right of a changeling to have or want the life of the person they are imitating. I have let the lines between me and Adda become too indistinct. She has every right to him and her life, the one I have been living for nearly four years. I swallow, pushing it down, all the uncomfortable feelings that have chosen this moment to rear their ugly heads.

"She's … fearless. Outspoken. She hates boredom – it's why she sought my services. She could never have been shut up in that tower for so long. Her father doesn't know her at all."

He doesn't say anything, so I continue.

"All her life she's been told what to do, and she chafed against it. The freedom she found these past few years made her truly happy. She knew it wouldn't last forever – she has a duty to Belforet that she won't shirk. But … there's a wildness in Adda that I don't think will leave her."

"You like her, don't you?" he says.

I nod, not looking at him. "We exchanged letters while I was in the tower. Other than Delphine she was the only person I talked to that whole time – the only reminder that someone in the world was thinking about me. None of the clients I've worked for have ever done that."

Fin was silent for a few moments. "How do I ... how do I do this?"

This can't be happening. I can't be giving romantic advice about another woman to the man I love.

But apparently it is, because I say, "You treat her like a real person, not a prize you've won. She won't like it, I've already warned you about that. But once she gets to know you ... I think she'll see."

See what a good man he is. What a good husband, a good king consort, he would make.

I can feel him looking at me but I keep my gaze straight ahead. I watch the rhythmic rush of the waves, crashing into foam. I try to ignore the weight, the squeeze, the feelings I don't want to face.

"Thank you," he says eventually.

We're quiet for a while. Even though I don't look at him I sense his movements as he lies back on the sand with a sigh. I stay sitting with my knees tucked up to my chin, holding myself tightly.

There is a shout on the wind from behind us. We both look around and see a servant from Brisebassier standing at the top of the cliff, waving his arms. It's not possible to hear what he's saying but I see the small figure next to him. A boy from the docks. My heart leaps as I know why they're here.

"Fin!" I say, getting to my feet and beating the sand from my gown. "Get up – it must be the *Nicolete*. She's come into port!"

23

My heart is drumming as the Prest carriage rumbles towards Brillermare. This is it, this is it. When I find Adda, my duty is done. I can shrug this skin off and move on – I've never wanted that more than I want it now.

Delphine is at my side and Fin is sitting opposite us, his legs spread wide in the kind of sprawl only a man can achieve. One knee bounces up and down unconsciously as he stares out of the window. The movement is distracting in my peripheral vision; I want to smack his leg to make him stop the nervous action.

The carriage stops on the main street, drawing a number of curious looks. It's a rare sight in these parts. It won't fit down the narrower streets so we get out and walk to the lodging house where Adda has a room. I rap sharply on the door and we all fidget while we wait for someone to answer it.

Eventually the landlady opens the door with a creak, one hand on her hip.

"Is she here?" I ask.

The woman nods. "Only just got back. She knows you're visiting?"

"Yes," I reassure her, "can we go up?"

She narrows her eyes at Fin. "Not him. I don't allow men in my house."

Fin opens his mouth as if to object but I give him a look. "Wait at the tavern. We'll find you."

After a moment he exhales sharply and his lips flatten into a line. "Fine."

I nod at the landlady and she steps aside, letting me and Delphine climb the rickety stairs. Up we climb, the floorboards groaning loudly with each step. I'm almost breathless with nervous energy by the time we reach the top. I knock on the door to Adda's room.

Silence. Then a creak on the other side of the door.

"Adda?" I call out, tension thick in my voice.

The latch lifts, the door slowly opens inward. And as soon as her blue-grey eyes meet mine, the nervous energy seems to fizz over and I fling myself at her.

"Aster?" she gasps as her arms wrap around me.

I hold her tightly, squeezing my eyes shut. Her hair tickles my face, I can feel the rise and fall of her chest against mine. It's her – it's really her. I found her.

"You're ok?" I choke out.

She pulls back in my arms, her expression still taken aback but also humorous as she stares at me.

"I'm fine. Although ... you seem to have taken better care of my body than I have."

My gaze runs over her face. She looks ... different. Her skin, milky pale before, is tanned a light golden brown that makes her blue eyes smoulder. The white slash of a scar curves over her left cheek. Her hair is wild and uncombed, falling in scraggly waves over the baggy tunic she wears, belted at the waist, that had gone a fair while without encountering a laundress. She's still beautiful and formidable, but now ... the outside reflects the wildness within.

"What are you doing here?" she asks.

I drop my arms from around her, realising that we're all standing on the narrow landing in front of her room. "Can we come in?"

Adda's eyes move to Delphine behind me and light up. "Delphine?"

"My Lady!" Delphine gives out a sob before covering her mouth with one hand.

I step past her and Adda wraps an arm around Delphine's shoulders, steering her into the bedchamber.

"I'm sorry," Delphine stutters around her sobs, "it's just ... I was worried that we'd never see you again!"

Adda's expression is confused. "I'm sorry to have worried you. The messenger didn't turn up to take my letter to Mother. We agreed that I would never move on without letting her know where I was heading next, so I ... decided to fill my time while I was waiting. I didn't mean to ..."

She stops talking when her eyes meet mine. I don't know what she sees in my face but her brow creases.

"What is it? Aster, tell me."

I take a steadying breath and sit on the edge of the bed. "A lot has changed since your last letter, Adda. Everything has changed."

She just stares at me with regal imperiousness, silently ordering me to carry on.

"About three weeks ago I woke up one morning, and ... someone had climbed the tower. A knight. I was so confused,

Being Adaliza

I hadn't heard anything from the outside world for months. He told me that our situation had changed."

I pause and swallow. Is there any right way to tell someone that their mother has died? I take her hand and grip it tightly.

"The plague did come to Throsne. Many people died, including ... including your mother."

Adda is frozen. She blinks once, twice. Her voice is strangled when she finally speaks. "What?"

"Your mother passed away nearly four months ago. And without her at the palace, no one knew that you were here and I had taken your place in the tower."

Adda shakes her head. I know I should give her time to process this, but there is so much more to tell her. Her hand is limp in mine.

"I'm afraid there's more. Your father was infected at the same time as your mother, and he barely survived. He must have felt vulnerable and wanted to secure the line of succession, because he decided to launch a contest for your hand in marriage."

Adda's hand twitches in mine at that, as if it rebels at even the thought of being promised to someone else.

"He decreed that whichever Belforetian nobleman could locate you first would be your husband. There have been knights swarming all over Belforet looking for you."

Adda's expression has turned from shock to outrage. I think it's an easier emotion for her to process.

"And one of them found you in the tower?" she says.

I nod. "Sir Finton Prest. He told me about the queen's death and the king's contest. And there was nothing I could do – I knew we had to switch back but I had no way of contacting you."

She nods, breathing rapidly. "So you came here?"

I dart a look at Delphine. "Well, not exactly ..."

I tell Adda everything that has happened since we left the tower. The Duc d'Eschecs' plot, Delphine's abduction, the revelation of my true identity, Rollo's illness and our journey to Brillermare.

"So ... where is this knight now?" Adda asks, distrust in her tone.

"He's waiting for us in the tavern down the street," I say carefully.

"He's waiting for us? Aster, do you really think I'm going to accept this ridiculous contest and be forced into marriage with the first idiot who scaled that infernal tower? I shouldn't have run away from it – I should have burned it to the ground," she fumes, pacing back and forth in front of the bed.

I raise my hands in a gesture of surrender. "I understand why you feel that way – really I do. But ... having one of them on our side is easier than fighting all of them alone. Fin is ... he's a good man."

Adda opens her mouth angrily but I cut her off before she can object.

"I'm not saying you should marry him. I know you don't want to. But ... won't it be easier if the contest is seen to be over? Fin is a good fighter – as good as any I've come across. Maybe when you get to Throsne you can persuade your father to change the prize to a sack of jewels of something. But at least you'll be back where you need to be without a horde of noblemen panting after you."

I know how much the idea of being "won" rankles her – it still rankles *me*. And I know that she finds the idea of running away much more preferable to cooperating with Fin. But Adda and Delphine need to go home to Throsne, and I trust Fin to help get them there – especially as I'm not planning to go with them.

"This is all so ridiculous!" Adda cries, throwing her hands up in the air. "How could my father think that this is the best way to secure the succession?"

It takes almost an hour – and a lot of gentle persuasion from both me and Delphine – to get Adda to descend the stairs and follow us to the tavern. She strides forward, haughty authority in every line of her body. How she has convinced the people she met that she isn't royal is beyond me.

The tavern isn't crowded when we enter. I squint through the darkness, locating Fin towards the back in a chair by the fireplace. He bolts to his feet when he sees us, his gaze widening as he stares at Adda. She is glaring daggers back at him.

"My Lady," he says, dropping into a courtly bow.

Adda folds her arms across her tatty tunic, her lips pursed in a moue of distaste.

"Sir Finton, I presume?"

Her voice is cold – far colder than I have ever made it, even at my frostiest. I want to shiver on Fin's behalf, but stop that thought in its tracks. This isn't my fight.

Fin's Adam's apple bobs. "That's correct, My Lady. I am glad that you are safe and we have found you at last."

Adda raises one eyebrow. "Aster found me. *You* are an unwelcome addition to this happy reunion."

"Adda ..." I murmur under my breath.

She glances at me, sighs and drops down into a chair by the fireside, her arms still tightly crossed over her chest. Delphine lowers herself into the chair next to her. Fin stays awkwardly on his feet.

"Adda has been caught up on our situation. She agrees that she needs to go back to Belforet as soon as possible – and that you should accompany her on the trip," I tell Fin.

Adda snorts in a most unladylike fashion. Fin blinks at her. I ignore them both and continue.

"You should return to Brisebassier and gather your belongings. Adda will stay in Brillermare and prepare to leave in the morning."

There's no way that we can just switch places immediately. Not only because I fear Adda would stab Fin with a knife at dinner – there's no way anyone would believe that tanned, scarred Adda is the same person who has been at Brisebassier for the past few days.

"You three will make your way south, using the same pretence we did on the road – you're a merchant, his wife and his sister."

Delphine frowns up at me. "Wait ... you're not coming with us?"

Fin and Adda both look at me in surprise, waiting for my answer.

"Well ... No. You don't need me. I came here to switch places with Adda, and I've done that now."

"But you've got to go back to Throsne. Why wouldn't we all travel together?" Fin asks.

Because I don't want to be present while you try to woo Adda. Because I want to put this whole mess far behind me. Because my heart hurts and I'm so tired.

"Of course you're coming with us," Adda says, as if her decree makes it final.

Delphine is studying me. I shy away from her gaze. She knows me too well.

"Please, Aster?" she asks softly. "We need you."

My heart tugs at her words. I feel the hesitation creeping in. Princess Adaliza's actions aren't my responsibility anymore ... but Adda is still my friend. Delphine too. They're my only friends. Am I being selfish, putting my secret heartache ahead of them? Turning away from them when they might need me just so I can mope in private? That doesn't feel like something I would do.

I chance a glance at Fin and immediately regret it. His gaze is bouncing from me to Adda, me to Adda, as if he can't stop his eyes from gravitating back to her. I *can't* face another week of that, of side-by-side comparisons and a front row seat to the disaster of a romance that will play out in front of us. I'm not sure what would be worse: Adda remaining hostile and me having to coach Fin through wooing her, or watching Adda fall for him like I had. Pain twinges in my chest. No, the latter would definitely be worse.

Setting out on my own would create a new set of problems. I have no horse and no money – I've relied on Fin for both of those essentials thus far on our travels. While I may be resourceful, I can't hunt like Fin can – which would rule out camping on the road to save money. I could make it back to Throsne, of course I could ... but it would take a while. I wonder how much I would regret my prideful decision to go my own way after days of stealing and fighting to survive.

I stifle a sigh, having made my decision. I know I'm going to kick myself later. I wish I wasn't such a masochist.

"Ok. I'll come with you."

24

Delphine is elated on the carriage ride to the Manoir de Sommette, where we head next. She chatters excitedly, requiring only the occasional input from me to keep her going. I understand why: Adda is safe and she's finally going home. Sometimes I forget how utterly out of the ordinary the past weeks have been for her. Fin is silent as he gazes out of the window, a slight furrow in his brow.

As we rumble up to the squat stone manor, I mentally prepare myself for what is likely to be a painful goodbye. We can't wait around for Rollo to be fighting fit – it might take weeks, even months, for him to fully recover. We have to leave without him. I will miss his easygoing company. Rollo had always been the buffer between me and Fin, first when I was trying to ward off his affections and then when Fin reacted badly to finding out my secret. Will *I* have to be the buffer now between Fin and Adda? I grimace at the thought.

Rollo looks better than he did the last time I saw him. He

has more colour in his face and an alertness in his eyes. I'm surprised by how well he takes the news that we're heading off without him.

"The quest is more important than I am," he says magnanimously. "The princess needs to return home."

His attempt at maturity makes me smile.

"I hope we meet again, Rollo," I say with genuine feeling.

"As do I. If I ever need a shapeshifting, multi language-speaking master fighter, I know exactly who to find."

I give him a gentle hug, careful not to touch his wounded shoulder.

"May I speak to Fin alone?" Rollo asks me and Delphine.

"Of course," I say, and we leave the room.

When Fin comes out a few minutes later, his expression is tight and grave. I wonder what Rollo said that would have affected him so, but I don't pry. Back at Brisebassier he is distant with me, and I try to ignore the uncomfortable tightness it brings to my chest.

"Fin," I say as he makes to leave me and Delphine in the entrance hall.

He turns back almost reluctantly, not meeting my eye. I scan his face, searching for some clue as to his change in manner.

"Is something wrong?"

He shakes his head, his attention clearly elsewhere.

"Nothing is wrong," he reassures me blandly. "I need to pack for tomorrow's journey."

He walks away. I turn to Delphine, who gives me a weak smile.

"Maybe he just needs some time to adjust to the new dynamic," she suggests.

I can feel the frown tugging at my brows. "He won't even look at me."

I cringe inwardly at how pathetic that made me sound. Delphine's expression softens as she considers me, but I cut her off when she opens her mouth to say something that will probably be all kinds of embarrassing.

"It doesn't matter. We have to pack too."

I start towards the round tower where our chambers are housed, blustering through the unwanted emotions. After a moment's hesitation, Delphine follows.

Fin is still withdrawn at dinner, which earns him a few concerned looks from his family. I try to make up for his mood with a brightness that I do not feel. I tell them that we'll be heading back to Throsne tomorrow and thank them profusely for the kindness they have shown me.

Fin's mother beams at me and takes my hands in hers. "It has been a delight and an honour to meet you, Your Highness. I'm so grateful that you visited us. I just know how happy the two of you will be together."

I fight to keep the polite smile on my face. Once again Fin proves himself to be a terrible actor. The furrow is back in his brow and he is still refusing to look in my direction. He excuses himself shortly after dinner and I don't see him until morning.

My sense of unease in Fin's company only grows the next day. I find it confusing. It feels like it did between us after the drama on the riverside – but I thought we had got past that. He knows who I am now. Yesterday we acted like friends on the beach. He had held my hand, asked my advice, valued my suggestions. Now ... now it feels like he doesn't want to be around me at all. Maybe meeting the real Adda made him remember those misplaced feelings he wasted on me – maybe he's embarrassed? My thoughts chase each other round and round as we ride to Brillermare. Fin and I share Alezan while Delphine rides her own horse from the Brisebassier stables.

Being Adaliza

I am relieved to see Adda waiting on the street where we agreed to meet. She looks more presentable today. She still wears a man's tunic and breeches but these are freshly laundered, at least. Her long hair has been washed and hastily braided back into a thick plait that snakes over her shoulder. She has a small pack with her that must contain all her belongings.

"My Lady, I have a number of your gowns from the tower. Would you like me to help you dress?" Delphine asks pointedly when we have all dismounted.

Adda pulls a face. "No, I've become quite fond of breeches. They make riding so much easier."

Delphine narrows her eyes at Adda's ensemble but I place a hand on her arm. "It's fine," I say.

"We're supposed to be blending in," Delphine points out.

We are wearing our travelling clothes again – me in my yellow kirtle, Fin in his green tunic. Delphine looks from me to Adda.

"And on that note, isn't a pair of pretty identical twins going to be quite memorable? Maybe it would be better if you shifted?"

She has a point. Adaliza alone is eyecatching – two Adalizas is likely to stick in the mind of anyone we meet on our journey. I close my eyes, briefly scanning through my mental library of faces for features I can use. I keep Adaliza's body, the one I have spent years honing and training, and the basic bone structure of her face. I change her mantle of mink brown curls for a shiny sheet of raven hair. It is pin straight and finer than Adda's, making it much less heavy and oppressive in the heat. My stormy blue eyes will stay the same colour as the lapis lazuli in my necklace, but I frame them with darker eyebrows and sprinkle freckles across the pale skin of my nose and cheekbones. I have a soft spot for freckles.

The last big change I make is Adda's mouth, which is narrow with rosebud lips quick to pout. I choose a more generous mouth that hitches a dimple in my left cheek when I smile. I saw it on a woman in Throsne and thought it was lovely. I wish I had a looking glass to assess the overall picture, but it feels right. Adda and I could definitely be sisters but we aren't so alike as to be remarkable.

"Oh!" Delphine exclaims when the transformation is complete. "It suits you!"

"It does," Adda agrees.

I glance at Fin and catch him staring at my face with a strange expression. He turns away before I can understand it. There is no blush in his cheeks to give away his feelings – not that I should expect one.

Adda hasn't yet acknowledged Fin's presence, but her eyes brighten when she sees Alezan. She approaches the war horse and strokes his long nose with gentle fingers.

"You're a magnificent beast, aren't you?" she cooes.

The destrier blows out a breath against her hand and she smiles.

Fin is holding Alezan's bridle with one hand. He clearly sees an opportunity in Adda's appreciation for his horse and sweeps his other hand towards her with a courtly flourish.

"My Lady, may I assist you into the saddle?"

I blink, frozen for a moment, and I'm glad that Fin has his back to me. It would have hurt less if he'd dealt me a physical blow.

There are only two horses. He must expect me to ride pillion with Delphine from now onwards. Of course he would want to ride with Adda. I'm not playing that part anymore – so why do I feel so devastated that he offered my seat to her? I hate that blasted destrier. And I hate my stupid heart for its infuriating, inappropriate, unwanted reaction. Why do I feel like crying? I need to get a grip.

I feel even sillier for caring when Adda throws a dismissive look in Fin's direction and replies, "Absolutely not. I'll have my own mount."

He pretends not to be taken off guard by her bluntness and stands with Alezan while she marches to the nearby stables to find an appropriate horse. The beast that is led out from the stable is a handsome bay that Adda clearly approves of. She pays the ostler from her own purse and the man's eyes bulge a little at the sum she hands over.

It's only when she has mounted that Fin seems to remember I'm here and reaches towards me as if to help me up into Alezan's saddle. I immediately turn away from him and stride towards Adda, compounding the snubbing that the princess has already dealt him. The leggy bay snorts at me and prances on the spot when I near. I grit my teeth. Now I have to start all over again with a new horse that hates me on instinct.

Adda shushes her mount before calling down to me cheerily, "Come on, scaredy cat. We'll make a rider out of you one day."

"Not likely," I grumble, but I take her proffered hand and manage to get my leg in the stirrup without the horse bolting.

Once I'm settled in the saddle behind Adda, she turns the horse towards Fin. I don't look at him. If he wants to be distant with me, then fine. Distance is an attractive prospect right now.

I don't have a chance to say a silent goodbye to the sea as we turn our backs on the port and head southwards – Adda's riding is far too distracting. She insists that her horse needs to run to rid it of its jitters and launches us into a gallop once the road opens up. I cling to her back and mutter threateningly into her tunic, reminding her that it's my presence that is making the horse nervous. Adda just laughs.

The sound is loud and bright, like the ringing of a bell. It surprises me; my laugh, the one that has bubbled out of me in recent weeks, is a lower chuckle like the burbling of a stream, less delightful but more infectious. I had assumed it was Adda's, something else I had borrowed when I took on her form. But ... maybe it's not. Maybe it's mine.

It's a thought that stays with me as we ride onwards. I watch Adda when we stop for rest breaks, I listen to her intently as we chat in the saddle, the conversation relatively private under the clopping of horses' hooves. Adda's voice is strident and expectant; mine is gentler and a little husky. She has mannerisms that I never had a chance to mimic. She twines the end of her plait around a finger absentmindedly while she talks. Her pursed lips are expressive and can be sly, coy or irritated depending on her quicksilver moods. I realise that I have lost the guile I originally practised nearly four years ago when I first met the princess. All this time I have barely been Adaliza at all.

The miles disappear under foot. I remember the conversation I had with Delphine on the tower balcony, back when she was first starting to trust me. She had asked me what I looked like when I wasn't impersonating anyone, and I had replied that I didn't have my own body. I had been self-conscious then, painfully aware of my own artifice, of a life unanchored and always drifting. But maybe ... maybe, all this time, there have been parts of me in every shift. The timbre of my voice when no one is listening, the laugh that escapes me when I can't keep it in.

These past few weeks with Fin, Rollo and Delphine have been the first in my life when I haven't had to pretend. And now I know – I am more than a series of impersonations. I have values and boundaries. I have quirks and idiosyncrasies. I have friends who know me and like me for *me*.

I am Aster Lemorque.

The last time I chanted that in my head I was shaming myself for caring what Fin and Rollo thought of me. Now it sounds like a revelation, a truth I have never truly accepted.

I am Aster Lemorque.

25

It's a long day. By the time we stop for the evening at a roadside inn, we're all tired and not feeling particularly talkative – even Adda.

The next day she's bright-eyed and chirpy when we go down to the taproom for our morning meal. We sit on stools and use a large barrel standing on its end as a table top. Delphine and I exchange mutinous looks over our bowls of porridge – it's too early for so much energy. I get the impression that Delphine found me a considerably less taxing Adaliza than the real version. Her plait, I notice, is sleeker and neater this morning. Adda must have let Delphine do her hair, at least.

Fin sits on the other side of the barrel, facing the three of us like a man on trial. It is more evident than ever that he is outnumbered, and I imagine that he is lamenting the lack of Rollo's company. He tries to join the conversation every so often but finds himself resolutely ignored by both me and

Being Adaliza

Adda. Occasionally Delphine takes pity on him and answers his questions, but it's awkward. I don't let myself feel bad about it. I was perfectly willing to be Fin's ally – he's the one who took umbrage with me for some unknown reason.

I notice Adda watching the dynamic between the three of us. When our bowls are empty and Fin has left to ready the horses, she turns to me with her lips pursed in a thoughtful pout.

"What's going on between you and Sir Clinton?"

I try to keep my expression as neutral as possible as my heart leaps uncomfortably in my chest, guilt flaring. There's no way she can know how I feel about Fin – because I'm refusing to feel it. I haven't said more than three words to him since we set off from Brillermare.

"Sir Finton," I correct, even though I know she knows his name. "Nothing."

Adda arches an eyebrow at me. She does it so artfully – it makes me want to mimic the gesture.

"When we first discussed travelling with him you were all, 'he's a good man, you can trust him', and now you can barely look at each other."

Adda is more observant than I gave her credit for.

"He *is* a good man. He just ... I don't know. He's different with me now."

I really don't want to have this conversation with her. Or anyone, for that matter.

"Since meeting me?" Adda asks.

I nod. She narrows her eyes in thought.

"It's fine, Adda. It doesn't matter. We just need to get you back to Throsne swiftly and safely," I reassure her.

She stands up, her stool scraping loudly against the flagstones, and marches out of the taproom. I look to Delphine, whose eyes widen, and we follow Adda out to the yard. She strides over to Fin, who has all three horses tacked up and tethered. He looks somewhat surprised by her sudden appearance.

"My Lady," he says, dipping his head respectfully.

Adda folds her arms across her chest.

"What is your problem with Aster?"

Fin blinks at her. It's the first time that she has directly addressed him since they first met in the tavern in Brillermare. I duck into the stables out of sight and pull Delphine with me. I'd rather not join in this conversation.

"W-what?"

"I'm sensing an atmosphere," Adda says accusingly. "I know you thought she was me at first. Is it resentment? Fairy prejudice?"

"What? No! I don't resent her—" Fin says quickly, but Adda cuts him off.

"Good. Because she's contractually obliged to keep *my* secret. She doesn't owe *you* anything. You're not supposed to be part of the equation."

Adda's words are so matter-of-fact that Fin doesn't seem to have a response.

"If you want to be angry at someone, be angry at me. But not her."

I hear Adda stalk off, her warning delivered. My heart is thumping as I lean my back against the stable wall. I'm not thinking about Fin. I'm thinking about Adda – her protectiveness, her fire. It brings a lump to my throat. No one has ever stood up for me like that, unprompted and unnecessary. It's just like her to think that tackling a problem head on is the best way to solve it. I should be embarrassed that they are discussing me, to have the friction between me and Fin highlighted, but the overwhelming feeling in my chest is ... gratitude. To have Adda looking out for me.

Delphine and I try to emerge subtly from the stables when we see Adda re-entering the yard. Fin is busying himself with the horses but I can see the fading pink in his cheeks.

"Ready to go?" he asks without looking at us.

"Yes," Delphine says, her voice higher than usual. She's terrible at keeping her cool.

I follow Adda to her bay horse, which she has named Cunstance. She fusses at the animal's head to distract it while I mount. The horse feels less solid than Alezan, more likely to startle or buck, but I trust Adda's skill as a horsewoman to keep us in the saddle.

We travel onwards, into the green hills and valleys that characterise this part of Belforet. It's cooler than it has been on our journey so far, with weak sunshine filtering through hazy clouds and the shifting leaves of the trees that overhang the road. It's the first week of September and I'm relieved that the year will soon turn into autumn. This summer's heat has been fearsome.

We've been riding for a couple of hours when I spy something unusual at the side of the road. The hedgerows and fields beyond are all wildly overgrown here, tall and fat with springy growth and an abundance of weeds. A mud track leads off the road to the left, also encroached upon by the untamed verge on both sides. A large cross, formed of two narrow branches lashed together, has been staked into the centre of the track.

"What is that?" I ask Adda, pointing to the cross.

"I don't know. Let's find out."

She pulls on the reins and clicks her tongue to encourage Cunstance to veer off at the turning.

"No," Fin calls from in front of us, "come away from there!"

"Why?" Adda shouts back.

We're already past the cross and heading down the overgrown track, swallowed by green. When I turn in the saddle I can't see Delphine or Fin, but I can hear the clip clop of their horses' hooves behind us.

The track leads to a village. A row of small houses – perhaps better described as hovels – lines the road in a curve, shabby and abandoned. We pass a farmhouse and then more cottages huddled around an overgrown green. It is eerily quiet. There are no people – no laughing children, no smoke from cooking fires, no rattle of cart wheels in the distance.

"What is this place?" Adda asks, her tone uncharacteristically hushed.

"It's a plague village," Fin answers quietly from behind us.

We both turn to look at him. His expression is grave.

"The plague swept through here about a year ago. There are a number of villages like this, where almost all of the population died from the sickness. The few who survived will have moved away. No one lives here now."

"Is it contagious?" Delphine asks, glancing around nervously.

"No, the plague has gone. But there has been so much death here – some say the plague villages are haunted."

I swallow thickly and turn back to survey the village. I don't believe in ghosts, but I understand why the place was abandoned and never revisited. With the local population so reduced by the plague, there is no need to rent these homes out to new tenants. Instead they've been abandoned and reclaimed by nature. Weeds choke the doorways, tools lie forgotten. I remember the cross staked into the track – it must warn people to stay away. The thought saddens me. How long will it take for all those victims, all those people, to be completely forgotten? Unacknowledged and unmourned.

Adda swings herself down from the saddle in front me, lifting me from my revery. She walks towards the green as the three of us dismount.

"My Lady!" Delphine calls out worriedly, but I lift a hand to stop her.

Adda kneels in the weeds and bows her head. She's praying.

"She hasn't had a chance to come to terms with her mother's death," I murmur to Fin and Delphine. "Give her some space."

Delphine's brown eyes are wide and sad as she nods. Fin and I make eye contact for the first time in what feels like an age. His expression is similarly somber and understanding.

"I didn't know," I say softly, my eyes still ranging over the abandoned dwellings. "We were shut away in the tower for so long and only came out when it had passed. I suppose the plague never seemed real. This ... this is very real."

Delphine nods her silent agreement, her eyes glistening, unable to put her thoughts into words.

When Fin speaks his voice is low and won't carry to Adda. "It was awful. Everyone was scared, from the lowliest peasant to the highest lord. The plague didn't discriminate."

It reminds me that, while I don't agree with the king's heavy handedness by locking Adaliza away for so long, his actions did protect her – protect *me* – from the plague. If she had stayed in Throsne, would she have died when the sickness infiltrated the palace? How did the Ruelle de Gargouille fare – if I had stayed in Throsne, would I be dead too? A number of times I have resented my family's lack of contact with me over the past few years. At no point have I entertained the possibility that they might not have survived the plague. That there might not be any Lemorques left in

Throsne.

I swallow that thought down and shake my head determinedly. There is no point thinking along those lines. I glance at Adda, who is still kneeling in the long grass with her head bowed. I approach on silent feet and drop to my knees next to her. I'm not religious but I close my eyes and bow my head, picturing the queen as I knew her. A regal woman with Adda's brown curls and steely-eyed determination. A devoted mother who risked so much to give her daughter the freedom she yearned for. A kind benefactor of marzipans and letters that made an unimportant changeling feel seen.

Thank you, I tell the queen in my mind's eye. *I hope you're at peace.*

My eyes are still shut when I feel Adda lay her head on my shoulder. She doesn't make a sound but I can feel the tremors of silent sobs through her body. I wrap one arm around her back and hold her clasped hands in the other, leaning my cheek gently against her hair. We stay that way for a long time, until Adda's sobs are spent and she can finally face the others.

There is little talk between the four of us for the rest of the day, even when we stop for breaks and meals. The mood is pensive. I try not to dwell on what I might find when I finally face the towering, black-and-white façade of the Maison du Lemorque.

There are no inns close by when the sun fades, so we make camp in a clearing just off the road. It must be a regular camping spot for travellers as there is a good-sized firepit and even a few leftover logs from the previous occupants. Delphine tends the fire while Fin sets out with his sling to catch something fresh for dinner and Adda and I forage from the nearby bushes. We're lucky that it's the most abundant

Being Adaliza

time of year. Our dinner of roast rabbit with nuts and berries seems to taste particularly delicious as we gnaw meat off the bones and lick the juices from our fingers in the flickering firelight.

I am feeling content and sleepy when out the corner of my eye I see Fin make the sign for 'star'.

Aster?

I cock my head at him.

Yes?

Delphine is rooting around in her horse's pack and Adda is facing away from us. Fin hesitates before his hands move again.

I'm sorry.

I frown a little at him over the dancing flames.

Why?

I've made a mess of things.

My stomach tightens at his admission. Adda's little speech this morning must have been playing on his mind all day. I'm not sure what to say. I don't want to be at odds with Fin – but I'm not sure I trust my traitorous heart to behave itself if he starts being nice to me again.

Let's just get to Throsne, I sign back.

Will you ride with me tomorrow?, he asks.

I shake my head.

I know Fin's expressions well enough now to read the dismay in his eyes and the unhappiness in his downturned mouth. I ignore the way it knots my stomach. I wish I didn't care.

When I glance away I notice Adda watching me. One side of her face is lit by the golden glow of the fire, while the other is in shadow. I can't make out her expression. I sit on my hands and give her a small smile, which she returns. She needs to be my focus here, not Fin. My gaze doesn't wander

                              Primrose Hugh

across the fire again.

26

When I wake at sunrise the next morning it is notably chillier than it was the last time we slept under the stars. I pull the blanket closer around me. A sheen of dew carpets the grass, glistening in the beams of frail sunlight that shaft through the trees. Birds, hidden in the canopies above, chirp and chatter loudly. I always thought that the city would be much louder than the countryside at night, but the birds' dawn chorus woke me every morning for months when I first arrived at the tower. Now I'm more used to it. I lie still for a few moments, cocooned in the warmth of my blanket, listening to the cacophony of birdsong. Savouring it. Savouring what I have left of my freedom.

    I don't often let myself comb through the tangled feelings I have about going back to Throsne. I want to see Adda home safely; I want to know my family is alive and well; I want to draw a line under the complicated relationship I have with Fin and put it behind me. But ... the truth is that my situation isn't all that different from Adda's. Both of us have responsibilities that we've run away from. I could have – maybe *should* have – found my way back to the Maison du Lemorque as soon as I could get myself free. My loyalty is to my family.

In quiet moments like this I can admit to myself that going on this quest was about more than just finding the missing princess. Along the way I found myself – and I know that will become insignificant as soon as I return home. I will be forced to wear a different skin, to learn a new life story, to act another person's part. Adaliza's form will become just another disguise in my mental library. That shouldn't matter to me – it was never mine to begin with. It isn't what makes me *me*. But somehow ... it does matter. I've never felt so at home in anyone else's body before.

There is stirring around me. The others are waking. We planned to set off early – we should be able to reach the ferry crossing on the River Fluet by the end of the day. I bundle my ravelled thoughts to the back of my mind and sit up, letting the blanket fall to my waist and shivering at the nip of the chill morning air.

Adda is chatty again in the saddle as the road wends through the green hills and valleys. Any vestige of the grief that wracked her yesterday has evaporated with the morning dew. She is carefree and playful as she recounts some of her more outrageous exploits over the past few years. I am reasonably sure that her ribald stories don't carry to Fin and Delphine over the clopping of the horse's hooves.

"— and I thought I had got away with it, until I turned and the fish slipped through my arms and flopped onto the floor," she laughs.

I can't help but chuckle at the mental picture and shake my head at her foolish bravado.

"That's when the man pulled a knife from his waistband," she continues.

"Is that how you got your scar?" I ask.

"No, no. That story is much less exciting. I was caught by the end of a rope when the rigging snapped during a storm."

Adda lifts her fingers from the reins to brush her scarred left cheek. The thin white line curves down and out from the centre of her cheekbone. It's hardly a deformity; the gash healed cleanly and didn't come close to damaging her eye. But well-bred ladies – especially princesses – are judged by the flawlessness of their skin.

"I'm not ashamed of it," she says softly, a little defensively.

"Nor should you be," I reply, keeping my tone casual.

"It's *my* skin. I don't want to be an unmarked canvas. I want to look in the mirror and see evidence that I've *lived*. And if that makes a difference to my eligibility – well, that says something about the people who no longer want to marry me."

Defiance and frustration war in her voice. I give her waist a small squeeze.

"Your skin is your own, Adda," I reassure her gently.

"Except for when it's yours," she says wryly.

"Yes, well, we've already established that I make a much better princess than you do."

She snorts. "You joke but it's true."

There is a pause before she speaks again. "What if ... what if I can't do it? Be Belforet's queen."

My response is instant. "Of course you can do it! You're clever and assertive. You love your kingdom and your people. There is no one I would rather see on the throne."

"They don't think I can – not on my own." Her tone turns sarcastic. "A woman can't rule without a husband. She needs a firm hand to keep her from spending all the kingdom's money on fripperies or running scared from enemy armies."

"We both know that any husband foolish enough to try to control you will find himself with a few of his own scars to mar his beauty," I retort.

My eyes drift to Fin, sitting upright and completely at ease in Alezan's saddle ahead of us. When Adda speaks next I realise that hers are fixed on him too.

"I know why you insisted he accompany us," she mutters darkly. "Better the devil you know ..."

I can't see her face but I imagine her mouth is twisted in distasteful assessment. My stomach lurches at the sentiment and my throat thickens. When I finally find my voice I force myself to speak evenly.

"He's a Belforetian nobleman. A knight dedicated to rescuing damsels in distress. Technically he has won your father's competition – he tracked you down before any other man. Twice, in fact. And ..."

My voice breaks and I swallow, hoping that Adda didn't hear the slight hitch.

"I don't think he would try to control you. He is fair and kind. There are far worse men vying for your hand than Sir Finton Prest."

It's true – I mean everything I'm saying. I love Adda and I love Fin. If that means letting them be together for the sake of everyone's happiness, I will do it.

"So you think I should marry him?"

Adda's tone is surprisingly even – far from the fiery refusals she has uttered so far when we broach this subject. Almost as if ... she's considering it.

"I only want the very best for you, Adda," I say, desperate to keep the strain from my voice.

"And *he* is the best?" she prods, nodding her head

towards Fin.

I blink rapidly, as if the action can clear my thoughts, clear my emotions. I'm glad that I'm sitting behind Adda and she can't see my face.

"Yes," I all but whisper.

Adda nods once thoughtfully. "I see."

In the mid-afternoon we ride past quite a spectacle. One of the large open fields has been commandeered by scores of wagons, tents and stalls lined up in rows, and the thoroughfares between them are thronged with people of all ages and stations. There are animals in pens, fine clothing displayed on racks, butchers, bakers, cheesemongers and winemakers all selling their wares from their stalls.

"It's a fair!" Adda says, delighted.

"We should carry on to Nortferry," Fin calls over his shoulder, not slowing Alezan's pace.

"It won't hurt to take a look," she mutters so that only I hear.

Adda has tugged on Cunstance's reins and is leading us towards the gate before Fin can turn around and object. I hear him give a heavy, long-suffering sigh behind us but both he and Delphine follow without further censure. We tether the horses and set out to explore the stalls on foot.

"We should stay together," Fin insists.

His gaze is wary as he inspects the crowds around us. He keeps one hand settled on his belt close to his dagger. I pat my pocket on reflex, reassured by the knife I always keep close at hand.

Adda rolls her eyes at him. "I doubt we're in any danger here. We blend in."

It's true – no one looks twice at us as we drift down the rows of hawkers. Adda and Delphine are immediately distracted by the shiny wares of a jeweller's cart. We pass smartly dressed ladies in elaborate headdresses promenading between the stalls, trailed by servants carrying their purchased wares, as well as haggard-looking villagers in roughspun tunics and grubby caps. All have been drawn in by the novelty of the fair.

Everyone seems in higher spirits than they are at a normal weekly market. Little children clutch corn dollies and sticky buns in their fingers, their smiles wide; ale-flushed men slap each other on the back and laugh uproariously; the jolly trill of an accordion and the beat of a tambourine carry over to us on the breeze. I follow the music absentmindedly, spying a gaudily painted wagon and a group of players dressed in motley. A beautiful young woman surrounded by a crowd dances to the music, the ends of her shawl swirling as she spins.

"Are you hungry?" Adda asks me, pulling my attention away from the players.

"Always."

She points at a tent where an entire roasted hog hangs from a spit. I sniff and inhale the delicious savour of hot pork, my mouth watering. We all buy a large pork roll, slathered in apple sauce and topped with crispy crackling. We drift beyond the hog roast to the next tent over, which occupies a sprawling plot among the smaller stalls. Huge casks of ale and cider sit on legs in the shade of the tent, and buxom serving wenches pass between the stools and tables with trays laden with tankards.

"We should sit while we eat," Delphine says, glancing at the bulging roll in her hands. Out of the three of us females, she's the biggest stickler for propriety.

Adda spots a free table and leads us towards it, lifting full tankards off a nearby tray and setting them on the table before she sits down. She gives me a mischievous smile as I sit down next to her. I can tell what she's thinking. She knows her days of wandering through fairs and drinking ale are numbered.

The men on the table next to us are loud and rowdy. It's not that late into the afternoon but they are already deep in their cups. One in particular has a gratingly loud laugh like the braying of an ass. I can't help but overhear their conversation.

"Where is he, then?"

"Off hunting the princess, along with all his brothers. Barely a handful of wits between the lot of them, there's no chance they'll find her."

I glance casually over my shoulder. The men aren't knights – they aren't wearing surcoats or carrying swords. I suspect they are servants of the local lord, gossiping like fish wives on their afternoon off. We're not in any danger from them. Adda catches my gaze knowingly, her blue-grey eyes sparkling with humour.

"That little harlot is leading all the lords of the realm in a merry dance," a different voice says.

Fin stiffens at the word 'harlot'; I place a steadying hand on his shirtsleeve.

"Let's just eat and move on from here," I tell the three of them calmly.

"I heard she's so ugly her father sent her away so he didn't have to look at her anymore, and he can't wait to palm her off on some stupid nobleman who's frothing at the thought of getting at her," one of the men cackles.

His suggestion is met with dirty laughs all round.

"I heard she's been whoring her way around Belforet to escape their notice. She loves a bit of rough," another declares.

Adda's eyes have turned flinty. Her hands are bunched

into fists on the tabletop.

"Adda ..." I warn under my breath, "they're not worth it. Ignore them."

"There must be something wrong with her. It's not right that *she* inherits the throne. Who ever heard of a female monarch? She needs a man to break her in ..."

Adda slams her palms on the table and jumps to her feet, her face like thunder. Fin is standing in an instant, his hand on his dagger, and I also rise, raising my hands in a placating gesture.

"Will you please shut your filthy mouths?" Adda rages at the men.

The group turns to look at her, some surprised and some amused by her anger. One blinks as if to focus his vision, one visibly sways on his feet with drunkenness.

"Nothing to do with you," one of the men says dismissively.

"It is when you're flinging that dung you consider conversation around for the whole fair to hear," Adda snaps.

One of the men folds his arms across his barrel chest and frowns at Fin.

"Control your woman," he orders dismissively.

Adda bristles at that, and Fin takes a step forward in anger. Delphine watches from the table, her eyes huge and terrified. I need to deescalate the situation before someone starts a fight.

"Don't you dare call me *woman*," Adda hisses, prodding her finger in the chest of the large man. "You've clearly spent too long in the company of idiots and animals to remember your manners."

The man gives a growl and bats her hand out of the way.

"Get your hand off her," Fin orders, barging his way between them and squaring up to the man with his jaw tensed in a hard line.

The other men jostle forward to lend their support, bumping the table and spilling ale from the tops of their full tankards, as the man scowls into Fin's face.

"You going to make me, pretty boy?" he dares through gritted teeth.

Fin shoves his shoulders in a quick, hard thrust that sends the man stumbling backwards into his drunk friends and unsheathes his dagger. His eyes dart between all of his opponents, quickly sizing up which is the biggest threat. He doesn't see the wink of a blade as one of the men pulls it from his waistband, but I do. I don't even think about what I'm doing. I move fast, just as he swipes the knife in a fatal slash to gut Fin – I step in between them, pushing myself against Fin, blocking the blade. Blocking it with my own body.

My belly.

I take the brutal slash, feeling the keen sting of the blade as it slices open my stomach.

27

A number of things happen all at once.

I clasp my hands to the wound in my stomach as blood blooms in a rising tide, dark red and sticky against the yellow linen. The pain almost knocks me off my feet. Fin's arms wrap around me from behind and he lowers me gently to the ground. Adda launches herself at the closest man, pummelling her fists into him with the fury of a wild animal.

"Aster!" Delphine shrieks from somewhere above me.

There is movement all around as the knot of men who had been squaring off to Fin and Adda quickly disperse. They must have panicked at the sight of all the blood.

I squint up and see Fin's face, pale and frantic, staring down at my stomach in horror.

"It's ok," I say faintly, "I'll be fine ... in a minute. Leave me, look after Adda."

The pain is intense, and my eyelids are heavy as lead. I

Being Adaliza

know I need to concentrate to heal the wound but sleep tugs at me and all I want to do is give in and drift off, away from the scream of damaged nerve endings and ripped flesh, the hot dampness of blood that pulses from the wound with each heartbeat.

"I'm not leaving you—" he insists, his arms wrapping around me more tightly, at the same time as I hear Adda order from close by, "Don't you dare leave her!"

I force my eyes open, seeing Adda's fierce expression as she leans over me and examines my injury. She's safe. I take a halting breath and force all my concentration into healing the wound, letting my eyelids fall shut. Magic floods my system; deep within me membrane knits, tissue closes, capillaries join, skin reforms. Once the wave of magic recedes I'm limp with exhaustion, but I won't die. It's very hard to kill a changeling, as our magic can heal all wounds and even regrow limbs. That's not to say it's impossible – a particularly motivated killer could succeed by decapitating a changeling or removing their vital organs. The only danger to me is blood loss, and I've sealed the wound now.

"Aster?" There's a warble of rising fear in Delphine's voice.

I squint through heavy eyelids and see the three of them all staring down at me.

"I'm fine," I repeat, and I can hear every ounce of exhaustion in my voice.

Adda's hands rest gently on my stomach, peeling back the slashed fabric of my dress to see smooth skin. Blood-slicked and gruesome, I imagine, but unharmed.

"You're healed?" she breathes in relief.

I nod. "The magic has taken it out of me though."

Fin shifts and I realise that I'm all but lying in his lap. He supports my back to assist me into a sitting position and then hooks one forearm under my legs, lifting me into his arms.

"We should leave before we draw any more attention," he tells Adda, who acquiesces without comment.

I peer at her from my vantage point in Fin's arms. Her tanned face is pale, her brow is creased with worry. I reach out with one hand – which feels so heavy I have to strain to lift it – and lay it on her upper arm. She glances at me. *It's not your fault*, I try to convey with a small squeeze. Her lips purse into the ghost of a smile, as if she understands but doesn't quite believe it.

I would protest at being carried but I very much doubt I have the strength to stand, let alone walk. Fin bears me easily, striding through the fair and ignoring the gasps of alarm as people notice my limp, blood-soaked form in his arms. When we're back at the horses he lowers me gently to the grass.

"Can you ride?" Adda asks.

"I'll take her," Fin says immediately, his tone brooking no argument. Apparently he doesn't trust Adda and her exuberant riding style.

"Wait," Delphine calls, kneeling beside me.

She passes me one of the uneaten pork rolls that I assumed had been left scattered on the table at the ale tent.

"Using your magic makes you hungry, doesn't it?" she says.

My heart warms at her thoughtfulness and I smile as I tuck into the roll. She's right – my stomach is a rumbling void, and if I give in to the sleep tugging at me then I will wake up utterly ravenous. They all watch in seriousness as I devour the roll, and then Delphine passes me a second. I try to refuse it, knowing that it's one of theirs, but she gives me a pointed look.

"Eat," she insists.

I don't have the energy to put up a fight so I eat the

second roll too, feeling pleasantly full by the time I'm finished.

"I'm done," I say before she can ply me with a third. "I'm ready."

I try to get to my feet but my knees buckle immediately – I'm embarrassingly weak. Fin catches me around the waist and holds me close to his side.

"You get on the horse, I'll hold her," Adda says, wrapping an arm around my waist from the other side.

Fin seems reluctant to let me go, but after a moment he leaves me in Adda's care and mounts Alezan. We hobble over to him and I manage to get up into the saddle, after some unceremonious pushing from Adda and pulling from Fin. I expect to ride pillion as I always have before, but he puts me in front of him. With one hand he holds the reins and the other arm curves around me to hold me against his chest. My head fits perfectly underneath his chin. If I wasn't beset by bone-deep exhaustion I know my heart would be fluttering at the feel of his arm around me and his chest flush against me, warm and strong and safe. Alezan starts to walk, and I assume the plodding pace is for my benefit.

"Relax, Aster," he murmurs in my ear. "Sleep."

I realise that I'm attempting to hold myself upright, to ward off the tiredness. I sigh and let myself settle against Fin, moulding myself to him, leaning my head back against his sternum and closing my eyes. His arm tightens a fraction, his bicep bulging. I'm so tired. Alezan's gentle sway is soothing.

"Why did you do it?"

His question takes me by surprise, thrusting me back to full consciousness.

"Do what?" I ask sleepily.

I feel Fin's swallow against the back of my head. "Step in front of the blade."

"He would have killed you. You didn't see it."

"He could have killed *you*."

"We're hard to kill," I insist weakly. "It's why changelings make the best bodyguards."

Fin is quiet for a long moment. I wonder what he's thinking, but there's no chance of me opening my eyes or lifting my head to see his expression.

"I thought ... when it happened, I thought ..." There is emotion restricting Fin's voice.

He feels responsible, I realise. Guilty, maybe. It's unnecessary. I didn't even think when I saw that knife blade flash – I just moved. To save him. Any other outcome was unthinkable. But, even if I could find the words to express how I had felt in that moment, I wouldn't tell him.

"I might make a habit of rescuing knights in distress," I joke weakly.

I feel him huff a brief laugh and shake his head. He doesn't say anything else – or if he does, I don't hear it. I am asleep within minutes.

I wake tucked up in a bed with a feather pillow under my head. Bleary and confused, I turn over and see Adda and Delphine lying next to me in the large bed, all of us sharing a blanket. They are asleep.

It's light outside, and considering everyone else is still sleeping I assume it's the morning and I've been unconscious all afternoon, evening and night. I carefully extricate myself from the bed so as not to disturb the others, assessing myself as I stretch my limbs and roll my head on my neck. I still feel tired, a little sluggish, but not the bone-weary exhaustion that dogged me after healing my wound yesterday.

I glance down; someone – presumably Delphine – must

have undressed me and changed my bloodstained clothes for a fresh chemise. I spy the yellow kirtle, now slashed and stiff with wine-dark blood, bundled in a corner of the bedchamber. My stomach dips a little with disappointment. I loved that dress. It was the first item of clothing I have ever bought for myself, Aster Lemorque. It wasn't the borrowed gown of another woman, nor a black, billowing houppelande, made for disguising and hiding. It was simple, pretty, the colour of sunshine. I sigh. Oh well – it's not as if I could wear it once I get back to Throsne anyway.

I glance around me. The room is clearly in an inn – presumably in Nortferry where we had planned to rest for the night. It's small and cramped with a ceiling too low for a canopy atop the four-poster bed, a construction far too grand for this modest room. The top of the bedposts have been sawn off. There is a mottled looking glass leaning against the wall on a sideboard. I peer at my reflection and find myself momentarily taken aback by what I see. Not Adaliza's face, the one I have grown so used to seeing. A new face: dark, straight hair, blue-grey eyes framed by black brows, a wide mouth. Pale skin that looks a little wan underneath a scattering of freckles.

A pretty face, less guileful than Adda's but not insipid. Delphine and Adda remarked that it suited me when I patched together attributes from various women without much thought a few days ago. I find that I agree. I give myself a small smile in the mirror and see the dimple curve in my left cheek. I trace the small depression with gentle fingers.

Someone stirs in the bed behind me.

"Aster?" Delphine says groggily.

I turn to face her as she sits up and blinks owlishly.

"How are you feeling?" she asks.

Adda rolls over, roused by her voice. Her sleep-mussed

hair is a tangled mess against the pillow.

"Much improved, thank you," I reassure her. "We're in Nortferry?"

Delphine nods. Her eyes trace me from head to toe critically.

"We'll need to find you a new commoner's dress."

"You can borrow some of my clothes," Adda offers. "At least you can be sure they'll fit."

Delphine makes a face of distaste.

"You might be comfortable roaming the realm in men's clothes, but that doesn't mean Aster should do it too," she grumbles, then blinks at Adda. "My Lady," she adds nervously.

I bite back my smile. Before she went to the tower, Delphine was a polite and respectful handmaiden to the princess. Since spending so much time with me she's more used to speaking her mind, and now seems to forget whether she's talking to me or the real Adaliza. I suspect that Adda delights in hearing her less respectful comments – she has never appreciated sycophants.

"Anything you have will be fine, Adda," I say. "I'd rather not delay any longer."

Adda smirks at me and shoots Delphine a triumphant look. We dress together, me in a pair of grey breeches and a mauve tunic. The men's attire doesn't bother me; I regularly used to don trousers for combat training and appreciate the freedom of movement that they offer.

Although it's early it's busy in the taproom as travellers prepare to catch a riverboat at the nearby ferry point. Fin is already up and waiting for us. His eyes fly straight to me, running up and down my body as if to assess me for injuries as we approach.

"I'm fine," I tell him for what feels like the hundredth

time. "I am well rested."

He nods, his expression serious. Then he turns to Adda and his mouth flattens in an expression of ... admonishment?

"Have you apologised yet?" he asks her.

I blink in surprise at his bluntness, so far removed from the courtly manners he usually displays in Adda's company, and find myself even more shocked by the look of contrition on Adda's face.

"No." She turns to me. "I'm sorry, Aster. The incident yesterday ... it was my fault. I shouldn't have let my anger get the better of me. I didn't consider the consequences."

I am taken aback by the apology – both Adda's meek delivery and Fin's insistence that she make it. They must have had words last night while I was unconscious.

"Adda, there's really no need. I chose to come with you to protect you. I'm all too familiar with the risks of the job."

I give her a knowing grin to reassure her that I'm not in the least bit angry with her. She smiles back in the mischievous, tight-lipped way she has, but Fin's expression stays stern.

"But please, for all of our sakes – no more impulsive stop offs before Throsne," I implore.

Adda gives a dramatic sigh. "I suppose I can agree to that."

28

The next few days pass without incident. We secure passage on a boat and follow the River Fluet down as it wends through the Old Woods towards southern Belforet. Secretly I'm grateful that I have an excuse to spend a whole day doing nothing on the boat, and find myself nodding off to sleep on more than one occasion. By the time we hit the road again the following day I am feeling fully refreshed.

The mood among our small group is a strange one. Adda still wears her bravado for everyone to see, but when no one is looking she slips into pensive silences that cause her to sit stiffly in the saddle. The run-in at the fair rattled her more than I expected. I'm not sure if it was the cruel words of her drunken subjects or the fact that she narrowly avoided a knife fight that continues to play on her mind. I try to broach the subject with her but she refuses to be drawn, dismissing my concerns with a careless shrug and a bright smile.

Fin is serious and vigilant, keeping his sword within easy

Being Adaliza

reaching distance. I understand why; my stomach clenches as we pass the place on the Forest Road where we were attacked and Delphine was kidnapped. This area isn't safe. As we ride south we pass parties of knights and noblemen – very few of them even acknowledge us, let alone take an interest in our party, but that doesn't mean we're out of danger.

Fin tries to persuade me to ride with him on Alezan when we first set off down the Forest Road, but I politely decline and stick with Adda. It's not because I'm still angry with him. The thought of edging close to him in the saddle, my thighs clasped around his, my arms twined around his waist ... I don't want to put myself through that kind of torture. In mindless moments on the road I find my thoughts wandering to the memory of riding away from the fair, of falling asleep against his chest with his arm wrapped tight around me. It's unfortunate that I was unconscious for hours and wholly unappreciative of that particular situation.

When I catch myself dwelling on it I give myself a firm mental shake. It feels like a betrayal of Adda just to think it. She and Fin act differently around each other now. He has finally abandoned his attempts at courtly wooing and treats Adda in much the same way he treats me and Delphine. I know she appreciates it; she no longer pointedly ignores him or attempts to embarrass him with barbed comments or insults, which is a sign of great favour coming from her. I tell myself that I am happy for them, that all the puzzle pieces are falling into place exactly how they should. The knight gets the princess, they live happily ever after. That's the way the story goes. It's nearly time for me to turn the page on this chapter and slink back into the darkness of the Ruelle de Gargouille where I belong.

There is only one strange instance that confuses this notion. When we got off the boat we agreed that it would be safer to camp in secluded spots on the road rather than expose ourselves to danger at the busy roadside inns. When we're just two day's ride from the city walls of Throsne, I wake as the night is lightening into dawn and our little camp is hushed all around me. I open my eyes and blink in surprise.

I am lying on my left side and Fin is facing me in a mirror image, close enough to startle me. We have drawn towards each other in sleep. Scandalously so, considering that Adda is sleeping just across fire. I should roll away, pull back, but ... I can't tear my gaze from his face. He looks so peaceful. My eyes trace the freckles across his nose and the shadow of new beard on his cheeks. I can't help but wonder ... would it be so wrong to lean in, just a little, and lay my cheek next to his? Just to be close to him, to fantasise in these secret moments before dawn that he chose me? That he wanted to lie down beside me?

Fin stirs and I close my eyes immediately, fighting to keep my breath deep and even as I feign sleep. I can tell from his breathing that he is awake. I expect him to open his eyes and flinch back, alarmed by the inappropriate proximity of our faces, our bodies curved towards each other, but ... he doesn't. It's almost as if he's holding his breath. Savouring the moment just as I did. No, that's a silly thought – a pathetic, dangerous thought that will help no one.

I turn as if just waking, rolling onto my back with a small sigh, and I hear Fin quickly mimic the action. When I rub my eyes and open them blearily, he stares straight up at the sky.

"Good morning," I say softly.

His reply is gruff and he clears his throat. "Good morning."

We are polite but distant with each other for the rest of the day.

Being Adaliza

The air is muggy and the sky is thick with grey clouds when we finally glimpse Belforet's capital city ahead of us. Towering stone walls encircle the vast sprawl of Throsne; hundreds of roofs are visible beyond, mostly tiled or thatched, as well as the tops of grand buildings that rise above the streets of houses and shops. I can pick out the spire of Throsne Cathedral and the stone towers and turrets of the royal palace in the central district. That is our destination. Although the royal court may be expecting their princess's return to be heralded with fanfare and a celebratory procession through the streets, Adda has insisted that we maintain our disguises until we're back at the palace. I suspect it's because she wants to put off discarding her breeches for a fine gown until the last possible moment.

The road has gradually grown busier with pedestrians, carts, riders and carriages all heading towards the city gates. Our pace slows as we near the imposing arch of the Porte de Marchant, where city guards inspect each group of travellers with varying degrees of interest. Sometimes carts are searched or riders interrogated, but most people are waved through with a bored sigh. We stay in the saddle as we approach the gate – Fin first, followed by me and Adda, and then Delphine. I glance up and see the lethal spikes of a portcullis hanging suspended above us.

"What's your business here?" the nearest guard asks Fin.

"We're visiting my wife's family," he says, pointing behind him to our horse.

The guard's gaze flicks over us in disinterest. He nods once to usher us past him into the city, but before Adda can heel Cunstance forward a voice calls out: "Wait!"

Another guard steps forward. He is an ugly-looking brute, tall and hulking.

"Dismount," he calls up to me and Adda.

It's unnecessarily rude and I know that Adda does not take kindly to barked orders.

"Why?" she asks imperiously.

"By order of the city guard, get down from your horse," he insists.

My heart starts to thud a warning in my chest. I've never been stopped at the city gate before. None of these men could possibly recognise Adda – even if they had seen the princess before, no one would suspect that this wild-looking woman in men's clothes is Princess Adaliza.

"Just do it," I whisper to Adda, and slip from Cunstance's back.

Adda gives a huff of displeasure but follows my lead. Fin also dismounts ahead of us, a frown on his face.

"What is the meaning of this?" he asks, striding over to us.

The guard puts a meaty hand on my shoulder, making a tingle run over my skin. I want to shudder.

"You're coming with me," he mutters.

I glance up at his face in indignation, which is rough hewn and mottled, and I freeze.

"Unhand her!" Adda demands.

"Sorry, Your Highness, she's coming with me," the guard says, more loudly than before but not loudly enough for it to carry to the other guards or travellers who continue to move on around us.

Fin immediately takes a step towards me with a face like stone, one hand on his sword hilt, and Adda tosses her head, fire in her gaze. Delphine has also scrambled off her horse and stands with them, her expression uneasy and her eyes large with worry.

"It's ok," I say to them, and the tone of defeat in my voice makes all their heads snap to me. "He's my brother."

Being Adaliza

Inigo Lemorque, my least favourite brother, smiles at Adda and Fin. I know that devilish grin. On a handsome face it is charmingly rogueish; on an ugly face like this one it's a leer with ill intent.

"You've certainly been off having fun, haven't you," he says to Adda in a mock-scolding tone that I know will immediately get her back up. Inigo has never had much tact. "Too busy playing the commoner with your knight to come home?"

Fin bristles, heat rushing into his cheeks at the lewd suggestion, and I speak before he can open his mouth.

"What are you doing here, Inigo?"

He turns back to me. "Tracking you down. Where have you been?"

"On a job," I say coldly.

"That job finished four months ago, as soon as *they* stopped paying for our services," he says, jabbing a finger in Adaliza's direction.

"Then you're not a very good tracker, are you, if it's taken you this long to find me?" I say, raising my eyebrows in challenge.

It's disturbingly easy to fall back into the spiteful oneupmanship that characterises our relationship. Most of my family – especially the males – can be real bastards.

His thick brows drop into a frown. "Grandmère has another job for you. You're needed – now."

I try to keep my composure even though my heart is racing. I turn to Adda, Fin and Delphine, all of whom are staring at me with varying degrees of shock. This wasn't what I was expecting. I had planned to say my goodbyes in the privacy of the palace, not in a very public place with city guards looking on.

"Ok," I tell Inigo with a small nod. "Ok. I'll come."

Adda immediately pulls me into a fierce hug, crushing us together.

"This isn't goodbye," I whisper in her ear. "When I'm done I'll find my way into the palace."

She nods. Delphine grabs me next and I lay my cheek against the top of her hair as I embrace her.

"Come on," Inigo snaps impatiently. "You know the protocol."

My arms drop from Delphine as I turn to him. "You can't be serious? Here?"

When we finish a job, it is protocol that the gemstone being used to disguise a changeling's eyes is returned to whoever was being impersonated. Inigo is telling me to take off the lapis lazuli necklace and give it to Adda, as a sign that our contract is over. Usually this takes place in the Maison du Lemorque, not outside the busy city gate of Throsne. If I give up the necklace here, my eyes will turn black and I will have to cross a city that loathes the faefolk before I can make my way to the relative safety of the Ruelle de Gargouille. The lack of disguise is unnecessarily dangerous for me. Inigo smirks.

"Finish this, Aster," he orders.

I swallow thickly and reach around to undo the clasp at the nape of my neck. The necklace feels heavy as I draw it away from my skin and hold it out to Adda. Her eyes are locked with mine; I don't see any change in her expression as she watches my eyes flood black as pitch, no surprise or revulsion. She takes the necklace from me, her fingers folding around mine and gripping tightly.

"Thank you, Aster," she says, her voice quiet but strong as steel.

"It's been an honour," I tell her, my eyes filling with tears.

I glance away in an attempt to disperse them and,

blinking rapidly, my gaze falls on Fin. The last time he saw me with my changeling eyes he was horrified. Now he stares at me with an expression I can't quite decipher, but I don't think he's judging my black eyes. It feels like he's looking past them – looking at me. The real me. I don't know what I was planning to say to him when we parted ways, but now I can't find any words at all.

"Enough. Let's get going."

Inigo throws something at me and our connection is broken as I catch it. A hooded cloak. I quickly don the garment, pulling the hood up over my head to hide my face. With a deep breath and one last look at my friends, I follow my brother and melt into the crowd that throngs the city entrance.

29

I follow Inigo through the city, hiding in crowds and slinking in shadows, taking the back alleys and cut-throughs to reach the Ruelle de Gargouille. The winding cobbled street, hemmed in on both sides by haphazard buildings with overhanging storeys, is gloomier than I remember. The shop fronts are dark and dirty, the air is thick with the smell of smoke and sewage. The people who lurk on the Ruelle de Gargouille can be divided into two categories: those up to no good, cloaked, wary and scurrying, trying to avoid notice; and those who watch them with a predator's cool gaze, contemplating thievery or violence. Some are fairies, most are criminals. All are bad news.

    The imposing edifice of the Maison du Lemorque emerges from the gloom. It bulges into the street like the stern of a great ship, rising level after level in a gravity-defying tower of black beams and greying, soot-streaked plaster. It's the only home I've ever known – yet I have to

Being Adaliza

force myself to step over the threshold.

Inigo strides straight through the shop front, tugging the bell pull as he passes.

"Wait in the parlour," he barks at me, then climbs the stairs without a backwards glance.

I glare at his retreating back – he can't tell me what to do. But there are creaks and groans from the floorboards above my head and I know that it won't be long before Grandmére appears and the berating will begin. I sigh and flop down on the settle.

"Aster," a rich, throaty voice declares as a woman sashays into the room.

Grandmére is wearing the form of a grand duchess she impersonated years ago and has since become one of her favourite disguises. She is handsome and graceful, her statuesque form complimented by the swirl of her black houppelande. Her hair is long and white, shining in twin rivers of ice that flow over her shoulders. I am surprised that her expression is mild, even jubilant. I expected censure over my absence.

"Grandmére," I say warily and kiss her cheek when she offers it to me.

Two other figures descend the stairs behind her and join us in the parlour. Both are women – despite their unfamiliar forms, I recognise them as my mother and her twin sister, my Aunt Calla. I blink at them, taken aback. It's rare that all three matriarchs of the Maison du Lemorque are present at the same time. Their assignments take them away from home for long periods of time and often overlap.

I bob a small curtsy in their direction and they nod back in unison. My mother wears the creased face of a peasant, sun-weathered and pinched. Aunt Calla has the pouchy, frog-like countenance of a pampered lady who hasn't been blessed with natural beauty. Both of them appraise me keenly with all-black eyes.

"I apologise for my delayed return, Grandmére. The death of the queen and the king's contest rather complicated matters—" I try to explain, but my grandmother dismisses my explanation with a wave of her hand.

"That's not important right now, Aster. Time is of the essence. You have a new assignment."

My eyebrows raise slightly at her unusually lax response to my disobedience. She clasps her elegant hands together in a gesture of excitement. I don't think I've ever seen her so animated over a potential job. I am immediately suspicious.

"What is it?" I ask.

"You're attracting quite an illustrious clientele," Grandmére purrs. "First Princess Adaliza of Belforet, now Queen Hemera of Orpho. You know of her?"

I nod. Orpho's aging king recently found himself a new bride. I have never encountered her in person but I know that Queen Hemera is forty years younger than her husband – around my age.

Grandmére continues.

"Queen Hemera summoned me to her palace in quite a tizz. It seems that she hasn't been able to perform her wifely – or queenly – duty. She and the king have been married for five years and she is yet to provide the requisite heir. King Nux is aware that he isn't getting any younger and is tired of waiting. He has given her until the end of the year to fall pregnant."

I frown. "Or what?"

"Or Queen Hemera faces execution."

I gape at my grandmother, who seems to be recounting the state of affairs with glee. It's barbaric – to think that the poor woman will be killed just because she can't bear that old man's child. The injustice of it pricks at me.

"The queen feels she is out of options. She has tried every apothecary's tincture and wise woman's charm but her womb won't quicken. The king has a number of illegitimate children so it's clear that the fault doesn't lie with him. She worries that she is barren. She has come to us in a last bid to give the king what he needs."

I frown. "I don't understand. How would a decoy help her situation?"

"She wants a young, fertile changeling to take her place in the marriage bed."

"What?"

I stare at the three women in front of me, my mother, grandmother and aunt. All of them simply return my gaze, unabashed. I feel like a dark, endless chasm has opened up at my feet. They can't be serious – they can't honestly expect me to do this? To lie with an old man and have his baby?

"This is the opportunity of a lifetime, Aster," my mother says, her black eyes gleaming. "If you bear the king a child, the heir to the Orphic throne will be a changeling. Imagine, a Lemorque on the throne! The influence we could have ..."

Any offspring of a female changeling would be a changeling too. I start to realise why the three of them are so excited. Queen Hemera has given them a way to infiltrate the monarchy, to seed their own particular brand of fairy anarchy in one of the most ancient royal houses. I am their only hope – the only changeling of the right age and gender to impersonate the queen. Of course Grandmére was anxious to get me back to Throsne. I am the Maison du Lemorque's most valuable asset. A brood mare.

If I get pregnant, I won't be able to shift without risking harm to the foetus. I would be stuck defenceless in Queen Hemera's body until the baby is born. And what then? Give up my own child to the real queen and head back to Throsne, my duty done, ready for the next assignment? Or stay in the royal court of Orpho to watch my baby grow up in the arms of another woman, waiting for the right moment to teach it how to shift and shape it into the weapon my grandmother envisages?

I shake my head and keep shaking it, unable to stop. "No."

Grandmére's gaze sharpens. "What do you mean, no?"

"No. I won't do it."

I have never refused an assignment. I never even considered the possibility that I could say no. But this – I can't do this. I won't. It's wrong of King Nux to give his wife this ultimatum; it's wrong of Queen Hemera to trick him with a changeling decoy; and it's wrong of my family to expect me to go along with the scheme. It's my body, my life. This is where I draw the line.

When she speaks, Grandmére's tone has lost its richness. It is icy, empty, sharp. "Aster, you are a Lemorque. You serve this family, as we all do. This is not a request, it's an order."

I stare at her, at all three of them. Their expressions are cold, their eyes are endless black. They are supposed to care for me. I never doubted it before – I never questioned how they could bring themselves to give me up to another family as a child, swap me in and out of situations as it suited them. They fashioned me into this creature of deception and violence. Grandmére is wrong; I do not owe any loyalty to the Lemorques.

The realisation doesn't make me feel angry or self-righteous. It makes me sad. So very sad. My grandmother must see it in my face, mistaking it for acceptance. She gives me a self-satisfied, feline smile.

"I will send a message to the royal palace in Kral and

request they send a boat to fetch you. Be ready to leave in three days."

"Three days?" I splutter, my heart hammering.

Kral, the capital of Orpho, is one of the other grand cities on the River Pompone. It is quick and easy to access by boat from Throsne.

"We've been waiting for your return for weeks, Aster," my mother says pointedly, as if the tight deadline is my fault.

It's not enough time. I need to find a way out of this. It's not as simple as just walking out the Maison du Lemorque and starting a new life away from my family. I don't have a gemstone to hide my changeling eyes – without one I won't be able to blend in with the human populace. My gaze flies to the hidden void behind the panelling across the room where the stash of unclaimed gemstones is kept, sealed with a lock keyed to Grandmére's magic.

I swallow and give a small nod.

"I want to see Princess Adaliza before I go," I say, hoping my swift acquiescence to the new assignment may have bought me some goodwill – and the opportunity to get my hands on another gemstone.

Grandmére shakes her head, lips pursed. "There is no need. You will stay here and prepare."

"But Grandmére ..."

She holds up a hand to stop me. "Enough, Aster. This misplaced allegiance to Princess Adaliza is wearing. Your assignment is over."

I fight to keep my expression blank, stifling a sigh of frustration. Is she planning to keep me under lock and key? It doesn't matter – I am resourceful. I will find a way.

"Yes, Grandmére," I say demurely, admitting defeat. Giving her everything she wants. "May I go up to my bedchamber?"

Primrose Hugh

She regards me warily for a moment before nodding her agreement. I bob a curtsy in the vague direction of all three of them and ascend the creaking stairs, my head down.

My bedchamber is on the third floor. The room is panelled floor-to-ceiling in dark mahogany, inlaid at eye level with carvings of fairy fables and beasts. A dragon spreads its scaled wings and breathes fire onto a human village on one panel; on another a ship is tossed in a stormy sea, beset on one side by a siren singing from a rock and on the other by a kraken bristling with spiked tentacles. There is a common theme: the suffering of hapless humans. My bed is a large, carved four-poster draped in emerald green hangings. Little light penetrates the space through the diamond-leaded window. It's dark and oppressive.

I light a silver candelabra that sits on a hulking sideboard by the door. Its candles throw a sickly yellow light over the scene. The glow is reflected back at me from a full-length looking glass that is propped up against one wall. Such large mirrors are very valuable and usually only found in the homes of the wealthiest lords and ladies, but changelings have a vested interest in their own reflection. I move to stand directly in front of the looking glass.

The young woman staring back at me is tall, her body slender and strong, her facial features even. Her dark hair is glossy, her lips are pink. A dimple will form in her left cheek if she smiles, but she doesn't. This dark room, this gloomy street, is not her world. She is a creature of sunlight and laughter, of friends and campfires and yellow kirtles. I change my form, shrinking my spine and limbs, choosing the sorrowful countenance of a lovelorn woman I once saw sobbing by a graveside. The colour seems to have faded from her: her ash blonde hair is limp, her complexion is wan, her all-black eyes are lifeless, their red rims the only colour in her face. I find it fitting.

30

The next morning – after a night of restless scheming and fitful sleep – I slip out the front door of the Maison du Lemorque, managing to avoid the notice of any of my lurking relatives. I don't intend to run away – not yet, at least. I need a gemstone first, and the chances of my grandmother opening the lock on our existing horde in my presence is slim to none. My best chance of escape is in Orpho once the decoy agreement has been made with Queen Hemera and I have her permission to mimic her eye colour. I will leave before I'm corralled into the royal bedchamber. Even the thought of it makes me shudder.

  I am escaping the house because I can't stay cooped up inside any longer. I need to be moving, need to be doing something, to take my mind off the panic beating its wings inside my chest. Grandmére told me to prepare for the mission, so that's what I'll do. I walk the short distance to

Being Adaliza

Madame Faucheuse's shop a few doors down the Ruelle de Gargouille. The lintel of the door is low and slanting but with my current stature I'm short enough to enter without ducking. A bell above my head jangles discordantly as I enter.

At first glance, the shop is incongruous with the dingy environs of the Ruelle de Gargouille. It is a treasure trove of finery. Gowns of all colours and styles are displayed on racks: sumptuous silks traced with embroidery, dark velvets trimmed with mouldering fur. Jewellery spills from small chests on various surfaces, chokers and bracelets and diadems. There are curtains and bed hangings, some emblazoned with the crests of noble houses. Odd pieces of furniture are scattered throughout the space. It's only the smell that lingers in the shop that hints at its sinister origins – the fusty, sour scent of death and misfortune.

"Aster? Is that you?"

The figure of Madame Faucheuse emerges from behind a clothes rail. She is a striking woman in her late thirties, plump of hip and bosom, with a mane of wild red hair that clouds around her shoulders.

"It's me," I say with a smile.

She doesn't recognise my face but she must have seen the black houppelande and my all-black eyes, and then worked out that I was the most likely Lemorque based on my age. Madame Faucheuse smiles in return, her eyes gleaming in the low light. Her eyes are human but her irises are coal black, hinting at her fairy origins. I suspect that she has banshee blood, based on her preoccupation with death.

"You've been gone a long time," she observes.

While I like the woman, I don't trust her. It would be foolish to trust anyone who plies their trade on the Ruelle de Gargouille.

"Indeed. And soon to leave again," I say vaguely.

"What do you need?"

I glance around at the clothes surrounding us. "Something ... regal."

Madame Faucheuse narrows her eyes slightly at me before giving me a tight-lipped smile. "I have the perfect thing."

She sweeps down the narrow pathways created by the profusion of wares for sale and I follow a few steps behind her. She pulls out a gown with a flourish and holds it out for me to see. It's a sheath of gold silk, traced all over with shimmering thread like spiderwebs. Madame Faucheuse drapes a green brocade overgown on top with long, dagged sleeves and selects a golden metalwork belt to match.

"Regal enough for you?" she asks smugly.

"Where did you get these?" I ask, stroking the fabric with my thumb.

Even I'm awed by the beautiful ensemble, and I had access to a princess's wardrobe for three and a half years.

"An old Throsne family. The whole household died. The plague was very good for business."

The woman grins wickedly, exposing teeth that are yellowed and slightly pointed. Her shop is filled with treasures pilfered from the dead and the unlucky. Madame Faucheuse haunts the grand houses of the city when there has been a death, picking at their belongings and secreting them away like a carrion bird stealing morsels from a carcass. The Lemorques are some of her best customers, as we regularly require all sorts of outfits at short notice with no questions asked. She also has a stash of palace uniforms, from guards' surcoats and armour to maids' dresses and aprons. I long ago lost any squeamishness when it comes to wearing a dead woman's clothing.

Being Adaliza

I nod at Madame Faucheuse. "I'll take it. Put it on our account."

The woman inclines her head and gives me a satisfied smile. She will probably charge a fortune for it but I don't care. I watch her unhook the heavy outfit and take it through to the back room.

"Are you supposed to be here?"

I turn around at the sound of the masculine drawl behind me. A young man watches me from the front of the shop, a smile quirking his lips. His arms are crossed over his chest and he leans against a dresser with a leonine grace that I recognise.

"Errol?"

Errol Lemorque, my other brother, pushes off the dresser and sidles towards me, effortless and arrogant. His irises, I notice, are brown, half-hidden under hooded lids.

"Is the whole family back in town just for my benefit?" I ask archly.

"You better return before they notice you're gone," he warns.

I cross my arms, mirroring him. "Grandmére told me to prepare for my next mission – that's what I'm doing."

Errol raises an eyebrow. "So this little sojourn has nothing to do with the news from the palace?"

"What news?"

"Princess Adaliza has been rescued, the heir has returned to her father, the wedding bells are ringing ..." he recounts, sounding bored.

My stomach plummets. I hadn't allowed myself to think of Adda or Fin, not when I had no way of getting into the palace without being seen in the next two days. My last promise to Adda – that I would find my way to the palace to say a proper goodbye – would need to be broken. And Fin ...

any words I might have for him would remain unspoken.

"The princess is due to be presented at court this afternoon," Errol continues.

I keep my expression composed. "So?"

Errol gives me a pointed look. "So ... I hear you requested to visit the palace before you leave, and Grandmére denied it."

I appraise my brother thoughtfully. Errol isn't like Inigo – he isn't needlessly cruel or brutish. He isn't particularly good or bad, and he rarely takes sides. No; Errol's weakness is a penchant for chaos. He sets fires just to see how quickly they will spread, and passes on whispers if he thinks there's a chance they could escalate into an argument. He will help me if I offer him the chance to make mischief.

My gaze fixes on his ochre-brown eyes again. His fingers are bare of rings and there is no bracelet on either of his wrists. He must be wearing a gemstone around his neck.

"Can I borrow your necklace?" I ask brazenly.

His brown eyes brighten with interest. "Why?"

"You know why."

"Why should I help you?" he asks silkily.

"Because I'm your favourite sister."

"You're my only sister."

"Your favourite sibling, then. Hell, your favourite Lemorque. It's not like there's much competition."

He smirks and tugs the cord around his neck, pulling out a plain jasper pendant. His eyes flood black and he lets the stone dangle in front of him, swaying slightly from side to side.

"What's it worth to you?" he asks.

I give him a level look. "I'll owe you one."

"One what?"

"One favour."

Being Adaliza

It's a dangerously open-ended bargain to make with one of the faefolk – and not a mistake I would make under normal circumstances. But that pendant allows me to accelerate my escape plans, and the minute I'm out of Throsne I don't intend to ever set foot in the city again, let alone the Ruelle de Gargouille. I will never have to repay Errol's favour. But he doesn't know that – I'm banking on the fact that he thinks me desperate. It will sweeten the deal for him.

"One favour of my choosing?"

Errol pretends to consider the offer, although I know he will agree. His midnight eyes are sparkling.

"To be reclaimed at any point after today," I confirm.

His smirk widens into a handsome, dangerous smile. "Done."

He pulls the cord from around his neck and hands it over to me as Madame Faucheuse reappears in the front room. When she sees Errol her gait becomes sultry and she licks her lips.

She doesn't look back at me when I speak. "On second thoughts, Madame Faucheuse, I'll wear the gown now."

Although my gown is quite breathtaking in isolation, it blends right in with the crowd ascending the palace steps. The primped and puffed peacocks of Belforet's royal court are aflutter with the news that Princess Adaliza has returned. I listen to their chatter and keep my gaze on my embroidered slippers.

"The princess was living in the *woods* all this time, can you imagine? How barbaric!"

"Who is this Sir Finton, anyway? I haven't heard of him ..."

Primrose Hugh

"It will be the wedding of a lifetime, I'm sure."

I wear the bland face of a lesser noblewoman who I know is currently absent from Throsne – neither beautiful nor ugly, all the better for my purposes. I hope no one studies me closely enough to notice that my ochre irises are not the right shade of brown to match her eyes. The jasper pendant on its leather chord is far too plain to wear with my outfit so I have it lashed around my wrist, covered by my voluminous sleeve.

I shouldn't be here. If I had any sense I would have snatched the gemstone out of Errol's hands and fled straight out of the city. But ... I can't just leave. Not without seeing them one last time. Not without knowing they're ok. Knowing they're going to be ... happy. I want that. I need that.

We file into the throne room, the din of the courtiers echoing off its lofty vaulted ceiling. The dais at the far end of the room is currently unoccupied. A large carved throne sits empty, as do the two tall chairs on either side of it. One for the deceased queen, one for the missing princess. Neither has been sat on for months.

The chatter dies down when a trumpet blares from the doorway, signalling the entrance of the king. As one the crowd turns and watches as the royal retinue processes into the room. The king leads the way, his pace slow and laboured. He has aged considerably since I last saw him; he is thin, almost waxen-looking, and he leans heavily on a walking stick. The plague has clearly taken its toll on his health. A few respectful steps behind him are his counsellors, all old men in sombre-coloured robes and hats. The crowd's eyes skip over them, focusing instead on the figures at the rear of the procession.

My heart leaps at the sight of Adda. She stands tall and walks with confident purpose, robed in resplendent purple trimmed with ermine fur. Her face is covered by a gossamer veil so that only the outline of her features can be seen underneath the filmy fabric. It gives her an heir of modesty and mystery, but I suspect it has something to do with hiding Adda's suntan and scarred cheek. Atop her head is a delicate golden tiara. She has never looked so splendidly regal.

Her left arm is outstretched, her fingers resting lightly on the arm of ... Sir Finton Prest. My breath hitches in my chest. Only his full title can do justice to the figure he cuts next to Adda. He looks just as he did the first time I saw him, although he seems significantly less hot and bothered than he was then. He wears his full armour and the surcoat of the Order of the Ivory Maiden, gleaming and clean and gallant. His shoulders are broad, his steps are sure, his free hand rests on the hilt of the sword sheathed at his hip.

They look so perfect together, the very picture of courtly romance. My throat tightens with emotion. *I'm happy*, I tell myself. *I'm happy for them. I can leave them now I know that they're ok.* I should sidle to the back of the room and slip away while everyone is focused on the dais. I should leave. I should.

The king has reached the dais, but he doesn't sit in his throne. He holds his hand out for Adda, who drops Fin's arm and clasps her father's hand. I can't see her expression so I can't tell what she's thinking. I know that returning to Throsne was bittersweet for her. Fin sinks to one knee in front of them both, his head bowed.

"It is with the greatest pleasure that I welcome home my daughter and heir, Princess Adaliza of Belforet, and her noble saviour, Sir Finton Prest," the king announces.

The courtiers applaud and make saccharin, fawning noises. I clap my hands, feeling ... I can't deny it. I don't feel happy. I don't feel happy at all. I feel empty and sad and hopeless and hurt. I feel heartsick and weary and lost and desperate. I know I have to leave it all behind – leave *him* behind. I don't even know where I'm going. All I know is that I won't find happiness here.

I haven't been listening to the king. He and Adda are now sitting in their thrones and Fin has risen from his kneeling position, coming to stand at the side of the dais with his back to the stone wall. Finally I will my feet to move. I slip through the bodies all jostling to get closer to the king and his favour. When I'm near the back of the crowd I can't stop myself looking back at the dais one last time.

Fin's gaze is scanning the crowd. Somehow, in the distracting sea of opulently dressed nobles, his eyes lock onto mine. It sets my heart hammering, even though I remind myself I'm wearing a different face, just another anonymous courtier in the crowd. But Fin continues to stare at me, and with his hands he sign the word for star.

Aster? he asks.

Yes, I sign back in astonishment. How on earth did he recognise me? It sends a thrill through me, rooting me to the floor.

His eyes stay fixed on mine, but his hands don't move. He doesn't know what to say – and nor do I.

I am so caught up in him for endless moments that I startle when someone lays a hand on my shoulder. The contact sends a tingle through me – a tingle as my magic reacts to hers. I know instinctively that it's my Aunt Calla. My stomach lurches with dread. *No, no, no,* I chant in my head, *this can't be happening. Not now.*

"Don't make a scene," she murmurs in my ear, her voice low and threatening.

I turn and see the severe countenance of a middle aged lady. Her bony hand is like a claw on my shoulder.

"Your grandmother forbade you from coming here, Aster."

I swallow thickly, defeat ringing in my ears like a warning bell. I shouldn't have come here – what did it achieve? Nothing, and it cost me my chance of escape. Of course they would look for me here – stupid, I'm so stupid.

I take a deep, shuddering breath and turn back to Fin. He's still staring at me from the dais.

I have to go, I sign with shaking fingers. *I leave in two days.*

His expression falls, his brow creasing. *Where are you going?*

My eyes fill with tears that I won't shed, not here. *Good bye, Fin.*

He still looks confused. He lifts his hands and then drops them again in hesitation.

Aunt Calla's grip digs into my shoulder, steering me away. As I turn, my hands raise again in front of my chest, seemingly of their own accord. Even though I know it's foolish and hopeless and ill-advised I sign one last thing in response. The words that Elinor taught me. The ones I never thought I'd say to him.

I love you.

Tears blur my vision and I turn before I have to see his reaction, as Aunt Calla steers me towards the door.

31

I lie on my bed, staring up at the heavy green hangings. I don't know exactly how long it's been since my aunt locked me in my bedchamber. Four meals have been delivered to me on a tray, my only way of marking the passage of time. The light that manages to penetrate the dirty leaded glass of my window has faded. Night has fallen. Tomorrow I will be sent to Orpho.

My restlessness dissipated long ago. With nothing else to occupy my time, I allowed myself to wallow in my despair. My eyes are sore and puffy, the skin of my face feels tight with dried tears. I cried for the injustice of my position, the betrayal of my family, the helplessness I feel that my body isn't my own. I cried for the path I have been forced to choose, the lonely unknown ahead of me, a life to be eked out as a changeling on the run. But most of all, I cried for Fin – for the man I love and the future we never had together. No one is around to see it or judge it. I can finally be as selfish and indulgent as I like.

Now I just lie on my back and stare upwards, spent and hopeless. I've watched the steady progress of a spider spinning her web between the bed posts, the gleaming thread so insubstantial. It billows in the stirring of a slight breeze, but it doesn't break. Back and forth she scuttles like an aerial performer at a circus, strengthening her web with every pass.

A noise – a muted bump against the outside wall beyond my window – makes me glance away for a moment, but I don't move. I can't bring myself to rise from where I'm sprawled over the bedclothes like a discarded ragdoll. What's the point? But another noise, this time a soft patter against the window glass, makes me look up again.

There's something outside my window. I sit up slowly, laboriously. Perhaps it's a bird? The latch rattles, but it doesn't open – it's locked from the inside. I frown and pad over to the window, turning the latch and pushing it open.

A shape moves in the dark.

"Aster?"

My stomach drops to the floor and my heart stampedes, because I recognise that voice ... I know what the hulking shape is on the other side of the window.

"*Fin?*" I gasp.

I pull the window wide and step out of the way as he manoeuvres through the small opening, dropping into a crouch inside my bedroom with the lightness of a cat. Luckily he isn't wearing his armour, which would have broadened his shoulders and prevented him from squeezing through. He's swathed in a dark cloak.

I just stare, frozen to the spot. Fin is here. *Fin* is here. What does this mean?

"What are you doing here?"

He looks up and his green eyes meet mine, sending a jolt

through me. "I'm rescuing you."

I blink at him, unable to speak, unable to give in to the hope crushing my chest like a vice.

"Your brother said you had another job lined up, and then in the palace you said you were leaving in two days, and we weren't sure if we could get it done fast enough, so I came as quickly as I could ..."

Fin rambles when he's nervous. His gaze darts around my bedchamber, and I feel self-conscious about what he sees. I don't like him being here, in the place where I am least human. He said 'we' – so whatever he's doing here, it involves Adda, too.

"Get what done fast enough?" I ask, trying to make sense of his presence.

Fin clears his throat and pulls an envelope with a purple wax seal from inside his cloak. As he holds it out for me I can see that his hands are trembling.

"I promised Adda I'd let her explain ... but there was no way to get her past all the guards to tell you in person."

I stare at the rectangle of parchment, because it's easier than looking at him. There's something sealed inside, a small, hard object weighing down one corner. I swipe a finger under the seal and unfold the letter, my gaze sweeping over the lines of familiar handwriting before an object rolls out of a fold and into my palm. It's a ring – a silver band set with a familiar lapis lazuli stone. Confused, I clutch it tightly in my fist and seek Adda's explanation in her letter.

Dear Aster,

I have so many things to say to you and hardly the patience to fit them all in a letter. The first is a thank you. I know I've told you before that I appreciate your sacrifice on my behalf, but I don't think I've ever expressed how much your friendship means to me. You

Being Adaliza

have cared more for me in the past month than anyone still living, even when you didn't have to. Which is why I can't let you stay at the Maison du Lemorque.

I know you feel indebted to your family but you're better than the Ruelle de Gargouille. I have an offer, although I won't be offended if you turn it down when a better one comes your way. Work for me – come and live at the palace. When I become queen I will need an intelligent woman on my council to keep all those boring old men on their toes. You don't have to change your shape if you don't want to. I give you permission to use as much or as little of my appearance as you like – my eyes are yours, if you want them. It's the least I can do for you.

But there's something else I can give you too – not that it was ever mine to begin with. Fin told me you came to court yesterday and said goodbye before my father's announcement, so I can only assume you're still labouring under a misapprehension.

I am not marrying Sir Finton Prest. Did you seriously think I would abide by the rules of my father's utterly nonsensical contest? He was resistant at first but when I told him about the attempted abduction by my uncle, he came to agree that my position as a female heir is too unstable. He will be changing the law to state that female heirs are no longer required to marry in order to ascend the throne, just like male heirs. It's about time, too.

Besides, there is no way I would marry Fin when it is so clear that you and he are in love with each other. In Brillermare it was a matter of hours before I could see you had feelings for him, and a matter of days before I confirmed that he returned them. It certainly wasn't me he made cow eyes at constantly – if you'd looked at him you would have seen it. I only played along to keep us all together in the hope that the two of you would realise and stop dithering around each other. I should have knocked your heads together earlier.

Now, by decree of your future queen, I order you to grasp that

man by his admittedly lustrous hair and kiss him like you've wanted to all this time.
    Yours ever affectionately,
    Adda

By the time I read Adda's swirling signature on the bottom of the page, the tears swimming in my eyes have breached the banks of my eyelids and stream down my cheeks.

    The floorboards creak as Fin takes a step towards me.

"Aster?"

    I glance up and the sight of him fills my whole vision. He is staring at me with intensity, a mixture of concern and hesitation and – perhaps, if I'm reading it right – *longing* carved in the lines of his face. He holds his arms at his sides but his fingers twitch as if he wants to reach for me. I'm not sure if I even dare to believe it. I try to blink away my tears as I look up at him.

    "Is it true?"

    He frowns at the letter briefly, as if he doesn't trust whatever it is Adda might have written. "Is what true?"

    "You really want *me*?" I ask in a half-whisper, still not quite believing it.

    "Yes," he says on an exhale, stepping forward to close the distance between us, cupping my face gently in his hands and brushing away my tears with his thumbs. "I want *you*, Aster Lemorque."

    I close my eyes at his touch and shift underneath his fingers, the act feeling strangely intimate – I've never had anyone touch me while I've changed shape before. It makes me feel exposed, self-conscious, but I don't want to face him as a stranger. I shift into the form that feels right, the dark-haired, dimpled version of Adaliza that could pass as her sister. I open my eyes.

"I ... I don't understand. Why? How?"

His thumbs continue to glide over my cheeks in gentle arcs, catching any stray tears that still fall. He speaks across the scant distance between our faces, his voice low and trembling with feeling.

"I loved you from the moment you woke in the tower, screamed in my face and demanded to know why I hadn't used the stairs. I loved you when you drew your blade on the Forest Road and fought off two grown men like a warrior knight. I loved you when you didn't flinch at dressing Rollo's wounds, when you asked me to teach you sign language, when you properly smiled at me for the first time and it took my breath away.

"Even when you broke my heart and I tried my very hardest not to, I still loved you. Meeting the real Adaliza only made me more sure that the woman I had fallen for was not the Princess of Belforet. And I'm sorry that I couldn't bring myself to say it earlier – that I let you think that I felt any differently. I thought ... I still wasn't sure if you ..."

I press my forehead to his, looping my arms around his neck. Adda's letter falls from my fingers and floats to the floor.

"Oh, Fin," I breathe.

He wraps one arm around my waist and his other hand sinks into my hair, cupping the back of my head. He holds me so securely and kisses me so deeply that I let myself *melt* against him, weak kneed and wanting.

If he had kissed me like this that first time we met, when I had awoken with his face hovering over mine, would I have surrendered to him there and then? No – this is a kiss forged of knowing each other, strengthened by the longing of all those kisses we denied and resisted. It tastes of desire and victory. It tastes of a new future, something sweet and bright and wondrous.

When we finally draw apart we stay close, fingers still twined in hair and clothing, our chests rising and falling with breathlessness. I feel giddy, lovedrunk, so happy I could burst.

"You have the ring from Adda's letter?" he murmurs.

I nod. I had slipped it on my finger to make sure I didn't drop it. Now I slide it into my palm and bring it between us. Fin takes the ring, which disappears in the cup of his much larger hand.

"This is why it took me this long to come to you. Adda found a jeweller and ordered him to remount the gemstone as quickly as possible, on pain of banishment from Belforet. I like to think she wasn't being serious."

I smile, easily picturing Adda making her demands. "It's beautiful. But ... why? Did she want to keep the necklace?"

"No ... it was for my benefit."

My brow creases in confusion but a moment later I understand. I watch aghast as Fin drops to one knee in front of me and looks up at me with an earnest green gaze, his chestnut hair tousled by my exploring fingers, the ring outstretched in his hand.

"Aster Lemorque, will you do me the very greatest honour of becoming my wife?"

I stare down at him in shock. I can't get my mouth to move, but my head nods and keeps nodding – yes and yes again.

Fin grins, the smile splitting his face from ear to ear and his eyes dancing as he reaches for my left hand and slides the ring on my third finger. I don't feel it but I know my irises have turned the grey-blue of a sea in storm. As soon as it's in place I throw my arms around his neck and he stands, lifting me off my feet and spinning me round as we share a heart-stopping kiss. They planned this together, Fin and Adda. It's a gift from both of them – a promise of trust and friendship, a symbol of love and commitment.

There is a noise from the corridor outside my bedchamber. I freeze in Fin's arms, my face still pressed to his. He slowly lowers me until my feet reach the floor and I hold my finger against my lips, signalling him to be quiet. Whoever is moving about the house passes by my door without stopping, the creak and groan of the old house loudly announcing their progress down the hall.

For a few heady moments I had completely forgotten where I was. I am still locked in my bedchamber, surrounded by Lemorques with a vested interest in keeping me in the family business.

"What was that you mentioned about rescuing me?" I whisper to Fin.

He grins and inclines his head towards the window.

"Let's go."

32

I climb out of the window first and balance on the sill, gripping with just my fingers and toes as I look down and assess the descent. My bedchamber is on the second floor but there are plenty of niches and protruding beams in the wonky façade of the building to use as hand and foot holds. I make my way down easily and quietly, my arms strong and sure.

When my booted feet hit the cobbled ground, my heart is racing; I can't believe this is happening. I'm leaving the Maison du Lemorque. I have a gemstone of my own, a gift rather than a disguise. I have allies who came to find me and offer me a way out. I have a fiancé. My entire life has changed in a matter of minutes and it still doesn't feel real – a girl like me doesn't deserve a fairytale ending.

Fin drops down next to me and I turn to look at his face. His smile gleams in the darkness and he takes my hand, his thumb brushing the slim band of the ring on the inside of my third finger as if he also has to prove to himself that this is real. My answering smile is wide and unabashed.

"Follow me," he whispers, leading me by the hand around the side of the Maison du Lemorque and onto the Ruelle de Gargouille.

Both of us scan the street warily. Fin pulls his hood up with his free hand and then settles it on the hilt of a dagger sheathed on his belt underneath his cloak. The vast pockets of my black houppelande are empty, and I realise that I should have grabbed a few weapons before I jumped out of the window. The Ruelle de Gargouille is a dangerous place at night, and there's still a chance we could encounter a Lemorque or two who might recognise me. We stride confidently, defiantly, as if we have every right to walk these cobblestones – just two more figures swathed in black, beneath the notice of the eyes I know are watching from the shadows.

I don't realise I've been holding my breath until we're streets away from the Ruelle de Gargouille.

"Where now?" I ask Fin.

"We're meeting an old friend," he says, and doesn't elaborate when I give him a puzzled look.

I understand his meaning when I see a familiar chestnut horse tethered to a roadside post, the small boy at its side dwarfed by its huge bulk.

"Friend? More like adversary," I mumble.

Fin chuckles and flicks a coin in the direction of the boy, who catches it skilfully and disappears with his earnings like a rat down a drainpipe. Fin must have paid him to watch Alezan while he was gone.

"I thought you two were on better terms now?" he says, reaching out to pat the destrier's thick neck.

I stand at Alezan's head and regard the horse. His nostrils flare as he takes in my scent but he simply stares back without a stamp, huff or neigh. I nod once at him in mutual respect.

"We have an understanding," I confirm, the corners of my mouth lifting.

I notice that there are full saddlebags strapped to Alezan's back, as if Fin is expecting a long journey. I haven't had time to consider what we are going to do next. I haven't led the kind of life that allows for long-term planning; my plans rarely extend beyond my next mission. Now my future – my future as a free woman, as Fin's wife – flutters ahead of me like a long streamer unfurled in the breeze. It dances and ripples just out of reach, bright and joyful but unpredictable. I don't know how to catch it, to pin it down.

I repeat my question, although this time it encompasses so much more. "Where now?"

Fin turns to face me. When he sees my expression he steps close, cradling my face in one hand.

"Where do you want to go, Aster?" he asks softly.

I don't have a home – not one that I want to go back to.

I trace the familiar planes of his face with my eyes. "I don't know."

I think of Adda's letter. She offered me a place at the palace. I picture that grand stone fortress in the centre of the city, the clamour and intrigue of court, the politics and preening. Her offer would have been a lifeline to me if things had turned out differently – but she knew I wouldn't take it. *I won't be offended if you turn it down when a better one comes your way.* She knew my heart belongs with Fin.

I think of the places I have felt at home in my life. The tower in the Old Woods, the trees all around it blazing in autumnal magnificence: back when it was a haven, before it felt like a prison. The hidden beach by the sea: the most beautiful place in Belforet, overlooked by a higgledy-piggledy castle on the cliff. Is it coincidence that Fin's home is the one place I can think of that could one day feel like my home too?

"Brisebassier," I say, intending to pose it as a question but it comes out like an acknowledged truth.

Fin's eyes seem to brighten, his hand cupped around my face tightens involuntarily.

"Really?" he asks. "You want to go to Brisebassier?"

I nod. I want to taste the salt on the breeze. I want to marvel at the size of the sky and stare at the place where it meets the sea at the horizon. I want rolling green hills and golden sand and blue ocean a few shades greener than the stormy blue of my eyes. With the gift of freedom at my fingertips, that's where I choose to make my home.

Fin brings his lips to mine, his gentle kiss so tender that it makes my stomach flip over. I press against him and deepen the kiss, letting him hold me upright, joyfully giving myself over to him completely. He steps back into the solid wall of Alezan's side, and the horse gives a snort of annoyance. Fin breaks the kiss, laughing.

"Sorry, old fellow," he calls to Alezan, but his eyes are still locked on mine and his smile is just for me.

I breathe in deeply, happiness infusing my body as if it's magic with the power to reshape my limbs. But then something occurs to me. It's not as simple as Fin and I riding back to Brisebassier and announcing our engagement. His family are under the impression that he's marrying the future queen of Belforet – that they met, hosted, *liked* Adaliza when we stayed with them.

"What about your family?" I ask, biting my bottom lip. "I lied to them."

Primrose Hugh

It had always sat uncomfortably with me. Now I imagine their distrustful stares, their disgusted dismissal when they find out what I truly am. I picture Elinor's disappointment, worn so honestly on her expressive face. I can't blame them for it – I purposely deceived them. I did the very thing that humans fear changelings will do.

Fin reaches inside his cloak and pulls out another envelope with a purple wax seal.

"Adda thought you might worry about that. She said to leave it to her."

He winces a little as he looks at the letter in his hand, as if it is a small creature that might try to bite him.

"Heaven only knows what she has written in there."

I smile. I imagine that the phrase 'by decree of your future queen' might feature in Adda's explanation of our scheme. I know she will claim all responsibility for it. I hope it's enough – that my and Fin's happiness together is enough to convince his family that I will be a worthy wife for him. That they will be able to forgive me in time.

"I can't offer you the substantial dowry your family is surely hoping for," I say, needing to ensure that he is making this choice in earnest.

"I don't care," he answers immediately, his eyes blazing, and I smile. I remember my first impression of him all that time ago, standing before me like a naughty child in the tower library. Young and gallant and idealistic. A romantic. All true, I know now – and how I love him for it.

"I also fear I will not be a quiet, obedient wife content to stay home at the castle," I warn. "If you go out rescuing damsels, I want to go with you. Perhaps I could join the Order of the Ivory Maiden and use my talents for good."

He gives me his wide Fin grin, probably picturing the same scene as me: some dreadful man thinking he has snared a maiden only to find a bloodthirsty changeling wearing her face. The more I consider it, the more I warm to the idea.

"I would expect nothing less," he says, placing a kiss on my forehead. "Are you ready to leave?"

Am I ready to leave this neighbourhood, this city, this life of solitude and subterfuge?

"Yes."

He takes my hand and turns to Alezan, but when his gaze falls on the saddlebags he pauses.

"Oh, I almost forgot ..."

He digs around in one of the satchels, pulling out a bundle of material and handing it to me.

"It's a gift from Delphine," he explains.

I shake out the material and hold it in front of me, my eyes widening when I realise what it is. It's dark in the street but I know the linen will glow buttercup yellow in the sunshine. It's a plain kirtle with laces up the front, just like the one I had to discard before we got on the ferry. I hug the dress to my chest, smiling. Delphine knew what this would mean to me. I can't wait to change out of my houppelande and put it on, but perhaps the street isn't the best place to do that.

"It's perfect," I say to Fin.

He takes it from me and folds it back into the saddlebag. Then he gives me a courtly bow and holds out his hand towards me.

"My Lady, may I assist you into the saddle?"

I roll my eyes at him but allow him to boost me high enough to reach the stirrup with one foot, then I swing my leg over the pommel.

"Shuffle forward," Fin orders, and mounts easily behind me in the saddle.

He immediately snakes an arm around my waist and

pulls me backwards into his chest, planting a kiss on the top of my head. Like before, my head fits perfectly beneath his chin and I revel in the feeling of Fin all around me, warm and strong and safe.

"You have no idea how much I have wanted to hold you like this these past few weeks," Fin murmurs in my ear, sending a shiver through my body. "That ride from the fair when you slept in my arms was heaven and pure torture all at the same time."

He picks up the reins with his free hand and nudges Alezan into motion with his heels. I still find it hard to believe that it was me he wanted the whole time. *Me.* Aster Lemorque. For so long I have worried that I'm nothing more than a cobbled-together creature of stolen body parts, lacking anything of my own. Being Adaliza taught me that I have my own mind, my own spirit. My own heart – although I have given that, wholly and willingly, to Sir Finton Prest.

My future – that bright, fluttering streamer – dances through the night air and we follow it as we ride through the quiet streets of Throsne towards the city gate.

EPILOGUE

Three Years Later

I smoothe the stack of crinkled parchment on my desk, flattening the dog-eared corners with a gentle thumb. All the sheets are covered in Adda's bold, looping handwriting. I smile as I look down at it. Three years of correspondence lies flat under my palms. Writing to each other regularly is a habit that Adda and I have kept religiously since we last met – which was years ago now, at my and Fin's wedding. There has been a lot to catch up on since then.

The door latch clatters noisily behind me and I turn to see Elinor enter my study, chestnut hair wild and eyes bright.

Here you are! she signs, her gestures big and fast with restless energy. *I've been looking all over for you. They've been spotted on the cliff.*

I give my sister-in-law a fond smile before answering, *I'll come down now.*

Elinor steps further into the room and cranes her neck to peer into the bassinet beside my desk. Her expression goes adoring and baby-addled, just as it does every time she sees her tiny niece.

Hello, little star, Elinor signs gently, then turns to me. *She's sleeping.*

I lean over to see the swaddled form of Stella, only her face visible among the blankets. It is peaceful in sleep; her skin is smooth, her cheeks chubby, the wisps of hair falling over her forehead soft as down. It's always an effort not to touch her when she looks like this – to stroke a fingertip down that plump, perfect cheek and wonder at the miracle of her.

I get to my feet and lift her out of the bassinet in the bundle of blankets. She stirs but doesn't wake as I hold her to my chest, breathing in her warm, milky smell. *Mine*, I think. For years I have resented my body's unnatural ability to change, to stretch and shrink and shift on demand, but I marvelled at the transformation she wrought on my body. My female relatives had described pregnancy as a prison, stuck in one form for interminable months as the baby grows, but I was content to feel the slow changes within me and watch my belly swell.

It's been three months since Stella's birth and every day I study her carefully for signs of change. She is bigger, plumper, heavier, just as she should be – but I can still see Fin in the shape of her face, the auburn sheen to her sparse cap of hair. She hasn't shifted. Her all-black changeling eyes are a sure sign that she has inherited my shapeshifting, but I don't know when the latent ability will surface.

It doesn't matter. I will teach her to use her gifts when the time is right. Fin and I will reassure her that it makes no difference to us what form she chooses to take. We will swaddle her so snugly in our love and acceptance that she never has to feel a shred of the insecurities that plagued me. I kiss the top of her head absentmindedly as Elinor and I leave my study and take the winding spiral staircase down to the main hall.

Most of the household has already gathered outside on the front steps: the Comte and Comtesse; Fin's older brother Quentin and his wife Alys, with their two little boys just old enough to toddle; Rollo, now seventeen, no longer gangly or boyish. They all smile at us as we approach. Their acceptance of me when Fin and I turned up at Brisebassier three years ago was immediate and enthusiastic – and wholly unexpected, on my part. I haven't stopped feeling grateful.

Rollo gives me a wide grin and a hug, careful not to jostle Stella. I notice that Elinor at my side is studiously ignoring him, high colour in her cheeks, and Rollo keeps darting glances in her direction. That's an interesting development.

Together we look towards the open castle gates, anticipating the riding party approaching along the cliff path from Brillermare. It's a few minutes before I can see the line of horses framed in the archway. I know who will be riding out front.

I feel an arm wrap around my waist and a solid body draw up against my back. I don't startle; instead I settle into Fin's reassuring bulk, lying my head back against his shoulder as he drops a kiss on my temple and reaches round to cup the back of Stella's head.

"She's still asleep?" he murmurs, and his voice, so close to my ear, still manages to send a little shiver through me.

"Yes – for once," I reply wryly.

"Well she better wake up once our guest of honour arrives," Fin says, nodding towards the gate.

The horse at the front of the approaching party clatters

over the cobblestones, the rider only reining it to a halt a few feet away from us on the steps. She swings down from the saddle, tossing her hair, and all of the assembled people sink into deep bows and curtseys.

I pass Stella to Fin, who hefts her in his arms, and grin as I run forward to greet her.

"Aster!"

Adda throws her arms around me and I hold her tight, even though I have a faceful of mink brown curls completely obscuring my vision. I pull back and take in her features – still blazing and wild and mischievous. Still totally and unashamedly Adda.

"My Queen," I say magnanimously, bobbing a swift curtsey, but she gives a huff of displeasure at the title. I'm serious when I add, "I'm sorry we missed the coronation."

Adda shrugs. "You had more important things to occupy you. Speaking of which ... I want to meet my goddaughter for the first time."

I turn towards Fin, who steps forward with a wriggling Stella in the loosened blankets in his arms, a grin for Adda on his face. But she isn't looking at him – her gaze is fixed on the little face peering out at her, midnight black eyes now open and curious. Adda doesn't look discomfited by those changeling eyes. She's enchanted by the baby.

My heart warms at her expression, the one I have come to recognise when people see Stella for the first time. She's been sheltered here in Brisebassier, surrounded by the fiercely protective household, but the few outsiders who have seen my daughter haven't been repulsed or fearful of her obvious fairy heritage. It gives me hope that she might have a normal future here, one in which she doesn't have to hide her true form. If she wants a gemstone to hide her changeling eyes when she's older, I will find one for her – but that will be her own choice, not mine.

"Hello, Stella Lemorque Prest," Adda whispers, reaching out to let the baby wrap a tiny hand around her index finger. "I'm your Auntie Adda."

Stella just stares at her, not understanding the importance of who is addressing her. Queen Adaliza, the first unmarried woman to ever take the throne of Belforet. In the past five months since her father died, Adda has successfully fought off a coup by the Duc d'Eschecs, strengthened ties with Ardhamra with a view to opening new trade routes, and single-handedly started the fashion for women's trousers. My chest feels fit to burst with excitement to see her again in person after all this time.

"Aster!"

I turn at the sound of my name and see Delphine, beaming beside her roan horse, with the hulking figure of Claude standing protectively at her side. I laugh and fling my arms around her, resting my chin against her golden hair. I can feel the roundness of her stomach pressing against me as I hug her. I pull back.

"You're ...?" I ask excitedly, and Delphine nods.

"Yes, expecting in May," she confirms happily with one hand on her bump, glancing up at Claude with adoring eyes.

"Congratulations!" I say, and quickly step aside as a short, round figure with a steely grey bun launches herself at Delphine and Claude.

"You're here!" Marie crows happily.

The old cook joined the household shortly after I did, once I had liberated her from the tower in the Old Woods. Her culinary skills were wasted there. As far as I know, the tower has sat empty since she left.

I turn away, leaving Marie, Delphine and Claude to their reminiscing. Adda now has Stella in her arms and is bouncing her, eliciting delighted giggles from the baby – Fin is looking on with a slight grimace, as if he doesn't quite trust what she's going to do next. I reach them in a few steps and take his hand, twining my fingers with his.

"So are you two going to carry on rescuing damsels now the little one has arrived, or will you finally move down to Throsne and join my council?" Adda asks me lightly.

It's not the first time she has tried to persuade me to take a position in her fledgling court. She is trying to oust the balding flock of old men who constantly circled her father. I understand why – those men advocated for both her isolation in the tower and the marriage contest that could well have got her kidnapped or killed. Replacing them with advisors she trusts is proving to be more difficult than she thought it would be.

I want to help Adda – of course I do – but I don't know anything about running a kingdom. Plus there's the fact that I would have to move back to Throsne to take a seat on her council, which appeals about as much as a bowlful of eels at the dinner table. I don't even want to be in the same city as my changeling family.

"Not for now," I answer Adda truthfully. "Stella's enough of an adventure for the time being, and we don't want to miss any of this time with her."

I look to Fin, who squeezes my hand and gives me a grin of agreement.

Adda pulls a face. "Urgh, you two. I forgot how sickly sweet you are together. Remember the days on the road when you could barely look at each other? I miss those."

Fin rolls his eyes but I nod towards Rollo, who is standing manfully with his shoulders squared and trying to catch the eye of Elinor further up the steps, who is doing her utmost to ignore him.

Being Adaliza

"What, like that?" I say under my breath.

They both turn to look and Fin's brow furrows.

"No ... Elinor and Rollo? They've known each other since they were babies," he says dubiously.

"So? They're not babies anymore," I point out.

"Oh, this is excellent," Adda says gleefully.

I put a hand on her shoulder. "No meddling, Adda."

"But look at them! They clearly need a helping hand from a well-meaning, benevolent monarch ..."

"No," Fin and I say at the same time.

Adda pouts at us but is distracted from the subject by Stella's squawking. She cuddles the baby close and starts to ascend the steps up to the castle, cooing to her as she goes.

"Come on then, little one, show me around your home ..."

The others follow her inside. I pause for a moment, watching them in the early spring sunlight against the backdrop of the castle I call home. I can't keep the wide, dimpled smile from my face. This is the family I chose: Fin and Stella, Adda and Delphine, Rollo and Elinor and all the assorted Prests and de Sommettes who have accepted me into their lives. The dismal dark of the Ruelle de Gargouille is far behind me.

I once believed that changelings like me don't deserve their own happy ending. Now I thank my lucky stars every day that I found mine.

Fin tugs gently on my hand and we ascend the steps together.

Primrose Hugh

A Note from the Author

I never intended to write this novel.

Usually my tastes, both reading and writing, run to sweeping sci-fi and fantasy with plenty of grit, politics and morally shady characters. BEING ADALIZA, my cosy fairytale romance, came out of a pretty extraordinary set of circumstances.

In February 2023 my life was going very well. I had just got married, my career in digital marketing was rocketing, I had a clear life trajectory and I felt like I was smashing it. Then, on the 18th of February, I had a migraine. That in itself wasn't unusual – I've lived with migraines for decades. This migraine, however, was different. It was by far the worst one I've ever experienced, and once the acute headache had passed I still felt ill for days.

My balance was off and I was constantly dizzy and nauseous, as if I was trying to walk the deck of a ship in a storm. I had another migraine a week later, then another, like aftershock earthquakes. My ears were constantly ringing, I couldn't shake the feeling of seasickness.

Two months (and 19 migraines) later I was diagnosed with a migraine variant balance disorder. It turns out that that first mega migraine back in February damaged my vestibular system – the part of your brain that controls balance – and my brain was now stuck in a vicious cycle of migraines and vestibular dysfunction.

I knew I had to make some big changes in my life. Many – in fact, most – day-to-day activities made me feel ill or triggered migraines. Reading, exercising, driving, going to the supermarket, looking at a phone or computer for more than five minutes at a time ... I had to stop all of it just to get through the day. I reduced my hours at work in an attempt to cut down on screen time, but I still averaged three migraines a week for months. Eventually, in October 2023, my health was so poor that I had to go on long-term sick leave. One month later I was told that I was being made redundant.

But worse than all that was the fact that I couldn't *read*. Attempting to read more than a few pages of a book gave me a blinding headache that inevitably led to a migraine if I tried to push through it. I couldn't write either, by hand or computer, for the same reason. Previously my life had been fuelled by stories; I couldn't bear the idea of having to give that up, along with every other thing that brought me joy.

In January 2024, in my third month of long-term sick leave and my final month before facing redundancy with a broken brain, I decided to make a change. Without the distraction or stress of work, I came up with a plan to teach myself to read and write again. I wanted a project with no deadlines and no expectations that I could use to ease my brain back into writing.

I didn't want to work on any of my previous novel ideas, most of which were sprawling and ambitious. At the time I found myself listening to a lot of romantasy audiobooks. It's not a genre I had really explored before but, when real life was particularly shitty for me, I craved easy listening and happy endings. I wanted to write a book that would be equally rewarding. Thus, BEING ADALIZA was born.

I published it chapter by chapter on Inkitt and Wattpad, posting every week to keep myself accountable. Almost the whole novel was written using a dictation app on my phone. It was so rewarding to see new readers finding my story every week, and I was bolstered by all their reactions and comments. Special thanks go out to Carole776608, smitch0787, Amitabh Sharma, bmad287 and Katarina Wrang – knowing you were reading along with me kept me going!

Primrose Hugh

I'm so proud of this lovely little story and all it represents for me: refusing to give up when life gets you down, spreading some positivity in the world and believing in the possibility of happy endings. I hope that reading it has brought you as much hope and joy that writing it brought me.

Rosie x

Join me on Instagram: @primrose_hugh

Being Adaliza

FORGETTING ERROL:
A Maison du Lemorque Novel

Errol is one of the Maison du Lemorque's most sought-after decoys. He's daring, deadly and – like the rest of his family – a master of disguise.

When he accepts a mission to take on the identity of Dr Fabian de Gris, nothing about the unremarkable man or his hairbrained quest gives Errol cause for concern.

There are rumours of a fell fairy beast hiding in the mountains of Paillevallee. The local lord has offered a reward for whoever can slay the creature. Fabian wants the honour for himself – which is why he has sought out a changeling to take his place on the quest. Who better to track down and kill a fairy creature than one of the faefolk?

Errol must blend in amongst a group of fairy-hating monster hunters, including one particularly prickly academic who swears she can spot a fairy trickster from a mile away. But will she spot the disarmingly charming changeling right under her nose? And can she and Errol work together to unravel the truth behind the beast's presence in the mountains?

COMING SOON

Printed in Great Britain
by Amazon